BLIND EYE

BLIND EYE

A NOVEL

MARTHA BURNS

atmosphere press

For Dennis E. Burns

> *"There is a limit to what a child can accept, assimilate; not to what it can believe because a child can believe anything, given time, but to what it can accept, a limit in time, in the very time which nourishes the believing of the incredible."*
>
> William Faulkner, *The Unvanquished*

Deputy Greenwood

Afternoon July 5, 2005

Lincoln County Dispatch had reached Deputy Rob Greenwood on the road. He was tired after the three-day holiday weekend but still on duty. Tuesdays were workdays too, and the Sheriff's Department never closed. He had turned off the highway right before the junkyard of failed sculptures onto unpaved County Road ED13 and knew he was in for a few miles of bumpy road.

Rock walls on the west shouldered the deputy in. Locals like Greenwood knew that no matter if the rich man named the ranch Bounty Canyon, this was no canyon, just a cleft between hills. Afternoon sunshine threw random shadows. A stunted tree did nothing much of anything to shade a half-wide. Abandoned foundations were scattered here and there, reminding Greenwood that Valley folks were optimistic on day one—or unrealistic, he might have added.

His Lincoln County unit was taking a royal beating, kicking up just enough dust to announce that the law was headed up to the 40,000-acre ranch owned by the celebrity rancher.

Folks came to their windows to watch Deputy Greenwood pass as if they too had been called by Dispatch and told to be on the lookout for suspicious activity. A woman in a housedress stood with the screen door to her ramshackle place propped open with the toe of her bare foot; the look on her face said that nothing amazed her, and she wasn't even that old. Greenwood was paying such close attention to her, making sure to acknowledge her with the New Mexican two-finger wave, that he never did see the tarp until it momentarily engulfed his truck, and he wondered at the timing of it, how many weeks it had been threatening to blow off something and take flight.

As Greenwood pulled up to the metal gate he saw the rancher climb down out of his truck and approach the gate, leaving it closed between them. It was a Texas-style gate with the rancher's initials, SD, on the iron bars and an arch above that boasted the name of the ranch in bronze block letters. The gate was intended to cut folks off from going any farther. Sam Duff stuck his polished boot in the gate, stood sideways so that his silhouette said more about him than his shadow, and waited for the deputy to navigate the cattle guard designed to keep livestock in and thin-legged wildlife out. Greenwood murmured a prayer of thanks for his big, flat, no-arch feet, but he still had to work to keep his balance on the slick bars while he visited with the rancher.

Quiet settled in. And then one crow in a group of seven circling above them let out a triumphant cry. Greenwood knew he'd been announced. The big name TV broadcaster and part-time rancher nodded as if he was, in fact, being admired, and started in with details and observations.

"I've not heard from my foreman, Luke Pruitt, in several days. It's unusual," Duff began, and then, as if reading from a script he had practiced, he explained, "Family of four. They signed on as a family unit."

Greenwood wasn't taking notes, didn't need to because he worked out of the Ruidoso office of the Lincoln County Sheriff's Department. He knew that Luke Pruitt, son of Payton and Linda Pruitt, lived here on the Bounty with his third wife, who had to be ten years older than Luke, and their two kids, one his and one hers. "Like the Brady Bunch," Luke was known to say around the Valley when he talked about his family. But the deputy let the rancher do the talking.

"It's unusual when Luke doesn't meet me at the pens when I come to see the horses. He's very attentive when we're in the headquarters area."

"Horses okay?" Greenwood asked.

"One's missing—a palomino filly that was supposed to be broke by now, and one dead-broke horse I thought I'd sold is back in my barn."

"But they're okay?" Greenwood repeated.

"Someone left them lots of hay. And pulled in extra buckets for water. Left them nearly full."

A breeze came up and the US flag on the thirty-foot pole to the left of the gate flapped fiercely.

"Anything disturbed?" Greenwood asked.

"Luke keeps a neat barn. I think I would have noticed," Duff said.

"Any vehicles missing?"

"The ranch truck is parked at the residence." Duff pointed behind him, up and over to the east, but the deputy didn't bother to look that way. Greenwood knew there was nothing much to see out here on this orphan land where little hills of rocks and mesquite could camouflage even a showplace, and surely Duff had built himself one of those.

And when Duff got to the part of his tale about how he had gone to the foreman's residence that very afternoon—after lunch—being concerned about the man's absence and all, he said simply, "An obvious crime scene. I observed a blood swath from the front door to the steps on the porch."

It had taken him so long to get to the blood.

"Just now, this afternoon, you saw this blood? Dry?" Greenwood asked, holding his voice steady. Greenwood nodded at the man's truck and gave him the country chin-nod that said, *Let's get going.*

It was July and Greenwood knew he could count on five good hours of solid sunlight, but something told him it was not going to be enough. Ink-black ravens, wings spread—a mated pair—soared overhead. He heard them before he saw them, but knew he didn't have time just then for bird watching, and they weren't vultures.

"I didn't get back here to the ranch till late yesterday afternoon," Duff said as he stepped up into his truck. "I wasn't even here this weekend for all this," and the deputy thought he heard him say the word "carnage," but the man was a good twenty feet away, and what with the noise of the truck starting up, he couldn't swear to what he heard.

Greenwood figured Duff must have punched a button on some doodad because the gate began to open, right to left. He stood watching while the man took a neat, practiced K-turn and started up the road. Then back in his Lincoln County truck, the deputy rolled across the cattle guard. The gate closed behind him, which put a smile on his face; 40,000 acres made that contraption a Texas-sized waste of time and money. But here he was, locked inside, being given an escort.

Greenwood followed Duff and pulled up to the north side of the foreman's house—a frame affair where Luke Pruitt and his family had been living for a few years now. He stepped out of his unit, looked around, and tasted dirt. The layout was nothing fancy: red metal-roofed house, a barn about thirty yards off from the house, stables and corrals picked clean of rocks, and a crumbling basketball court—a rusted hoop but no net and a sorry plywood excuse for a backboard. He wondered if the big deal rancher couldn't do better than that for the family working his ranch.

"No watchdogs?"

The man shook his head.

"A family vehicle?" Greenwood asked.

"Yes, a blue Ford truck. Four-door. F-150. Almost new."

"Dark blue?"

"Just blue."

"Missing when you and your family returned? Yesterday, you said? The Fourth?"

"Yes, from Santa Fe."

Greenwood didn't hear the rest. He was doing a roll call in his mind of the pickups that had been parked shoulder to shoulder at Capitan's Fourth of July Smokey Bear Stampede Saturday, Sunday, and Monday. Year-in, year-out, he worked the Stampede from parade to fireworks. The entire Lincoln County Sheriff's Department was called in for the holiday weekend, and most would have admitted it didn't seem like work really, not that some roughhousing couldn't break out with some of the young cowboys—especially those who rodeoed.

"Men know boys," was something he often said to the one female investigator he worked with in the Lincoln County Sheriff's Department. She'd always nod and say, "Good to know."

The basketball rim was in fact bent, would have distorted some of the best shots. The kids who lived here were not the apple of anyone's eye. There was a warped plywood box next to the court filled with balls and things. A scooter hung off the side of the box. All of the things had been left out too long in the weather.

"The All-American Ranch Family," Duff said when Greenwood bent to inspect the toy things. "They came recommended by the manager at the Diamond Crown. It's up the highway a bit." He was only getting started.

"Yes, I know," Greenwood said and headed up the gravel walkway to the house.

On the porch, Greenwood could see a trail of what appeared to be blood from the front door to the south side steps. He stepped up on the porch being careful not to disturb what he knew by then to be evidence. He opened the screen door and saw a large pool of congealed blood in the living room. There was no mistaking it, and there were drag marks.

Duff—wide-eyed now—said something about a boundary dispute Luke had jumped in the middle of. But the deputy brushed Duff aside, happy to have an excuse to ignore him, and yet Greenwood had to wonder if this man had manipulated the discovery so that the law would be here to testify to his shock. Greenwood didn't like that one bit.

Sunlight from the west flooded the room, and Greenwood had a sense that everything he needed to know was right here in front of him, like the paperback left open on the sofa, pages yellowed. He got close enough to read the title, *Valley of the Dolls*.

Suddenly he wished for pitch dark and his county-issued flashlight so he could focus inch by inch on the scene, could set the beam on the gun safe sitting there in plain sight.

Keep that locked, does he? Greenwood wanted to ask someone who didn't have a horse in the race, but just then he did not know who that could be. "Stay there," he said and, gingerly setting down each big flat shoe, he did a walk-through of the place.

Everyone who lived here had left quickly, he decided, in the middle of things like reading a trash novel. He seemed to remember not from the novel but the movie that dolls were pills, all based on a true story, he seemed to recall.

He backed out of the house, and when Duff did not follow

his lead he said, "Let's the two of us step outside. Wanta wait over there by your truck while I secure the scene?"

Greenwood didn't ask for any help with taping off the porch. He didn't want Duff seeing anything he hadn't already seen, and he sure didn't need any more crime scene contamination. When he finished, he turned his back on the man and said, "I'll make calls from your place."

Someone left here in Luke Pruitt's blue F-150 was what he wanted to say to Dispatch when he called in, but it didn't seem the smart thing to be saying just yet, not standing here in the grand living room of the Bounty Canyon Ranch with Duff and now his wife listening in. He played it safe and requested backup. He told Dispatch to contact the State Police Crime Team and his boss, the Lincoln County Sheriff, who was out sniffing around graveyards, hunting bones from the Old West Lincoln County War, and doing his darndest to exhume the body of Billy the Kid, as if dusty bones could tell the tale of that kid.

"Hold on just a sec," Greenwood said to Dispatch and put his hand tight over the receiver. "Do you have the license plate number for Mr. Pruitt's personal vehicle?"

Sam Duff's expression said, *Why would I?*

Duff was on his high horse for sure, but Greenwood knew he had learned more than he had asked. He wouldn't be needing any APBs anyway, not in this valley. Valley people always had their own truck, and even if people didn't know much about their neighbors they knew the make, year, and color of the vehicle their neighbor drove.

Still, he decided he might want to give Duff another chance to be helpful. He'd had a shock after all, and so Greenwood asked, "Now...when was the last time you saw the foreman and his family?"

"Saturday morning," he said, and his wife, who had taken a seat on a sectional sofa, nodded. He and Duff stood as if in a face-off.

"And when did you leave the ranch?"

"Like I said, day before yesterday. Sunday. Early." Husband and wife nodded in agreement with each other.

Greenwood returned to the call. He thanked Dispatch, got the gate opener from Duff, and returned to the foreman's place. While he waited for help to arrive, he did more taping and then walked over to the barn and opened the door. Light flooded in. He heard the horses before he saw them. He talked to them and then left, closing the doors, and walked around to the side of the barn where equipment was parked. His eyes fell on a yellow backhoe. The grading bucket was dipped down. Balanced on the edge of the bucket was a pair of glasses, looking like someone had just placed them there while they attended to something.

He went closer. In the bucket Greenwood saw what appeared to be blood, and what looked like tripe floating in the little bit of rain water that had fallen in the early morning: not that tripe was the word he said to himself. That was Incident Report talk. He backed away.

Something bad happened here, he said to himself and followed the pitted path the backhoe had left down to the manure pit. A backhoe was nothing like a bulldozer, which left a signature scrape. The pit had been dug pretty deep—*maybe six feet*, he thought. Ranchers did that so that the pit wouldn't flood out in a downpour. The pit was surrounded now by wild sweet peas, and in early fall sunflowers would begin each day facing east, ever hopeful.

It was all so clear. He saw the one arm, stiff now, flung backwards as if someone was trying to catch themselves in a fall. It was a man's arm and there was a woman's leg too, in jeans smeared with manure, bent in a painful direction at the knee. Greenwood had never minded the smell of cow manure—a manure pit was part of a ranch. But this was foul; this was human.

Greenwood bent over and tried to get a breath, and then tied yellow tape on a mesquite bush and walked from bush to bush circling the pit. Then at a brisk clip unlike him, he walked up the hill to the backhoe. He took the glasses and put them in his shirt pocket.

He climbed in his truck, thought a few seconds, put the eyeglasses into his glove compartment, and then he drove down to the gate to wait for backup. He didn't have to wait long. The young deputy had been driving in from Carlsbad and was a few miles south of Roswell when he got the call from Dispatch to get to the Bounty Canyon Ranch—fast.

"Hear there was a shooting," Deputy Darrell Conley said after he drove across the cattle guard and pulled his unit up window-to-window with Greenwood and stopped.

"Now where exactly did you hear that?" Greenwood asked, but didn't wait for an answer. "Here's what we know," he began. "There's a family of four missing—the foreman, his wife, and two kids—a teenage boy and a girl about eleven or twelve. There are at least two bodies in the manure pit."

Greenwood watched the younger man lean his head on the steering wheel and weave back and forth like a stubby bush in a New Mexico windstorm. It could have been an act.

"The family vehicle is gone too. There are pools of dry blood in the family residence. A backhoe is sitting out back of the barn with blood and what is probably brain matter in the bucket. The walkway to the house is gravel. Hell, the yard is all blow-away dirt so forget footprints. The rancher, Sam Duff, said he saw nothing and heard nothing, for sure not a gunshot."

"Got it," the younger man said. "Crime scene secured?"

Greenwood didn't bother answering him and resisted the urge to point a finger at him. Instead, he said, "Now let me tell you what we do not know."

"Sir," Conley said.

"We don't know for a fact what Mr. Sam Duff saw or heard. And we don't know who's buried out there."

"Yes, sir."

Greenwood started up his truck and hit the button to close the gate behind them.

"Up ahead, you can't miss it. I'll follow you. Pull up on the north side. Stay off your radio."

"We need to establish a timeline," was the way Greenwood put it to the celeb rancher and his wife when he went back up to the ranch house to get a formal statement. The two of them had been sitting there waiting on him for some time now. They made that pretty darn clear the way they each looked at the bottom of their empty cocktail glasses before setting them aside. But they had eaten dinner. Greenwood figured that out when he walked in. Homegrown beef, center cut, he didn't have to be told.

"Let's begin with the last time you saw your foreman and his family," the deputy said.

Duff started in. "On Saturday about noon. I heard some pounding at one of my guesthouses and walked up to where the pounding was coming from. I met Luke on the porch hammering nails in some porch planking. I noticed he was using pine, not maple, so I told him the work should stop until he could get the right materials. It's hard to get, but I like polished maple."

"His wife and kids with him?"

Duff held his fisted hand to his mouth and acted like he was going to bite his knuckles. Greenwood didn't think he'd ever seen anyone other than a cartoon character do that. Duff looked up at the beamed ceiling, as if making a calculation, and said, "Just the boy, Leeland."

Greenwood got that all down. Duff said that he and his

wife had left the ranch on Sunday, the third of July. He took time to explain that it was his wife's fiftieth birthday. Said they'd returned to the compound, which was the way he put it, around five p.m. on Monday in time to watch the nightly news.

Duff's wife signaled to him with her index finger to her bangs, which hung in her face. Duff touched his toupee, getting it set straight.

Duff carried on with details, and the deputy had to hold his hand up to signal him he needed a minute to catch up. Greenwood figured he didn't need to be a shrink to notice the man's willingness to talk was him trying to shake off the nightmare of sudden news—getting the fright out of his system.

When Greenwood thought he had gotten it all down, he said, "Let's talk about relationships in the foreman's family." Out of the blue, he pictured the King of the Cowboys, Roy Rogers, and his wife Dale Evans. He'd had a Roy Rogers fringed jacket as a little kid, but there was no time for such small talk, and Duff was off and running again, saying something about one of his longtime Mexican hands who had gotten sideways with Luke over a boundary dispute, something to do with the salt cedars that had taken root along the northern fence line of the Bounty.

"I had to step in to keep the peace," Duff said, and before he could add what he'd taken a breath to say, a cuckoo clock Greenwood had not noticed earlier struck the hour. Eight shrieks followed and Greenwood watched as a frenzied little carved bird broke through double doors with each shriek.

Duff's wife stood and crossed the room to grab and calm the pendulum.

"A souvenir of our honeymoon in the Black Forest," Duff said.

"Titisee Lake," she said.

And so Greenwood went ahead and said what had popped into his head, "Yes, home of the Brothers Grimm, I believe."

Greenwood could see that Duff regretted the honeymoon detail because he went back to the story he was crafting about the Pruitts. He took another breath and said, as if he was an authority on the subject of marriage, "We never saw anything to indicate a problem between the foreman and his wife. Deona is his third wife, you know."

Greenwood didn't recall asking that question.

He thought again of Roy and Dale, which was funny because he knew those two had a big number of marriages between them. But he was back to taking notes, what with the information flowing. That's when Duff's wife spoke up and said, "The hand's wife—you know the Mexican hand my husband mentioned—well his wife told me she thought the children might be physically abused."

Without looking up, Greenwood wrote that down, but when he did look up to nod at her to go on, she just shrugged her shoulders, and his heart did that plunging thing it always did when he came upon an accident where kids were involved.

"Ever see a need to call the sheriff before?" Greenwood asked.

Duff quickly answered this time, "Sure, for predators. Coyotes can thin a herd once they taste blood."

"About this family...a call about the Pruitts?"

Duff shook his head as if the answer was obviously no and then added, "You know how it is with western people. They take care of their own."

Out the Duff's big picture window, Greenwood saw the generators used for night jobs that he'd requested from the Highway 70 repair job. They were fired up and lit up the sky like the midway at a county fair.

Back inside his pickup he called in on his radio and told Dispatch to hold off on any APB for the Pruitt truck. As he drove back down from the crest of the hill where the ranch house sat, he saw the yellow backhoe—backlit now, the bucket dangling, making it look like some traveling carnival ride. And now, in the dark of that summer night, he realized that living miles in from the highway could sure enough isolate kids; make them think they were helpless.

We

July 5, 2005

At suppertime we started hearing it. Trouble up at Bounty Canyon Ranch. Two Lincoln County Sheriff vehicles and at least three New Mexico State police cars had turned off the highway and headed up—some of us saw the dust clouds they kicked up—leaving us thinking, *Not my fault. I'm not the bad guy here.*

We were all part of it—all knew it had been brewing a long time. Trouble is, we'd seen it coming, and stood by watching it the way we'd watch a dry storm approach across flat land— always thinking we had more time.

Someone had been hurt bad up there at the Bounty Canyon Ranch, because the State Murder Team had been called in. If the Lincoln County Sheriff's Department called in a K-9 Unit for a foot search, it never got reported, but at our supper tables we were taking calls, making calls as we scraped half-eaten dinners off plates for yard dogs.

What had we expected? We'd been privy to a lot of bad

stuff about Luke Pruitt. We'd known his dad, Payton Pruitt, who'd started out fresh, even got a big deal foreman job but still turned out despicable. We had to wonder if Luke Pruitt ever had a prayer. Sure, back in the 1990s we'd read Luke's mom's columns in the *Ranching Weekly*, posted them on our refrigerators. We'd eaten up her ranch wife humor about her husband Payton and her boys. She wasn't a careless writer, so we sensed most of what she wrote was written through gritted teeth. Maybe somewhere in her weekly missives she'd put God's honest truth. We should have caught it because neighboring is what we do in the Hondo Valley.

Then Luke was back in the Valley working over his own young son with a rope, calling the boy a pussy and a faggot. We had known in our guts that nothing was right on the Bounty Canyon Ranch. Summertime was the worst.

Now as the sun set in the Valley, the glow was lifting from beyond the hills, making us feel foul.

Our fault. Cowards, all of us. We weren't going to escape this story.

Luke

1992

Luke could have called his worthless landlord at one a.m.
when his furnace blew out. His wife had called him at the plant
and said, "It's like freezing cold in this house and Leeland is
gonna get sick for sure with this heater out. It'll be your fault."

And so Luke decided to call his mother instead. Linda
Pruitt knew people who'd gladly make the trip out to East
Grand Plains, south and east of Roswell, just cause next she
might call them out to the Diamond Crown Ranch. That was
the deal when you worked for important people, and his folks
worked for the fanciest rancher around. He'd call his mom at
sunup.

He'd been married four years, but it was his mom, not his
wife, who came through for him. She'd offer to pay for the
repairs but might take the time to tell him something like how
the Good Lord came through when man had given up, or she

18

might try the one about grown men still needing to keep their dreams. That was a tough one when you were twenty-three and working at Leprino Foods cheese plant.

He couldn't tell you why he'd married Corrine; why he'd married anyone at nineteen. It sure as heck had not been innocence, not about married life, but he couldn't remember asking her to marry him. She'd been a disrespectful little thing with long hair, good legs, and big ideas. Luke's mom liked her from the start, and it crossed his mind that was it, that and Corrine acting all wild about him when she really only wanted a ticket out of Roswell, and New York sounded grand. Now he was working graveyard and they had a kid, nearly two. The kid gave him *watching you* eyes every chance he got; it was Corrine turning the boy against him.

Luke and his wife had tried a stint in Albuquerque after he was discharged from the United States Army in New York, but an auto parts store two hundred miles from family to help out with their kid didn't work. He knew that was a sorry excuse for being back in a town that bragged about its smiling alien artwork, and how it kept coming back from the dead over and over as if that was something to be proud of.

During his first break at three a.m., he took a nap with his head on the table in the lunchroom. He didn't care about food in the pitch-black of night. The only thing he ever dreamed about was being alone on horseback, and sometimes in those dreams he'd find himself the boss on his own outfit. He was a better man on a horse which, not being all that original, was something not even his mother with her western ranch wife wisdom was ever gonna put into print. But waking up was pitiful. He'd wake suspended in the stench of sour milk. That catastrophe was not worth the dreaming. Leprino ran product sixteen hours a day, followed by eight hours of cleaning, and some Roswell people, once hired on, planned on making a job at the plant their career.

Luke had four more hours ahead of him on the cleanup shift, and he planned on hating every minute.

But we could have told you Luke didn't have his eye on a cheese plant life. Sour grapes was what he was. We'd see him in town, maybe at the hardware, and we'd pull the brim of our hats down, like a mask, and try to avoid him, didn't want to hear him disparaging ranch life. We'd honest-to-God thought he'd gotten out for good. Who would have thought he'd come back here and put himself smack dab in his dad's neighborhood? He even looked like his dad.

Luke lived with his family in a peeling stucco house out past the turnoff to Bitter Lake, and he was headed that way now. Corrine was waiting for him to come fix what was broken and there was always something busted. The clock on his dashboard said 8:30. He hadn't had time to change out of his uniform and he smelled like milk gone bad. His heavy work boots stuck to the accelerator pad, and he punched it, and the truck took a five-foot skid on the icy road. If the repair dude got to the house before him he'd be making time sizing Corrine up. Luke hadn't bothered to call her to let her know the guy was coming out. It didn't matter. She'd have been in her sleeping getup no matter if she was expecting anyone or not.

He turned off the highway; the one he could have taken heading north, could have made a straight shot up through New Mexico, passing through Santa Fake to Colorado. He'd given that some thought now and then. A left, not a right, and he'd be on his own. He could get lost up there in Colorado and do cowboyin'.

Today he didn't have time to take the detour that avoided the dairy farm. He closed his eyes as he passed through the acres of black and white cows. Four hundred head, he figured. They weren't cattle, they were prisoners. And when he opened his eyes they were still there, a mass of them and not just a few with deformities. They'd already been milked and were facing a day of standing and waiting for the next go round. He said under his breath—something he'd learned to do as a kid— "I'll never drink another glass of milk if I can get back on a ranch." He had a plan. He'd get himself a herd of day-old calves. He'd bottle-feed them and then let them graze. It was the only way to get started in beef raising unless you had an oilman daddy passing you a herd and giving you a leg up.

Luke found the repairman in his kitchen saying, "Ma'am, yes ma'am," and "Ain't that the truth?" Corrine was handing him a cup of coffee, and Luke recognized the belittling look his wife shot him.

"Done some jobs for your dad out on the Diamond Crown Ranch. Always enjoy working on that place," the repairman said while offering his free hand in a silly crossover type of affair. And then he smiled like they both knew something that had not been said, and Luke didn't know if it was about the handshake or his meaner-than-shit father, Payton Pruitt. Luke shook the man's hand only because of his mom. Noticing then that the back door was open and Leeland nowhere in sight, Luke said to his wife, "Are you stupid?" He took two steps to his left and slammed the door, and he could see that he'd unleashed something worse than belittlement. He didn't care. He'd been up eighteen hours, wasn't gonna see breakfast in this kitchen. Luke glared at Corrine and whispered, "Say a prayer."

The repairman heard him and smiled a mouth full of short teeth and said, "Say a prayer for the hard-working people." Damn, it was a goofy thing to say.

"The furnace is not in the kitchen," Luke said and headed down the hall, hearing a few more "ma'ams" before the man followed him. He could hear the tools jangling on the man's belt. Luke opened the flimsy door, stood back, and watched the man get down on his knees to inspect the thing.

"Hey man, can you turn the thermostat up to eighty, get it to something that demands heat."

Luke did as he was told, and when he returned his son came galloping down the hallway, which was narrow and curved like a miniature racetrack at both ends. The boy was wearing only a diaper. *He was born galloping,* Corrine liked to say and wrote it in a letter home to his mother, who'd of course used it in her *for the world to see* newspaper column. Linda Pruitt's columns made it sound like she lived in a bed of roses, which was not the deal out on that part of the Diamond Crown where the owners had parked the foreman's trailer. The weekly column, more than anything else in his life, told Luke that the truth is what you can get someone else to believe.

"You own this place?" the man asked. "Cause maybe it's your landlord who should be footing the bill. This pilot light is not going to stay lit. I can tell you that much."

"The wife is cold," was all Luke was willing to offer the man, who was on his back now with his face up in the dirty furnace as he held a dirty finger to a red button.

Luke had told Corrine about ten times already that all she had to do was check the pilot. How hard was that?

Before either of them could go on judging the other, the boy came down the hall again, shouting something about Trigger, and the way he was moving looked to Luke more like prancing than galloping.

"Kids can be a trial." The man pulled his head out of the heater to say that, sounding just like a preacher.

Luke had his belt off and wound around his hand like a bandage before his son made it through the front room, the dining room—which was only the bottom of the "L" shape of the front room, through the kitchen and utility room, and back into the hallway stretch. The child was heading right for him.

"You shouldn't have done it. Shouldn't have come back

around," Luke said to his son.

The kid didn't do that thing that most kids do. He didn't freeze and cry for his mother. Instead, he turned and ran, and Luke headed after him in his big mean boots with the belt ready to be hurled out. Luke heard the repair guy scrambling and knew when the man was on his heels, but it was already started and he had the kid pinned. He heard the repairman yell, "Lady, you're gonna have to help me pull him off the boy."

Suddenly the repairman got him by the collar of his uniform and bashed his head into the cabinet beside the refrigerator. Twice, Luke thought. And then the man backed him out of his own kitchen without using so much as a fry pan. Luke might as well have put his hands up and surrendered. The repairman shoved him onto the sofa, which slid back hard into the wall. Luke lay there breathing and it occurred to him that he and the repairman were both on alert, waiting to hear a sound from the kitchen. And then they heard the boy take a big long grab of breath. He began to cry. Luke could see that it had taken the punch out of the repairman.

He knew what he was supposed to do; get in there and get some ice and say sweet things to his wife and his kid, who would not even remember this, but Corrine would. Damn right. But he was freaking hungry and afraid he'd fall asleep if he stayed there on the sofa with the furnace kicking in at eighty, and so he said something to himself about whose fault it had been. And then he was thinking again about those spent cows. It was monstrous the way they were treated, and then he got up and thought about going north on the highway.

The repairman had just left him there in the living room like he no longer mattered, and now he was telling Corrine that she needed to report this, needed to call the county sheriff.

"Leave it. I'll take care of my husband," Corrine said.

And so Luke took off. Driving helped. His truck was his and his alone, paid for by the US Army and all those *Yes, sirs.*

He didn't know what the repairman would say had happened, but there'd be talk. The man would probably get on his radio and broadcast it all over the damn county.

"Stay out of my business," Luke said aloud.

What got back to Luke was that it was "no way to treat a human being." We all said that for starters. It was Luke's mother who repeated to him what all she'd heard, her eyes gone cold like a scared animal, making Luke wonder just who was being talked about. She said that good people would be pointing him out on the street if he weren't careful.

But as days went by no deputy sheriff ran up behind his truck to pull him over. Corrine cleaned up her act—put on decent clothes in the morning—and didn't complain, not once in the next week, about the GD all-American town they'd moved back to.

"No way. Not again," was what his mother suggested he say to himself when he got flustered, and he tried saying that each morning when he turned right, heading home on Highway 285.

But in any event, he never did take off for Colorado—not that any of us knew it was a card he almost played. But he should have gone and gotten himself lost.

> *As soon as someone said, "Who did...?" I said, "I did," because it was easier to take the blame than to try to explain why it was done that way, whatever it was. After a year or two as the wife of a cowboy, I got the hang of things and really started to enjoy myself. I even got brave enough to say, "Not me!" when someone said, "Who did...?"*
>
> Linda Pruitt, *Ranching Weekly*

Luke

1993

Final Decree, the two-page thing was called. Luke was the petitioner, which he figured made it clear he'd been the one to get up and get it done and file the first piece of paper, the *Petition.* He read aloud to his mother, "The Court has ruled the petitioner is entitled to the divorce."

"Which part of getting hitched didn't you pick up on?" his dad asked when he pulled open the screen door and found Luke there at the kitchen table in the house trailer out on the Diamond Crown.

"The Court requires a parenting plan," Luke said, reading again from the paper. He looked up and held his dad's mean eyes, looking for the irony to dawn on him.

"Cleaned you out, did she?" his dad said and stood at the kitchen sink gulping water down from cupped hands. Luke's mother got up and pulled the screen door tight and closed the door—it was January.

"I'm going back out," his dad said, but his mom was in no way going to participate. She'd made that clear.

"Maybe there is more than one way to skin a cat," Luke said to his dad's back, not knowing what the heck he'd meant by that. He'd read the saying in his mother's column a few weeks back. He knew he'd only said it because he'd outgrown his dad, and the relief made him say things, stupid things.

"Save it," his dad said and then turned to his wife and said, "Unless you want me to have the shakes, you better put some food on the table." And then he left by the back door, leaving it open and the screen swinging. Luke could hear him out in the yard making trouble for the green hand who'd come on after Christmas. His mom heard it too, but she was pretty good at letting it go.

"The surname of the respondent shall be changed to her maiden name," it said on the last line of the second and final page. His mom was standing behind him with her hand on his shoulder. She pointed to the page and said, "Corrine okay with that?"

"She'll have to be."

"Don't get me wrong, Luke..." she started, but he interrupted.

"From the day I got that damn furnace fixed, Corrine turned up the heat and left it there."

"Wore it out, did she?" His mom smiled and squeezed his shoulder, which he read as affection.

On January 21, 1993, Luke Pruitt climbed the first set of steps to the courthouse. It faced Main. He turned around to check his back. The cottonwoods and willows, which owed their size to the Pecos River, stood bare. A thirty-foot white fir tree, pulled out of the Capitan's for the holidays, stripped of decorations, waited to be hauled off. Luke picked up its citrus odor. He took the second set of steps, which were covered with a thin coat of clear ice, without stopping and said under his breath, "Crown jewel." The courthouse had been there since statehood, maybe, he couldn't really remember dates. Its green dome and columns made it look like a monument—all show.

Luke knew how it looked when people headed up these stairs. Had we seen him that day we wouldn't have taken him for a stranger doing business at the courthouse, but we wouldn't have been as hard on him as Luke suspected—wouldn't have taunted him. He'd served his country, and getting a second chance at twenty-four was nothing. We could have humored him even, reminding him that marriage, being like it is, is like buying an animal at a stockyard auction. You never know what you're getting.

Standing there, leaning against one of those columns, he would have looked dwarfed, but we didn't see him that day; and if we did, we didn't take notice.

"Meet me in the rotunda," his attorney had told him, but there was no place to sit and Luke had no intention of standing there as if he were awestruck by the light that filled the place like a mist. He went looking for a bench, a place to blend in. He knew he was average-looking and, what with his Wranglers all pressed and his hat, he'd be hard to pick out, except he looked like his dad, and lots of Roswell folks knew Payton Pruitt—square cut with the same smirk. At least that's what people said. His mom said that *his* son, Leeland, was different. He had a grin.

Yeah and a stupid lisp, Luke thought, as he spotted a bench at the end of an empty hallway, but he still double-checked around him. People talked about his wife, her stripping and all, and that lisp Leeland had. It wouldn't end.

"Cat's out of the bag?" he'd heard a woman he recognized

say a month earlier in the three-acre grocery store. He'd been picking up a bunch of things on the list Corrine left him that morning. He remembered the diapers balanced there on the top of the groceries like some sort of trophy. He'd walked off and left the basket; likely it stayed there, frozen dinners melting, all morning.

He sat on the bench and tried to brace himself but his boots were slick-soled and he kept slipping, and so he stood up and leaned up against the wall. He rolled up his paperwork and held it under his arm.

His attorney came around the corner with an exasperated look that Luke spotted twenty feet off. If Luke had been the type to wear a watch he would have checked it to make a point.

"You're late," Luke said, because he was the one paying.

"It's final, you know," the attorney said and took the rolled-up paper Luke held out to him at that particular angle that said, *Here, take it.*

Luke looked away and said, "Is that a question?" and then looked back at the man who had tucked the end of his tie between buttons three and four of his wrinkled shirt. "Because it damn well better be final."

"If the judge asks you why, you answer, 'Sir, we are incompatible.' Nothing more. Simple as that."

Luke was a good mimic and he repeated, "Simple as that," but the attorney ignored him as if he had a tight schedule and had to keep to it.

"We're talking judge here, Luke. Any smart stuff and you're on your own."

"I showed up, didn't I?" Luke said. "You see Corrine here? That woman was looking for an easy life and when that didn't happen she turned on me, that's the way it happened."

Luke heard himself, knew he had gotten himself going just like his dad, and thought maybe he should have let his mom come along. He glared at the attorney to get himself stopped, told himself that this man did not matter. Then he gave him the Pruitt smile—all teeth—and said, "As long as the judge understands I keep my property and that bitch doesn't get my name."

"Watch it, Luke. Try to be sensible for what—an hour more? Corrine doesn't want your name. You can take that for granted. And take off the hat in the courtroom."

The judge was Mr. Business. He looked over his glasses at Luke's attorney and said, "I'll speak directly to the petitioner."

"That's you," his attorney whispered.

"Got it," Luke said and waited.

"You sure have a long list of allegations, Mr. Pruitt." The judge kept right on talking. "You understand what joint custody means?"

"Yes. Sir," Luke spoke the two words as if they were two different sentences, and the judge took notice of him, finally.

The attorney squirmed.

"You understand and agree to the parenting plan?"

Luke nodded. It was a nod that said, *don't be messing with me*—a sideways nod, eyes closed.

The judge went still, and Luke felt his attorney drive his pen into his side. And then the judge took up his pen and scribbled something, handed the document to the woman sitting next to him, and said, "See the clerk at the payment window."

Luke headed for his truck, his property now that'd he'd paid her for half of it.

For what? he asked himself again for the umpteenth time. *Paid her for what?*

Without a wife looking for him to come home, he didn't know why he didn't head north. *Just drive*, he told himself as he gunned it.

Deputy Greenwood

Daybreak July 6, 2005

Deputy Greenwood took the turnoff to the county road at 5:15 a.m., just before first light, just as he had planned. Growing up in New Mexico he'd come to accept all the foolishness about New Mexican sunsets being the best, bar none, in the world. Dust was a big part of it. But he favored first light and thought now, as he often thought when he was on the road early, that first light was a uniquely personal event. The way it worked, he figured, was that if measurements were precise enough, a person could pinpoint the singular moment in time and place that first light hit them. Sunsets weren't that way. They were big impersonal events happening far off at a point that had nothing much to do with you.

He was five miles in at 5:28, according to his dashboard clock, when his moment of light hit, and he saw four pickups parked at the ramshackle place where he'd seen the barefoot woman in the housedress the day before. A single yellow bulb lit the place now. He bet the woman had called in her family for the big event up the road.

As he passed, he turned off his headlights and slowed further while watching out for the tarp off to his right. He had to think it had wound up tangled around some bush. But he didn't see it. He glanced to his left because he'd been taught to scan right and then left, and he thought he saw it off about one hundred yards, he figured, tucked neatly around some sort of lean-to.

He knew he'd found the kids.

He pulled his truck off the road just past the last of the pickups, letting it coast nose in and at an angle so that anyone coming up the road might not identify it as a Lincoln County Sheriff vehicle. He was still several miles from the Duff gate but could hear the generators working, and he hoped they had masked the sound of his arrival. At least he was pretty sure the woman had not been at her door watching.

He was suddenly certain that the kids, if they were holed up there in the lean-to, would have a gun.

He was always sharper at daybreak, and without thinking too much about it he reached under the seat and felt for his bulletproof vest. He didn't know the last time he'd worn it and had been meaning to turn it in for an extra-large. "Men grow thick," his mother had said kindly to him, as if all the weight he carried now at forty was not his fault.

He had to step out of his truck to pull the thing on. He had his gun holstered and he grabbed his flashlight from under the dash.

A light came on at the woman's home, and he broke into a trot but still counted his steps. He'd been right to put it at about one hundred yards.

Greenwood walked around the lean-to, saw that it actually had a door that faced north toward the ranch. He squatted and let his heart go soft. He heard nothing, and so he went closer. It wasn't a tarp really, just an old used drop cloth, perfect as camouflage in these parts where matted tans and muted greens were the usual paint choices. He'd have to remember that. Near the door he stopped, hands on his hips now. A name was painted on the door—Richard Parker, it said in a cartoonish script. He breathed in slowly and called out in a voice a friendly neighbor might use: "Mr. Parker, anyone home?"

Nothing. The morning was full of the noise of humming-birds and baby quail—fledglings learning to fly. Here in the Hondo Valley hummers were fed and quail were hunted. He never would get people. The sun was still not up. He looked at his watch—5:46 a.m. He moved back away from the lean-to. There was no real cover for him. He said, "Leeland, I'd like to talk to you and your sister. I'm a Lincoln County Deputy. We'll just talk, you and me."

A minute later Greenwood knocked, heard nothing, and opened the door. He stepped in and propped the door open behind him with a lava rock that had been left there for that purpose. He looked up toward the ranch. He could see the road cut through the hillside that led from the foreman's house to the big ranch house. Over to his right he spotted the flag and a bit of the gate.

This was a safe place. Kids would know when someone from the ranch was about to pass by. And then sure enough he saw a pickup pulling a single pink horse trailer down that little piece of hillside, and he heard it too, knew it was loaded with a horse by the sound it made passing over the cattle guard.

He'd have to look into that.

The place was neat. There was a small broom in one corner near two rolled sleeping bags. In the other corner was an old flare, the type used at highway accidents. One small table and three stools were the only furniture and looked like they had been made in a high school shop class. He ran his hand over the top of the table. On it were placed a box of jumbo matches and a Tupperware jug of water. A thin layer of silt sat at the bottom. There was also a spiral notebook labeled "Summer Homework," and a new-looking Leatherman in a belt holster. A kid wouldn't want to lose such a prize.

He used the flashlight to study the walls. There were two posters taped to the corrugated metal walls. One said Bear Country and featured a big, friendly-looking brown bear. "Cloudcroft," he said aloud. He got up close to the other one. It was a travel poster of an island paradise in colors he had never seen in New Mexico. Someone had printed over it in marker in the same cartoonish script as on the door, *Island of Despair*.

That was not going in any report. But he knew who he was looking for now. And with some relief he closed the door tightly and put the rock there on the outside to secure it.

He got back to his truck in a fraction of the time he'd taken to get there. The bug light was off now on the porch, and a group of six people, all men except for the woman he'd seen the day before, crowded the porch. One of the men held back a square-faced dog on an honest-to-God chain, like the dog was something out of Dickens.

"Morning," Greenwood said, and two of the men waved. The one with the dog stepped back inside the house, dragging the dog, and letting the screen door bang.

"Appreciate it if you folks can keep an eye out on the club house," Greenwood said and pointed. "Took an inventory and will send my deputy out to collect things," he pointed again.

They all just hovered, and Greenwood said, "Seen any kids out this way?"

The woman put her hand to her mouth, covering it, and shook her head to indicate *no*.

"Thanks again," Greenwood shouted. "I'll have my deputy check in with you, ma'am, before he heads out to Mr. Parker's little house." He pointed again and thought he saw one of the

33

men flip him off.

"Fine, I know now who I am dealing with," he said not quite loud enough for them to hear.

He had suggested to Deputy Conley that they meet at the gate at six a.m. But Conley wasn't there and Greenwood was thankful it had only been a suggestion and not an order. The young deputy would be along.

There was a duty officer in a Lincoln County SUV parked at the gate and another car off to the side of the road. Next to it stood a camera on a tripod all set up for sunlight to flood the place.

"No chance of getting in, sheriff?" The woman manning the camera said.

Greenwood nodded at the officer and strolled over to the reporter. They shook hands. The woman had a name badge that hung around her neck. She was from Alamogordo. Newspapers always gave what they called *tragedies* priority. She had to be an up-and-comer. The word grit came to him.

"Deputy Greenwood," he said, and she smiled but didn't give her name.

He took a look at the shot she was aiming for, nodded at the gate.

"Heard there are bodies buried in a shallow grave," she said and looked through the viewfinder. When she got nothing from him, she said, "My editor spoke to Mr. Duff last night. He said he'd hold a press conference at noon at the compound and release his statement then." She paused and then added, "Said the sheriff would be attending."

Greenwood was sure he had seen a little smirk.

"I can tell you, Miss, that so-called grave is a manure pit back behind the barn at the foreman's place. And it's not all that shallow. But don't quote me, just something you heard."

She held up her name badge, offered her hand in another handshake.

Conley was pulling up, and Greenwood pointed at him. "You need something, he's your man."

That got a real smile, but he decided he'd have to think it over to know why.

"Is Mr. Duff a suspect?"

"Couldn't say," he said, and they shook hands a third time, because it was the way he'd been raised, and she was a New Mexico girl. He stopped himself with the girl stuff. Yep, that was the cause of the smile. Things kept changing even here in the Hondo Valley. Women did not necessarily need a man to help them out. "Check," he said aloud.

"Hope you brought water," he said to Conley. "You're going to need it. Keep an eye on the reporter there. No one, including her, goes in unless you get my okay, or if I am not here, the crime scene commander. I'll get his name for you. And first things first. A pickup left the ranch about fifteen minutes ago. It pass you? White. Heavy hauler pulling a pink horse trailer."

"No, sir." Conley shook his head as if he meant it, and Greenwood had to wonder why the younger man did not question why he had not stopped the truck himself. *Tells me something about the both of us*, Greenwood thought.

"See what you can find out from the duty officer, and after he briefs you, send him home. Been here all night."

"Yes, sir."

Conley was charged up and wide-eyed.

"Radio silence, sir?"

Greenwood nodded and stepped back into his truck, but before he could start it up Conley asked, "Sir, do I need a vest?"

Greenwood had to like this young man. He patted his chest and shook his head slowly. He'd forgotten the damn thing. He wondered what his mother would make of that.

Linda

1995

Linda Pruitt's column, *Views from the Ranch,* went to press once a week. Linda was a genuine ranch woman. She knew her livestock and her sheepdogs and could put a sturdy meal on the table. The *Ruidoso Ledger* referred to her as a local girl, a graduate of Ruidoso High School. Neighbors seemed to have no inkling trouble was brewing in Linda and Payton Pruitt's marriage; said they were shocked by the deaths.

Her final column appeared in *Ranching Weekly* on February 23, 1995. A person could find the *Weekly* lying around all over southeast New Mexico, but especially in Roswell at the livestock auction. A close-up photo of a single cow was often featured on the front page, making us think there had to be an artistic type calling the shots at that paper.

"A person who is real observant," she wrote in her June 20, 1991, column, "can tell cowboys apart, even on a distant hill, by the way they sit a horse. No two ride the same. I can tell my three, plus some of the guys that help from time to time. We call it seeing what you see. Sort of like when you see a cow, you should see the whole cow; if she's calved or not; if she's been sucked or not; if her nose is snotty or not; if she's limping or not. All in one glance. Seeing what you see."

Linda was observant, even about herself. It made us think we knew her like a sister. She gave a lot away in her columns, probably making her husband and grown sons, Stralin and Luke, a bit touchy, especially when she got close and personal in another 1991 column:

"In 1964, I was probably the happiest young girl around. I was going to marry that cute cowboy that had been chasing me. Aren't they cute? And those tight-fittin' jeans with perfect creases down the legs and polished black boots. What a sight! It hasn't dawned on you that soon it will be you struggling and sweating to get those creases straight and those boots clean again."

It was that happy young girl—over the moon about her guy—we were thinking about in February 1995, when Linda Pruitt turned up in the news.

She would have gotten up that bitter cold February day determined to put her column to rest. Anyone who cared about her would have figured out she was on deadline that day and would need to drive the column fifteen miles into Roswell, so it'd be on time for the March 2nd issue of the *Ranching Weekly*. It seemed like she never missed a deadline.

Likely she would have told Payton before he headed off in his truck that morning that she'd be ready early afternoon to go into Roswell. Any one of us could imagine him saying, from across the dirt yard, something like, "Tell that to my boss."

Her readers, who picked up on counterfeit sentiments pretty fast, understood that sometimes Payton Pruitt's better-half got short-changed.

Payton didn't need to take their personal vehicle that

morning; the company pickup was, sure enough, sitting right out back behind their barn, but he was the only one authorized to drive the company truck.

For the last fifteen years, Payton Pruitt was with the Diamond Crown Ranch, thirteen years as foreman.

That's how the *Ruidoso Ledger* reported the plain facts about Payton Pruitt, a reliable man.

As she submerged her cold, hardened hands in the hot suds that February morning, she would have looked out the Plexiglas window while she waited for the feeling in her hands to return.

"The world was never out to ruin you, Payton Pruitt," she'd said aloud to Payton the night before as he came in the back door of their trailer, smelling of manure, looking for his supper. He'd rubbed the back of his baked red neck and screwed up his stiff face like she was a nut job. Then she whispered to his back as he went down the stubby hallway, "You did that all on your own, cowboy."

Living all those twenty-seven married years, fifteen miles from nowhere, Linda Pruitt finally came to a point. Nothing scared her in those weeks after she decided, not even seeing her sons with their loaded .38 Specials on their hips. Well, she'd agreed to raise them around loaded guns, and an unloaded gun was no better than a rock, Payton said, so who could she blame? A peace that she could not describe settled in on her. That was good, because she had plenty of things to get done.

The way she had it figured, there would be no county deputies with shield-shaped badges coming out to the ranch to gather evidence, no detectives plotting the case against her. No courtroom reporters who, God knew, loved murder. There'd be no *nothing but the truth* testimony with her sister and sons pulled apart up there on the witness stand—no courtroom performances. In her plan, her boys would finally be safe from their father and wouldn't lose the only thing Payton Pruitt had to leave them, his good-for-nothing *Pruitt* name.

Besides, if she took the stand she wouldn't have stood a chance with the not-yet-cold ghost of Payton Pruitt hanging around in the courtroom, smelling of barns, convincing us all that she had a good motive to kill him. *She had her reasons*, neighbors and town folks would offer sympathetically in her defense—which was no defense at all when it made her out to be a calculating killer.

Even if she'd actually made it out of the Hondo Valley on her own, south to Mexico to start her life over, the talk would have been unleashed.

There was one surprise. Not expecting a future was a burden lifted, it was like the best part. In those weeks the stars each night out there in the Hondo Valley had never been deeper. Each night she'd look up at them and say, "Goodnight stars."

Now, from her kitchen window, she looked past the little piece of Chaves County off into the neighboring distance of Lincoln County. Her window had been pelted with so much sand over the years that you'd think the yard would have eroded to rock, and nothing would be left to turn to mud when it finally rained. But there'd be mud again even if she weren't there to slosh through it.

What she could not see, but knew was there, was the three-story, nineteenth-century territorial mansion of the longtime oilman owner turned rancher. It rested out there in the cool shade of his Lombardy poplars. This gentleman farmer rancher—Payton's big boss—had arrived in the Valley in the late fifties and planted the long row of fast-growing—short-lived—poplars to stand guard over the ranch, and put up simple steel gates at each cattle guard. People were always talking about how he restored the mansion, how he registered it as a National Historic Building, and moved his wife and happy family of three boys and four girls in. In Linda's mind it was a boastful home.

She'd heard that back in the early days the ranch attracted the likes of Truman Capote. Folks said that they saw him cavorting out in the acres of well-tended apple orchards, sporting his fur-felt Open Road Stetson. That was long before her time, but surely Capote's interests would not have extended to salt-of-the-earth ranch hands living in a metal, mobile home, standing in a patch of rocks.

The decision came to her weeks earlier when she was sitting in her recliner in the middle of that winter day, watching Court TV, when she should have been outside keeping an eye on the mothers-to-be. She remembered her heart hammering. The plan came to her whole, which was the odd thing because with so many bosses around she hadn't had much planning experience. She'd decided her first project was to start telling all the good, kind, and innocent animals in her care goodbye. That part of the plan calmed the hammering. She'd learned out here on the Diamond Crown that if you watched out for the animals and did your best for them, they'd do their best for you.

So, in those next few weeks, she spent time remembering many of the ones that were already gone, like the herd sire-bull she wished she'd named. And especially the wild ones who had stood broadside to her and let her admire them, their own hearts hammering. She had not been born to ranch life, but she'd loved so much of it.

And she'd made it her business to see her three little grandsons one last time. She wished that they were old enough for her to explain that most of the stories she had told were make-believe, but that didn't mean life couldn't turn out that way for them. Of course, they were still little boys, and all she could hope was that they'd remember her voice. Now, little Leeland, well everyone liked that curly-headed kid, except for maybe his own dad, her second son, who didn't seem to be able to abide Leeland's impetuous nature. When Luke and Corrine brought him back home to New Mexico, already a one-year-old, Linda could see he'd been born smart and determined, nothing sluggish about that kid. His hair curled western-style around the back of his head and ears. A cute kid, everyone said. But his dad had been a darn cute kid too, running around in an oversized cowboy hat and tooled-leather boots. Luke was rougher stock than his brother— hardened. We all spotted that.

What was hard for her in those last weeks was stealing from their ranch hand, Osvaldo. Planting evidence against herself was easy—too easy—her being the bookkeeper for the Diamond Crown. All she had done was turn Osvaldo's $26.00 check for his part of the phone bill into $626.00 and then cash it. It was only a straw man, that stealing thing she did, giving people something to talk about. After it was all over, her sons would settle up with the ranch hand.

That morning, minutes after Payton left, Osvaldo came to the back door. He propped his summer cowboy hat, which was the only one he owned, up next to the door. He held his brown leather work gloves in his hand. She didn't ask him in. He told her about the bank sending his check back, telling him he was responsible for the money. Keeping his eyes down, he asked her outright if she had changed the numbers. She didn't deny a thing, but the betrayal made her skin crawl. He was a Spanish speaker. She had learned the language early on and told him, in Spanish, that it was a mistake and was being taken care of. She told him that the "boss," which she said in English, was aware of the situation and that after the gather he'd fix things with the bank. Osvaldo wasn't to worry.

At the sink, Linda looked, not through the window, but at it. God, she hated this trailer nearly as much as she hated the scorpions with their poison-tipped tails that sauntered in on all eight legs out of the cold at night. There was no way to stop them. She swore they glowed in the dark, but Payton refused to believe it. He wouldn't kill the damn things. "Let 'em wander off," he said anytime she begged for that little bit of help.

She had wanted her own house and a real glass window over the kitchen sink. She didn't need the land to be hers. That was a silly way to think anyway. Just her own house with a big, east-facing picture window and one room she could paint green. But she was not a cattle queen, and there was zero chance she was going to have that. She wouldn't miss this sad excuse for a house, but she would miss calving season. No two calves were ever alike, and all the mamas, fierce defenders, knew their own.

She dried her hands. It was already ten a.m. As she gathered things up from the counter, sorting clean silverware, she flipped the radio on. She got the local news; listened to the old story about the river of cocaine flowing north from Mexico, running night and day. That sketchy story made her think of the Stubbs, neighbors about her age. They'd been gunned down in their own kitchen—not that far up the road from Penasco. A pretty, rock place with shade. Judy Stubbs had gone into Ruidoso on her own whenever she darned pleased. She liked stopping off at the Hollywood Lounge. We all heard the talk.

Lincoln County residents were stunned by the shooting deaths of Tyler "Cotton" Stubbs and his wife Judy. The brutal slayings occurred in the Stubbs home about twenty miles south of Penasco. The bodies were found Thursday morning by a friend and a neighbor.

The *Lincoln County Gazette* went on to quote the sheriff, who said it was a "cold-blooded execution type murder." That was enough to make Hondo citizenry think it was a payback kind of thing, especially since hearsay evidence from the UPS man was that nothing had been stolen.

A story, old and grown cold. No motive, the *Ruidoso Ledger* reported, before it went all silent on the story. Linda looked at the radio, thought about the gag order the district judge had put in place, and smirked—which she often did when she was alone, even though she hated that about herself.

"People talk, gag or not," she said to the radio.

The Lincoln County Sheriff made no promise of any quick or dramatic solution. Even now at public events he'd sometimes be asked about it. Linda had heard him say that there were no viable suspects. Folks in Lincoln County knew that Judy Stubbs' sister thought different. Linda turned the radio off.

To calm herself down after Osvaldo left that morning, she turned on *The Today Show*, and sat and watched the daily recap of the O.J. trial. The day before, Eunice Simpson had been in the courtroom sitting in her wheelchair in her yellow dress, listening to a detective testify that Nicole Brown Simpson was attacked first that night, before Ronald Goldman, and that it appeared that Goldman put up a fight. Linda got up to stand close to the TV, which was a two-foot deep contraption that attracted dust like a magnet attracts lead. She wrote her name in the dust absently—there was always dust. She was watching to see if she'd spot Nicole's sister, Denise Brown, in the courtroom. Of course, Denise was there. Day in, day out the Brown family sat as a unit in their assigned seats. The camera didn't always linger on Denise, but sometimes when it did, she looked disgraced, and then she'd glance at the camera and turn her face the other way.

Linda had been watching the trial whenever she could get away with it. She saw the trial through Denise's eyes, through the affection Denise had for her sister. Denise knew what she knew. She knew that O. J. Simpson was one hundred percent guilty of abusing her sister, long before he murdered her. Sisters see things other folks miss and no way in hell was she going to turn a blind eye.

Denise had witnessed Simpson pick up Nicole and hurl her against the wall. It had taken a long time to get that telling done, what with Simpson's attorney trying to force her into simple yes or no answers, and because Simpson's defense team kept objecting and conferring with the judge as Denise sobbed. Sitting there on the stand waiting to go on—a careworn woman—she'd looked so very angry and so terribly sorry.

It was one of Simpson's dream team guys—Alan Dershowitz—a smart man, Linda thought, who had said, "Only a fraction of women who are abused by their mates are murdered." Linda tried to make a roadmap in her mind out of that statement. It was as if the man, who had a Boston-type accent and intensely honest eyes, was giving that as a defense for his famous client.

It was that statement of half-truth that had started Linda's heart pounding; that day three weeks earlier was the exact moment her world changed. That smart man had overlooked the tiny fraction of women who were long past being able to forgive and weren't going to wait to get thrown against the wall one more time.

Linda took a step away from the sink and sat at her kitchen table, turning her thoughts to her column. She loved pencils and paper. She licked the lead and tapped the page as she read what she had rearranged, reassembled, straightened out, and finally typed the day before. She didn't make a single mark. She settled the pages and paper-clipped them. Then she reached underneath the one-legged table that flipped out from the wall, and never stood steady, for a blank piece of paper. The ream was nearly gone. *Fine*, she thought as she switched to pen and wrote on the top of the page, in her pretty Sierra

Vista Primary School hand, "Dear Luke."

It would have been easier to start with the letter to her oldest son, Stralin. With Luke, she never knew what mattered to him—land, yes, and cowboyin'. But he was on a downslide; living in town, working nights at the cheese plant. Divorced and remarried—two years in now—to Angie, a thick-tongued gal without a temper. Linda pushed the pen and paper aside.

She needed air, and she knew as sure as she knew her real name was Lindalean that Payton would not be back in time to take her into town.

She opened the kitchen drawer. She had insisted on calling it that even though her sons liked to call it the junk drawer. She pulled out a plain white envelope and felt for her roll of thirty-two-cent Love stamps. She took three of them and placed them carefully side-by-side on the envelope. She addressed the envelope to the *Ranching Weekly* in Roswell, folded the pages of her last column neatly, and slipped them into the envelope. Then right below the stamps, she wrote AIR MAIL in block letters, and she laughed for the last time in her forty-eight years. Nobody heard.

Linda stepped out the front door of the trailer and whistled for the dog. Cattlemen and woolgrowers were pretty proud of their dogs, but not Payton Pruitt. He never did give the best dogs much credit. And this dog was hers.

She had bundled up real good, which was smart because even with the sun nearly overhead it was good and cold. She knew that the sun never sat directly overhead in New Mexico. But she'd never once left New Mexico and wondered if this was normal for the sun.

"Shit, nothing's normal," she said. The dog heard her and poised to scat as if Linda was giving fair warning that Payton was close by. The dog lived in fear of him and got lost every night when Payton turned off the highway onto the dirt road. Linda took off a glove and stroked the collie's fine head. She'd had a healthy litter of five puppies that fall. Linda tried to give one to Luke's son, but Luke didn't want Leeland having a puppy.

Linda had a pretty good idea where she'd gone wrong with her two sons. She'd let her boys see her face be bruised and blackened by their father's hand. It wasn't right, what she had done to them.

"Here's the plan," Payton had said when he sniffed out the puppies in the barn. "I put them freeloaders in a bag with rocks and toss it into the Rio Hondo. You want them to live, use your yellow journalism money to feed them."

Linda had right quick called a friend in Ruidoso, and when she said, "I can't give Payton an excuse to drown another living creature," the friend drove out to the ranch to get them. We all heard about those pups. It might have been what wrecked her.

If Payton had kept the job he had doing maintenance at the Ruidoso Downs racetrack, back when Stralin was a baby, they might have had something of their own by now, a house with real walls to paint. She could have worked and brought some cash home.

"Goodbye to all that," she said because she liked talking to the dog.

It was nearly two thousand wide steps on the rutted road to their mailbox. She'd taught Luke to count by making that mile-long walk. As always, the dog stayed right with her. Linda called her Trixie. Payton didn't believe in naming dogs.

Linda tucked the envelope way back in the box, lifted the red flag, and sat right down on the dirt with her back up against the post. Then she started wishing real hard for someone to come by. She considered counting her blessings and even started with her grandson, Leeland, but quit, because what she kept remembering was driving down this unpaved, sunbaked road with Payton, their sons in the back of the extended cab—telling him to stop for the mail, and Payton reaching his thick arm across her, opening the door and pushing her out. Well, sure enough she *had* waited too long.

She needed to get back home to feed the horses and see about supper, but Trixie moved close, checked the narrow loop road left and right, lowered herself down, and leaned against her. And because there was no way to tell a dog that her pups were safe, Linda whispered in her ear, "Hush now."

Linda did not have to tell her hand to pull the trigger of the cold revolver. She was grateful for that and grateful for the few hours she would have all to herself that night. And, of course, grateful not to be worried about one single thing. Payton was gone, a gunshot to his left temple. He was right-handed, and she didn't want any confusion for the Chaves County Sheriff. The evidence had to point to her as the killer, that she was the only one to blame.

She had simply said, "Goodnight, Payton," and thought of a green room, and then she shot him, but no one would ever know that tantalizing tidbit.

Linda Pruitt, 48, and Payton Pruitt, 49, were found Friday in the master bedroom of their trailer on the Diamond Crown Ranch.

That was the *Ruidoso Ledger* weighing in on the true facts. Linda would have smiled to read that. Master bedroom was stretching it.

She tasted blood and closed the hollow bedroom door behind her, then stepped into the tiny bathroom to splash her face with cold water like her mother had taught her to do whenever she was feeling flushed.

And so out on the rawboned Diamond Crown Ranch, in the little piece of Chaves County that the ranch spilled over into, the part of the ranch devoid of windbreaks, she looked into the mirror and said, "Lindalean Pruitt waited until her husband was tucked away in their bed, and then she killed him."

The Pruitts each died of a single .38-caliber gunshot wound to the head consistent with a homicide and suicide, according to information from the sheriff's department. A blue steel handgun was found at the scene.

Linda had never considered poison. Shooting him close up like that felt justified and inevitable, natural-like, even if it was the dreadful side of a natural thing. And for a few seconds, standing there before the veined bathroom mirror, enthralled maybe with her own clean face, she toyed with ideas for her column, ways she might write about that perfectly natural thing she'd done. Then she told herself that this topic, even if she turned it into a fairy tale of self-reliance mixed with dedication to family, would be too grim for her readers, and she got her mind off that quick.

How she'd loved her readers.

She wished then that she could tell them that this last night she was doing exactly what she wanted to do in her own home. It wasn't really hers. She knew that. It was the Diamond Crown Ranch bookkeeping office, nothing fancy, but tonight it felt like hers.

She took the Tylenol bottle from the kitchen counter and dug in her purse for the tiny prescription bottle of Valium and crossed to the living room to put them both on the table between the two ratty recliners.

"Decoys," she said.

Most nights Payton fell asleep in his chair, but not tonight. She'd gotten the Valium down him and sent him down the hall without as much as a "thank you, ma'am." She'd slipped him quite a few pills since they'd been prescribed for her, a woman going through her changes, on her way to becoming an old lady. There'd be none of that now.

Just then, when she found herself squeezed between Payton's monster of a chair and the sharp-edged table, the phone rang. She put her hand to her mouth and felt a well-known panic. Any little noise in the night and her husband could not get back to sleep. Then she remembered what she'd done and pounded her forehead with the palm of her hand as if to say, *silly me*. But she still lurched for the phone and got it at the end of the second long ring.

It was Nathan. She'd known him for years and always knew he'd end up being one of Payton's bosses. He'd called about Payton's back problems, and so he didn't seem surprised to hear that she'd already put Payton to bed, even though nine was his bedtime. Folks on remote ranches knew things like that about each other, like they knew Judy Stubbs had often stopped at the Hollywood Lounge before heading home.

"If Payton's back is hurting and bothering him he doesn't need to mess with the gather tomorrow. We can get by without him," Nathan said.

Linda knew better than to smile. Smiling always gave away the girl in her voice and this was still Payton's boss, and he wouldn't know what she knew for hours. So she started in, saying, "No, Payton's feeling really good," and then she did smile a real honest-to-God smile, because she was the one feeling really good right then. By the time she hung up it was nearly 8:30 and she had the whole night all to herself.

The sheriff entered through the front door of the residence. He noted that the television set was on and the ceiling fan in the living room was on. The television was going at a pretty good volume. Other lights were on, inside the residence. He observed, on the table between two recliners, prescription-type bottles—the lids off.

The sergeant out of the Roswell office got that all down in the Incident Report, sounding like good, solid evidence.

It was apparent that both individuals were deceased and medical attention was out of the question.

Linda had gone over to the front door and turned off the yard lights. Then she opened the door just enough to slip through and not let too much light out. She needed to see the stars. She tried to coax Trixie over. The dog gave her the eye, the same look she always used to control the stock back when Payton let her do her work, and then crept on her belly right up to Linda to sniff her hand.

Linda said, "You've seen the last of him."

Trixie took off, circled the yard clockwise and then counterclockwise, let out one plaintive wail and headed up the road to the gate. Seeing Trixie take off made Linda sad. She should have tied her up. She closed the door but didn't lock it. The front gate wasn't locked either, only dummy locked. It saved all the hands a lot of trouble.

She went into the kitchen and looked out the window to the front gate and saw Osvaldo coming home. He almost always went to eat supper with relatives after work, always returned same time. He crossed the barnyard and went into the bunkhouse. He kept his eyes on his feet, away from her windows. Good hands had good manners. He never even turned a light on in his place. He'd be up and working by five a.m. the next day.

Linda made herself hot tea and wrote two letters, one for each son. She folded them and placed them on Payton's chair.

She'd written Luke letters when he was in the army in New York but never any to Stralin. He'd never gone away. It was a shame. You could say things in letters you couldn't in person. Not that it had done much good with Luke.

The letters weren't suicide notes, but they'd get called that. There'd be a lot of detective-talk here at the ranch headquarters the next morning. Nothing she could do about that. Her home would be a crime scene.

Reporters would come out to do their tantalizing job—leaving no stone unturned.

But it was her job, as a mother, to explain the $600.00, and how she couldn't bear to live with what she had done, stealing the money from Osvaldo and all that. This was the only way out, she'd explained to each son. She blamed it all on their recent money problems. It was a pretty lame cover story, she knew. A person did not have to have an off-the-scale IQ to know that all she had to do in such a situation was kill herself. Why their father?

After she finished up with that one last part of her plan, she listened to the night highway noise up on the road she couldn't see, heard the approaching 18-wheeler, and then the next, and then she didn't hear any noise anywhere.

In that silence, something dawned on her that must have made her feel like the happiest person she had been in forever. She opened Luke's letter and wrote on the bottom: "Son, find Trixie and give her to Leeland to protect. Let the dog teach the boy how to look out for an innocent creature, and you watch out for that boy. See what you see."

She got up and turned up the heat and turned on the ceiling fan. Payton hated that fan stirring up the air in the living room. He had a point. It really mostly stirred up dust. She settled into her chair and let her mind drift. Being caught up was not something she was used to. She dozed off, and when she woke she knew in an instant that Payton was dead. It occurred to her that she wouldn't be attending a memorial service for her husband, having to listen to stories of how he sat a horse. And she was grateful for that too.

Readers of Linda Pruitt's column will be saddened, as we at Ranching Weekly *were, to learn that Linda and her husband, Payton, passed away last week. Many of our readers identified with Linda's column because she related so sincerely the pleasures and frustrations of ranch life. Hers were the heartfelt observations of someone who'd been there and done it, and who'd do it again in a minute. Payton Pruitt had been employed by the Diamond Crown Ranch of Roswell for fifteen years, and Linda wrote her "Views" column for the* Ranching Weekly.

The March 2, 1995, issue of the *Ranching Weekly* featured that piece on their front page, right beneath a photo of a single cow standing in a mushy winter field. Linda probably would have seen something in that photo the rest of us missed.

> *There are some sayings that I just love. They are never used to mean what they say, but if you are familiar with them you don't have to ask anyone what they mean. "You saddled this bronc, son, now let's see if you can ride it!" "You signed on tough, now's the time you prove it." "It's time to put this old dog to bed," etc. I could go on and on, but I'm sure you get the idea.*
>
> Linda Pruitt, *Ranching Weekly*

Luke

1995

It was raining hard that spring morning when the two Pruitt boys pulled into the overflow parking lot at the Vista Baptist Church of Roswell. "Classic backdoor front. Saw these storms in New York state," was the only thing Luke had to say to his brother on the drive over from the funeral home.

As Luke locked his truck he looked east and said, "Yeah, coming out of the east." He figured that by parking across the street from the church, afterwards he'd be able to get out faster and avoid visiting with people who were there to hunt gossip.

The brothers took off in the downpour in a slow trot. Stralin shouted, "I thought there was supposed to be some sort of calm before the storm."

It had been a full two weeks after the whole murder thing before Pastor Trent had called Luke and said, "Know you boys are grieving, but let's do this the right way. We all put stock in

Linda's opinions, and now is the time to do right by her. Put her to rest."

"Did you ever meet her?" Luke asked. He almost hung up on the man but didn't and instead agreed to call his brother. They'd set a time to come by the church.

And so there they were, sitting in the church office when the pastor asked them who the pallbearers for their dad would be. Luke lost it. "Not me," he said. The preacher got that *I understand* look on his face. Luke hated that look.

"Regardless, we will be needing six men," Pastor Trent had pronounced.

"No caskets in the church," Luke said right after Stralin had told him to stay calm.

"There are ways to do things," the pastor said. "You need to understand that Baptists are congregational; each church has its own way of doing things, and in this one, we always carry the casket out to the hearse."

"Do we need to take this deal someplace else? 'Cause no one will be carrying Payton Pruitt's casket," Luke said.

"Fine," the pastor said and made a note on the yellow legal pad he'd been carrying around all morning. "Just so you understand, we won't be doing any prayer service."

"Didn't ask for one," Luke said, mimicking the preacher's solemn voice. Stralin took his two-tone, open-crown, straw cowboy hat—the American—off his lap and put it back on as if to say *meeting over*. But it wasn't over. The preacher had his finger on the next item on the legal pad. Luke had noticed earlier that the items were numbered.

Luke said, "A funeral here for our mother with pallbearers and a gravesite deal for our father. Easy as pie."

"Not gonna fly. Your parents were members. Records say they were baptized as teenagers."

We could have told Luke and his brother that preachers pride themselves at turning things around. These preacher men come from a special species of vanity, and we could have saved the Pruitt boys some time if we'd shared that bit of wisdom.

That morning as the brothers ran across the parking lot, which was hard to do in boots, Luke shouted, "I'd put these winds at thirty miles an hour." Luke knew his brother was a man who liked talking about the weather. As they got close to the back door of the block-long church, a man in a suit, with a white carnation in his lapel, pointed to empty parking spots and said, "Pruitts, right? We need you to park close in so we can get you up front in the procession to the graveyard." Luke and Stralin stepped inside. The man went on, "We'll be putting up roadblocks."

"No," Luke said. Two young women handed them each a red rose. One of them said, "For Linda."

Stralin said, "We're family," and tried to return his rose, but the woman got busy ushering them down the hallway. "The parlor is where you need to be," she said and pointed.

Luke's wife, Angie, was sitting off by herself with Leeland. She had Luke's four-year-old son all cleaned and pressed. She stood and waved Luke over so that they could group together as a perfect family.

We will see about that little show, Luke thought.

He started in on the boy first thing, telling him he'd need to be acting like an adult. "You are not getting another warning," he said.

"That's enough, Luke," Angie said. And because he could see that his mother's sister was on her way over, he let it go. His aunt grabbed his hand and Leeland's at the same time and squeezed. Luke could have sworn she was the only one in the parlor who was red-eyed, and she looked hungry in the way his mother looked at times. She said to Leeland, "Just look at you. Your grandmother loved you something fierce."

"Yes, ma'am," Leeland said.

"Speak up," Luke said.

"It's his inside voice," Angie said and put out her hand to shake the woman's hand.

In those first days after the murder-suicide, Luke tried to talk his brother into burying their mother at the Diamond Crown. "That's if we ever get her body back from the medical examiner," Luke had said to his brother.

"So, you're gonna be the one to ask the big wheels out there on the Crown?" Stralin asked, sounding just a bit hopeful, which was the way he was. They were sitting in Luke and Angie's kitchen on Hummingbird Lane. Stralin was teetotaling as usual, and Luke was on his second beer. Beer wasn't something Angie allowed in the house, but neighbors had brought a couple of six-packs by with casseroles when they first started hearing the news about Luke's parents.

When Luke told Angie to get him another beer, she left with Leeland to go outside, saying they'd be tying some more strings above the kitchen window. She'd trained honeysuckle to climb those strings and it grossed Luke out the way the vines crept up walls like they had their own simple minds and intended to cover the windows next. But he wasn't looking out. He and his brother were hunched over, heads between their knees.

Finally Stralin said, "Truth is, Luke, they're not gonna put her in their private cemetery out there on the Diamond Crown. No matter how long she lived there and worked that place, they just won't allow it. We never were family." The brothers raised their heads, and Luke saw that the cleft in his brother's chin was wet with tears.

Still, Luke thought he had it figured, and he explained that it was his plan to put their mom in the stand of Lombardy poplars along the river. "Scatter her ashes out there," he said softly so as not to upset his brother any more than he had already. That plan never went anywhere.

Those of us waiting in the mega-church that morning for the service to begin—four full weeks after Linda Pruitt had killed her husband Payton and herself—got a chance to check out the folks gathered there. We spotted the Mexican hands who had driven in together from Hondo. They were sitting in the back. It would have been Payton's boss at the Diamond Crown who had given them the morning off. We each had reasons for being there, just like they did. But most of us reckoned we were there to join ranks with Linda; give the town fathers a chance to say, "The community always comes together in times like these." Well, that was a lie. And we sure weren't there to get her story told. We were there to guard it and keep it secret, and go on our way.

Luke didn't appreciate being paraded into the snooty church with everyone who called themselves family. He could see in a glance that the church, which Pastor Trent called the Praise and Worship Center, was full. He put it at about three hundred people. He made that calculation the same way he could look at a field of cattle and pretty much know the head count. He spotted his ex. She was with her whole family crew—a freckle-faced bunch. She was in her US Navy dress uniform. *Clothes don't change the person*, he wanted to say loud and clear over the organ music that he just then noticed. Pastor Trent had been all about the sob-story music. It wasn't anything his mother would have ever bothered to listen to.

Luke looked up to find the big deal organ, but the stained glass behind the altar had a blinding effect. *Family is the foundational institution of human society*, it said over the doorway that Pastor Trent came through in his long-sleeved shirt and Wranglers; there was a hush, and all the whispering, that Luke had not realized was going on, stopped.

"Redemption," the pastor said the moment the last family

members took their seats.

Luke dug his elbow into his brother's side and said, "Here's where he turns it all around for us." Leeland was on Luke's other side and Angie beside the boy, and now she reached across the boy and took Luke's hand. Luke let her. His mother had liked Angie okay. She'd said once that Angie never missed an opportunity to keep her mouth closed. "Make that up yourself, Mom?" he'd asked. He let go of Angie's hand.

The talk started up again, was competing with the wind and rain. Luke could hear the roll of the voices, each person using his own precise language to describe what they were seeing and smelling. "Microburst," Stralin said loud enough that even the pastor nodded.

At the close of the service, the family was let out of the church through the doorway with the inscription that read, *Man is the special creation of God, made in his own image.* It occurred to Luke that he had not heard the preacher mention his mother's name, or his father's for that matter. We'd taken note of that too. The Baptists could be like that, but you'd think there'd be something personal said about the two people who had died, and not just their God. Even though the Pruitt boys were grown men, *dust-to-dust* was not going to be enough for them. It was a damn shame that preachers had to be told as much.

Luke pointed Angie and Leeland to his truck.

"Way over there?" Angie said, which was something his mother would never have said to his father.

When everyone was in line, the procession took off and turned onto Main.

"Is this zero visibility, Dad?" Leeland asked. The boy's wool jacket was soaked and he was doing a little head-shaking thing where his jaw was chattering. Angie got the jacket off and held it up to the heater. She fooled with the knobs.

"Zero visibility is when Angie turns the heater up full blast and turns it into a radiator with that wet, smelly thing." Luke cracked his window and watched as Leeland put his head in Angie's lap. A baby still at four.

A cop directed the procession into the cemetery, and as they pulled up to the gravesites, two men suited up in raincoats and rubber boots to their knees were shoveling mud away from the patch of dry ground under the white tent. Tarps anchored with painted white rocks covered the open graves, but the wind was doing a good job getting underneath them, puffing them up like little domes.

Angie said, "There's no place for the water to go in a downpour. They keep talking about digging a trench out here."

Luke said, "We're not putting my mother in a swamp. Stay in the truck."

Suddenly the tent came loose at three corners all at once and whipped around like a kite held by someone strong. Pastor Trent and Stralin were standing there with their mouths open, watching it all come apart. Trent held his hand up to the two mismatched hearses, which had pulled up. He did it professionally like a traffic cop.

"Call it off," Luke said.

"You're right, son. These storms are hard to forecast."

"Really?" Luke said and turned his back on the preacher and his brother.

"Please join us in prayer," Trent said, but Luke was on his way back to his truck.

He called back to Stralin: "Meet me at the courthouse. I'll drop Leeland and Angie off home first."

As Luke walked back to his truck he saw his ex arriving with her entourage. They were in three cars. Corrine was first to get out. Her brimmed cap, designed for the sea, was doing nothing much to protect her from the deluge. He had to admit she looked sharp, that eagle—wings spread—on her cap and the skirt just short enough. And she knew it.

"It's over. You're too late," he said and got right in her face.

She'd always called him on everything. But he could see she was through bothering, and then he saw in her big, dark pupils a tiny image of him dangling there like a puppet.

She said, "Let me take Leeland today. He can stay the night. Might be his last visit before I ship out."

"Ship out? You're out of luck. I don't see any ship, Corrine." He wanted to get back to his truck, out of the storm and out of her line of sight. Instead he just stood there. "Go ahead," he said, surprising himself. "But you'll have to take him back to the house to get his stuff. Take Angie too while you're at it. Stralin and I have things to do in town."

As Leeland climbed out of the truck Luke heard him say to Corrine, "They never rang those big bells for grandmother. She liked bells."

Luke slammed his door. He reset the knobs Angie had messed with, but he didn't start the truck. Instead, he banged his fist on the dash. It was supposed to feel better with Payton Pruitt gone. Luke knew that was his mom's orphan plan, but it felt like nothing had ended.

He felt for his wallet. The manager at the Diamond Crown thought he was doing them a big favor when he suggested the yard sale at the trailer his folks had lived in; where he and Stralin had grown up. The sale was a huge hit because Hondo Valley folks and even people from Roswell got to get onto the Diamond Crown and nose around.

"We know you boys will step up," the ranch manager said when he handed over the money they had taken in at the yard sale, and now they had to go pay off their parents' debts. He and Stralin were still waiting to get the cash his mom had tucked away in the trailer. She'd left six hundred dollars there in the junk drawer. Her intentions had been pretty simple.

"That might take months. It's evidence you know," the

county deputy had said.

At the Chaves County Courthouse, the storm had ripped off dozens of the newly leafed willow branches, making the grass underneath look like a field of switches. Willows bloomed early in southeastern New Mexico and stayed a yellow-green color until it got blazing hot. Luke took a place in line at the county clerk's payment window. He wasn't the only one dripping his own personal puddle of water on the slick, polished floor. The building was overheated for April, but after the soaking his feet had taken—right through the ostrich skin boots—he didn't mind.

"The gravestones weren't ready anyway," Stralin said when he joined Luke in line.

"Right," Luke said and smiled at his big brother. Those stones had been a fight from the get-go with the Baptists. Luke argued that if you put the same date of death on those two stones, February 23, 1995, then complete strangers would make connections and read things into the Pruitt story, things they thought there were seeing. *Oh, poor things, they died together in an awful accident.*

No accident, Luke thought.

He'd suggested to Stralin *Baked-in Bad* for their dad's grave marker, knowing that when he later suggested putting only their dad's name on the thing that Stralin would agree. On their mom's stone, which was a pretty granite that Luke had found from driving out to the quarry west of town, they'd put her name and the date of her birth and death. *Beloved mother, sister, daughter* would be carved there too in the granite.

"Put a little calf there in the corner," Luke told the dusty old man who'd promised the granite would not erode.

Luke's head ached. He'd have to punch in at work by six.

"Pastor Trent promised he'd have them buried by suppertime," Stralin said.

"Better," Luke said.

Stralin was doing the little head-shaking thing now.

"The last time it flooded out there graves washed away," Stralin added.

"Gee, thanks, brother."

"Just saying things work out," Stralin said.

The brothers moved up slowly in the line. Luke turned to look out one of the vaulted windows. He saw clear sky. He'd sleep in the truck, he decided. No one would be missing him. He'd move the truck over there behind the courthouse by the statue of the lawman Pat Garrett. His mom liked that stupid statue.

Ride to Destiny, the bronze plaque at the base of the statue said. Luke never did get her liking the statue of a man who'd killed Billy the Kid, who really was a kid and the town Favorite Son, even if he wasn't all that innocent. They'd had a rare picnic there once, in the grass near the statue, just Luke and his mother.

Thinking about that picnic lunch, it dawned on him that he was hungry. He'd go eat instead. A real meal.

Luke had made it clear to the preacher that there would be no lunch—no gathering at the church following the burial. It would not have been that hard to put a meal together for just the Pruitt family, something substantial. We should have thought of that. Looking back now it might have been Luke's outright contrarianism that kept us clear of him. That too was a type of vanity, but for us, a damn poor excuse for doing nothing.

Deputy Greenwood

Early Morning July 6, 2005

Greenwood drove up the hill to the foreman's house slowly, checking for movement on each side of the road. He had daylight working for him now. He backed up to a spot on the north side of the house knowing he'd probably be leaving for interviews once he had the scene nailed down here.

He saw that they'd been busy with yellow tape when he'd been up at the ranch house the night before. He had arranged for the generators to be turned off at daylight, and suddenly he took note of the silence that hung heavy. He stepped out of his truck, struggled out of his vest, and tossed it on the passenger seat.

The basketball court had been taped off. A New Mexico State Trooper car sat broadside to the south side porch, and as Greenwood started that way, the state trooper, clean and pressed, stepped out of the vehicle. Greenwood recognized the man—placed him at an accident scene on Highway 380 two years back. Flooding on the two-lane highway was where the blame was placed for those two deaths.

"Quiet night?" Greenwood asked.

"I'd say so. But with that generator going it felt like I was the only one alive for miles." The trooper hesitated and then said, "Sorry."

"I can imagine," Greenwood said.

"But the phone in the house started up at five this morning. There must be at least two extensions. Of course I didn't go inside."

"Of course," Greenwood said. "I'm going to head up to the ranch house and make some calls off radio. And I'll get an officer to sit at that phone as soon as the scene is cleared."

Greenwood did a 180 on the heels of his big feet and took a few seconds to order his thoughts.

"Crime scene team will be back at seven with their commander. Of course, they took control of the scene last night."

The trooper nodded and said, "Greenwood? Right?"

"Yes, sorry," Greenwood said, and they shook hands.

"Hoyt," the trooper said as he smiled with just his eyes. "We've worked together."

Greenwood nodded. They were about the same age and had seen some of the same things that changed a person—like the accident on Highway 380 in San Antonio where everyone on scene was too messed up to eat the burgers the Owl Bar kept bringing out.

"The medical examiner will be here by nine a.m. No later is what he told Dispatch. He's coming in from Santa Fe. I've got a couple of questions for you, but I want to get on the phone with the judge first off." Greenwood nodded at the trooper who was nodding at him.

He really did not want to see Duff and wished then he'd gone ahead and bought himself that tiny little flip phone he'd seen at the Walmart. The investigator would be bringing hers, but these calls couldn't wait.

Over his shoulder he said, "Investigator Paula Magliaro will be here soon. Go ahead and brief her, would you?"

But he was nearly in his truck when he realized what he'd forgotten and, feeling like a bit of an idiot, he backtracked and said, "Officer Hoyt, did you get a chance to put eyes on that truck that left the ranch around five-fifty this morning?"

"No, parked over here at the house, I didn't see much. As soon as I heard what I knew was a truck passing I charged after it on foot. From what I saw in the twilight he was hauling a beat-up one-horse trailer with a bubble top. The driver popped the gate open himself though, made some racket crossing the cattle guard, and just kept on going. I knew not to leave this scene."

"Couldn't see inside the trailer, I'm guessing."

"No, but he might have had a load in there seeing as how he took it slow going down to the gate." He stopped and then said, "Hoyt's the first name."

Greenwood nodded and took his notebook out of his back pocket to jot down times on the timeline.

"Pass you on the road?" Hoyt asked.

"I was stopped at that ramshackle house about a mile down the road—lotta porch watchers there already."

Hoyt nodded and said, "Neighborhood eyesore, that place."

Greenwood's radio started buzzing before he could start the engine of his truck. It was his favorite dispatch officer, Fay, over in Carrizozo, at Lincoln County headquarters. Knowing that it was not yet seven, he knew she had clocked in early. She was good. She read off a list of names to him, people who had called in wanting to help.

"Keep logging," he said. "As soon as I reach the judge for the search warrant, I'll get on the phone to those folks. I'm going to make calls, for now, at Sam Duff's."

"Let's hope he knows to put a pot on. Okay, I'll let you go."

Greenwood always pictured Fay with a cup of coffee in her hand as she talked. She drank cup after cup of coffee, and when the fancy coffee shop opened in Carrizozo, she did her best to keep them in business, but of course folks in Lincoln County favored a simple cup of coffee and Styrofoam did just fine. He kinda missed the fancy place with its hi-top tables.

Duff explained when he met Greenwood at the front door of his ranch house that his wife was still in bed; she'd had a fitful night. Greenwood followed him into the kitchen where coffee was, in fact, on, but he had to ask to get a cup.

As Greenwood stirred in the sugar and cream he asked, "Think I could use one of the guesthouses to make some calls?"

Sam turned his back and said, "You can use the den phone." He headed that way.

So be it, Greenwood thought and followed. He'd have to add the guesthouses to his search.

It didn't take but a minute to get the judge on the phone. She said she'd been waiting for the call. She'd fax a copy over to the sheriff's office in Carrizozo, she said, and she'd get the kid who was picking apples out back in her yard to drive the original down the thirty miles from Ruidoso to the Bounty. "Give him thirty minutes," she said. "Just get Duff's permission to search the rest of the property."

He'd grown up with the judge, graduated Ruidoso High School in the same class, so he knew this part of his morning would be easiest. He took his notebook out of his pocket and called Fay back for phone numbers. Then while he talked first to the postmistress, Rosalie, at the Hondo post office, he started sketching out the Pruitt family tree. He would have liked to finish up the callbacks, but he didn't want to leave Sam Duff too much time to start with his two-plus-twos.

But then the phone he'd just set in the cradle rang, and he picked it up before it could ring a second time and bring Duff back to the den. It was Fay. She'd just spoken to Leeland's stepmom, Angie, over near Roswell. Angie reported that Karmen, the twelve-year-old girl, was safe and sound at Luke's brother's house. "Follow me?" Fay said.

Greenwood pulled out his notebook again and added to the growing family tree. "Who called who?" he asked.

"Near as I can figure, Luke's brother's wife called Angie, Luke's second ex. You do know that the word is out across two counties," Fay said.

"Okay now," he said and thanked her. He didn't have to tell her to keep it quiet.

"Say, Mr. Duff," he said as he returned to the kitchen, "I'll be needing your permission to search the rest of the property."

"It's a big ranch," Duff said.

"Sure is," he replied and nodded, pointing his index finger at the big deal rancher in a friendly manner before writing a note in his notebook. He clapped it shut and thanked the man, although nothing really had been agreed to.

"And can you tell me who left the ranch this morning in a ranch pickup? Hauling a trailer?" He was guessing on the ranch part of that question.

Duff pulled his chin up into his mouth and tucked his bottom lip into his mouth. It looked as if he had some sort of lockjaw. "Alfonzo," he said through his clenched mouth.

"He haul a horse outta here?"

"No idea," Duff said.

"Well, when you get a moment, I need you to take a look down in the barn and see what's missing—saddles, tack, tools...horses."

Duff rolled his eyes, and so Greenwood decided to say more not less.

"Listen, Mr. Duff, we have two bodies and two missing kids. I don't want to find two more bodies." He raised his eyebrows up at the rancher the way his mother had done when she'd had enough and was making her final point. "A crime scene officer will be there to walk you through the barn. I'll let him know to expect you."

Greenwood spotted his coffee cup in the sink. Full.

"Think you or your wife could send some water down the hill in one of those contraptions you ranchers carry in the bed of your trucks? This place will be crawling with investigators in another hour."

"Okay," Duff said.

"I hear you've called a press conference. How's that going to work?" Greenwood asked and picked up the coffee cup from the sink. The coffee was stone cold.

Duff wasn't going to answer and so Greenwood said, "Well, you'll need to host it outside the gate. Surely you can understand that the Bounty is an active crime scene now, and it's gonna be that way for a while."

He put the cup back in the sink and thought he was going to have to show himself out. And so, he played with the man, thinking now was the time to ask a question he already knew the answer to.

"Luke Pruitt have a temper?"

Duff started to fold his arms across his chest but instead nodded toward the door before saying, "Look, Luke worked for me two years without an incident."

Greenwood didn't budge and said, "This Alfonzo, is he the Mexican hand your wife mentioned? The one whose wife thought she saw some abuse? I'll need their home phone number."

Duff left him there while he went for the number. Greenwood emptied his coffee out and poured himself some water. He looked out the window over the sink, watching for any sign of life. It was stone quiet. There were no guests at the Bounty Canyon Ranch that day.

Paula was already following leads when he got back down

the road to the crime scene, which meant she was working the phone. She held up her hand to indicate she was in the middle of something and he took advantage of the time to compose his thoughts.

The Crime Team had arrived, or at least those with the tent, which they were erecting at the basketball court. It was white with side flaps that could be raised or lowered and looked like a chapel with the basketball hoop standing there like an ancient Christian cross. The box of balls and random things kids played with had been emptied, and the contents were laid out in a straight line. *Looking for a gun in all the wrong places*, Greenwood thought.

"First on scene?" a man in civilian clothes said to him. A ring of keys hung from his belt or otherwise he would have passed for a super-fit insurance salesman. He approached with his hand held out. They exchanged titles: Deputy and Commander. Greenwood looked at his watch and said, "Search warrant should be here for you by half past seven."

"Perfect," the commander said. He stood back and studied the layout of the house and barn and pointed when he saw the camp chairs being set up under the white tent. "Let's take a seat," he said.

Greenwood saw that Paula had finished up her call and he waved her over. "District Court Investigator Magliaro," he said by way of introductions. Paula leaned up against one of two metal tables, and now she pointed at the chairs, and the men sat. Greenwood filled them both in on the details of the night before—the Pruitt family stuff that the crime scene might not disclose.

"A blended family," Paula said.

"Here's the only good news so far," Greenwood said. "The boy's stepmother called into county Dispatch a little bit ago." He saw confusion. There would be plenty of that today.

"She's Leeland's first stepmother, Angie. Luke divorced

her to marry Deona. She lives over near Roswell. She told Dispatch that the Pruitt girl is staying with her aunt and uncle off on a ranch near Corona. That would be Luke's older brother, Stralin Pruitt, and his wife. The aunt and uncle took her to the Capitan Stampede on Sunday, and then took her home with them for a visit." Greenwood took his notebook out and said, "Her name is Karmen with a 'K'."

Paula smiled and Greenwood didn't know if it was relief or if she had already heard this news.

"Hmm," the commander said as he studied Greenwood and then said, "So?"

Greenwood ordered his thoughts only as the words came out. "Any number of people could have come in here on Sunday after Luke's brother and his family left, and who would have known, what with Duff being away and it being a holiday weekend? Or on Monday for that matter. Let's say someone came in here. Killed Luke and Deona and took off with the boy."

"Hmm. It's possible. But realistically, could they be in Mexico now?" the commander asked.

Greenwood liked a man who could ask a question he genuinely wanted the answer to. He and Paula nodded in unison.

"But you don't think so—do you? Wait. Don't say. You do your job and I'll do mine. But do this for me...Tell your officers to forget what they think they saw and describe only what they saw. Big difference, if you get my nuance." He gave them both a serious look. "For example, you see a pale, bald head in a pit of manure, and you say that man's hat is missing, must have fallen off in that pit. Wrong. You see a pale bald head period. No hat and no missing hat. That's it."

There was a silence and the commander closed his eyes. Paula nodded and then said, "Got ya."

Then the commander stood up and looked over at the

Pruitt house and said, "And tell me one more thing. Did Mr. Duff turn on or off any lights or open or close any doors when he happened on the scene?"

Greenwood had to think before he could answer, and he wondered then why he had not asked Duff if Luke or Deona wore glasses. *Damn*, he thought, and then answered that he'd watched Duff pretty closely and had not seen him touch anything. Well, if experience counted for anything on a day like today, he was getting a dose of that.

Greenwood was more than ready to head out after he'd talked to all the Lincoln County officers who'd shown up, but he wanted to wait for the medical examiner. Technically, he knew he could leave. The scene was not his. But it'd be important to see what the ME saw.

The ME arrived in a Honda Civic at eight a.m., followed by two ambulances. Paula knew the man and went to get him briefed. While they stood at the open hatchback, she showed him the copy of the search warrant. She made the introductions to the crime scene commander by way of pointing at the man who was standing on the porch, hands in blue gloves. From the way it looked to Greenwood, the men were well acquainted.

The doctor had a pocket full of saltine crackers, which he began to munch on before he even got to the manure pit, and he didn't ask a single question after he got to the pit. But he was talking all the time into a small recorder he held up close to his mouth.

A group gathered as the doctor circled the pit. The man looked at the sky, and then clicked off his recorder and shouted in what was a well-cared-for German accent, "There is the matter of the downpour that is predicted. We have to get these bodies exhumed quickly to beat it."

Greenwood noticed then that the sweet peas were dancing in a breeze that seemed to come out of nowhere. He turned to

Paula and pointed his chin toward his truck. They weren't needed here and besides, Hoyt was there at the back side of the pit gagging, and couldn't seem to quit. Greenwood was backing away from the pit when the commander startled him by taking his elbow.

He said softly, "What can you tell me about that spackled wall in the kitchen? It's fresh. Did Duff say anything about that?"

"No, but I didn't let him get that far into the house." Greenwood wanted to say that he didn't think you could see into the kitchen from where he'd told Duff to wait. But he stopped before going there. "I didn't take note of that in the kitchen. And I was there."

The two men walked back toward the house. Greenwood nodded at Paula. She had a backpack hanging off one shoulder as she headed to the trucks.

The commander seemed to be watching her while he sorted something out, and Greenwood gave him time. Finally, the man said, "Listen, I've read the statement Duff gave you last night, and I've decided I don't want to be asking him any questions, I'll leave that to you."

"Of course, and we'll call in on the half hour," Greenwood said.

He climbed into his truck, and as he reached across to unlock the door for Paula, he grabbed the vest and pushed it under his seat. If she had spotted it, she didn't say.

> *Ranch kids do seem to grow up with a healthy respect for everything alive and our environment. They have usually seen human nature at its worst during hunting season and at its best while caring for sick and injured livestock. I have seen these kids cry over a dying lamb but wolf down meat from a calf they have helped fatten for the freezer. It just seems to me that by the time they have reached adulthood they seem to have all their priorities in place.*
>
> Linda Pruitt, *Ranching Weekly*

Corrine

1997

Corrine was twenty-seven years old and had been in the US Navy for two years and gone from Roswell most of that time. Her leave home had been a long time coming; she'd put the Leave and Liberty request form in back in January. Life in the United States Navy agreed with her, and she'd had no problem with the discipline of life in uniform. She liked thinking she could be responsible, but it was after eleven p.m. when Corrine drove up to her aunt's house on Fourteenth Street. Her Aunt Sally was sitting on the porch in her one plastic patio chair. Waiting up, while two doors down music was blaring from an open garage.

The porch had a yellow bug light burning; it mostly attracted moths. Corrine had kept her son out late, overdoing it, she knew.

The yard, protected by a chain-link fence, was overrun by heartleaf milkweed—descendants of the same weeds that had

covered the yard when Corrine was a kid. She'd warned
Leeland, like she'd been warned, that the sticky milk that
leaked from the weeds was poisonous, but her aunt protected
the damn weeds because she swore those weeds were the one
single thing a monarch butterfly needed to survive. Corrine
couldn't argue with that, and Sally made us all believers
because come early spring her yard was always a haven for
the black-veined butterflies.

"They're intelligent," Sally insisted.

Corrine knew she wasn't going to get past her aunt
without a full explanation of exactly why she was getting
Leeland home so late.

"People will be watching," her aunt had warned when she
left the house that Sunday evening with Leeland. But things
were actually going well. Corrine hadn't gotten into it with
anyone since she'd arrived in Roswell at the beginning of the
week, not even with her aunt's church people who'd given her
the evil eye when she and Sally took Leeland to the Wednesday
night potluck.

"I get the idea we're not welcome," Corrine said to her
aunt, who'd refused to leave before the coffee and pie.

"They have a lot to get past—like the Gentlemen's Club,"
Sally said.

Now Corrine was still getting the particulars of her story
down as she stepped up on the porch. *I was only showing my
son a good time,* she'd start in. *I picked a wholesome movie,
but I let him pick where to eat. The only problem was filling
him up.*

"Too late for a first grader. Let's get him in the bath," was
all her aunt said.

Sally was going on about how Leeland no doubt had a head
full of spring dirt, telling Corrine she needed to get that curly
hair washed.

"Your ex probably doesn't know how to wash a boy's hair,"
Sally said.

"Angie gives him his baths," Corrine said and Leeland nodded.

Leeland suddenly became modest and crossed his skinny arms tightly in front of his bare, little-boy chest and said, "I'm six, Mom."

"How about you step out, Auntie?" Corrine said sweetly.

Sally stationed herself in the hallway and Corrine plugged the tub and started running a warm bath. Keeping her back to her son, she gave him time to finish undressing. She could smell his now bare feet. She had locked herself in this bathroom more than once. She remembered sleeping off a bad drunk in the tub after she'd tried to count the tiny black and white tiles to stay awake. She'd only gotten to one hundred.

God, he was still a little guy.

"Come on, Leeland. Get 'em off."

She pivoted without standing, sat him on the toilet seat and, taking the cuffs of his jeans in her hands, said, "Here we go," and yanked the way she had when he was a toddler. It was funny what came back to you about mothering. And she laughed the way she had when she was a kid without a care. *Listen to me*, she thought.

"Road dust," she said as they watched the dirt and pebbles settle on her aunt's tile floor.

Leeland was giggling. She had not expected giggles. She thought he might take off for one of his famous butt-tuck runs around the house, which had been their bath time game when Luke was gone from home, and he was gone a lot. But now Leeland just stayed there planted on the toilet seat in his baggy briefs. They looked like hand-me-downs.

"Get those off too," she said as she threw the jeans into the hallway.

It was nearly midnight, and if they didn't get the lights turned off soon the neighborhood watch would be reporting that Corrine was out partying when she should have been taking care of her kid.

What did they know?

"Hop in or the water will be cold," she said. Leeland stood and his briefs pretty much fell to the floor. He made a quick move for the tub, but she still saw it. The bruise on his backside looked like it was growing.

"Who did that to you?" she asked. That was all it took to get her aunt into the bathroom. Corrine knew it was wrong to ask that question of her little boy when she knew exactly who'd done this.

She'd gotten a bruise the same exact color when she was in boot camp. She'd been stupid enough to leave a piece of equipment loose, and it'd rolled into her leg, got her right above her knee. It could have been so much worse. Her first thought was that her mistake would ruin things for her, but no one had asked her who'd done it to her. "Take blame," the officer on duty had said and added, "Train, train, and train some more."

She sat on the toilet seat while her aunt worked to get Leeland bathed. The water turned a swampy color, and Corrine thought she should never have taken him out that night, all dirty like that. The two women had him toweled off before either of them said what they both knew was obvious.

"This is business for the sheriff," Sally said in her smoke-damaged voice—all flat now, no girl left in it.

When Sally opened her front door at 12:30 a.m. Deputy Spatz said he'd been dispatched to take a look at an injury. He came into the house and got a good look at the bruises on the boy's rear. Then, right there in front of the deputy, Sally asked Leeland what he'd been spanked with and Leeland said, "A white board. It has splinters."

"Who spanked you?" Sally was relentless.

Leeland looked at his mom and his eyes sparkled with tears. "Dad," he said.

That's when the deputy said with authority that Corrine mistrusted, and urgency she believed, "A doctor needs to see the injury, at the ER. Needs to be tonight."

Citizens tuned into a police scanner in the middle of that night might have started right in slinging mud at Luke Pruitt. Up to now we'd stayed clear of the man and look where that had got the boy. That night some of the blame was directed at Corrine. "School night," is how some folks started out when they repeated the story. And after all, she'd up and left her boy with her mean-as-shit ex.

But in the five days since Corrine had been back, we could see she'd changed and that was a hard thing for a Roswell girl to pull off. Her hair was brown again and shiny, and we would have bet it was wavy when she let it down, but she didn't, not that any of us had seen. You couldn't help but notice that girl. Back in the day her spiked, milky white hair and bug-black eyes pulled us in, and when we could we grabbed a look back over our shoulders. "There goes trouble," was a common comment on the character of that young mother heading into the Gentleman's Club or running into the Walgreens for that matter. It was just simpleminded, harmless gossip. It's not like we didn't know that the boy had a decent stepmom now and was in a good school. But we'd turned our back on that kid. Damage done, plain and simple.

For a good hour, Corrine sat in the ER waiting room. A sign over the door that the one and only nurse kept going through said Area 51. Stupid jokes did nothing to brighten the place as far as she could see. She could smell Leeland's clean hair.

He has no business being here.

The nastiness of the other smells—of boots caked with manure and foul body odors—made her ashamed to call Roswell home, but that was nothing new. Living with Luke in upstate New York, before she had even turned twenty, people would hear she was from Roswell and get all interested, but mostly it felt like they were making fun of her. Now she told people she was from New Mexico and left it at that. Some went right for the Indian stuff and spirituality—asked about Santa Fe and turquoise. No one mentioned aliens unless you gave them more information or acted spooky.

The tough, dirt-caked, sun-branded couple huddled in the corner, who were paying zero attention to the infant they'd left strapped into the banged-up car seat, convinced her that no alien with any sense would have chosen Roswell, New Mexico as the one town in all of the world to visit.

Sally rolled her eyes over at the couple and whispered, "I hear that family lives in one of the abandoned Atlas missile silos."

Corrine shrugged her shoulders and said, "No sign of intelligent life there."

"Sticks and stones," her aunt said, but Corrine knew she hadn't meant anything by it.

Leeland had fallen asleep, his head in Sally's lap. Corrine thought a six-year-old would be bigger and sturdier. His arms were like saplings.

When the detective came through the door to the ER, Corrine saw that he had intent written all over his face. He wasn't in uniform, but he might as well have been. People in the ER knew a Chaves County detective by the way he entered a room. He had a camera slung over his right shoulder, positioned for grabbing. She'd seen this man before. He hadn't been one of the regulars at the strip club where she'd worked, but she'd seen him strut into the place. She remembered that he'd handled rage with rage and arrogance with arrogance.

He crossed the room, and the couple with the baby moved the car seat out of his way. He knocked on the window at the registration desk. Deputy Spatz suddenly appeared from behind a closed door where Corrine figured he'd been sleeping.

Looking over the sampling of people in the room, the detective pointed at Corrine and said, "Only one family member comes back with the boy."

Sally said, "He's a kid."

But Corrine left her aunt there and walked with Leeland behind the nurse, the detective, and the deputy to a curtained-off, cell-like room. It had a sink and a bed way too high for Leeland to climb up on. A nurse got Leeland undressed, sat him on the bed, and stood back while the deputy showed the detective the evidence on Leeland's backside. Corrine imagined the bruise darkening on her son's tender skin. The detective took his time doing the inspection.

Experts now in bruises.

The two officers never asked the nurse a thing. The detective took pictures, and Leeland smiled when the nurse told him he could get under the white sheet and sleep while they waited for the doctor. Corrine thought to smile at the nurse for being kind to her son, but she felt sorry for the woman wearing that silly uniform that made her look like a preschooler. It had bears in pastel colors swinging on rope swings.

Ridiculous, she thought. Such an embarrassment when the deputy wore a gun on his hip, and the detective sported a coat and tie.

The deputy touched Corrine's elbow all respectful-like and called her Mrs. Pruitt. He said the case now officially belonged to Detective Craig Reynolds. He nodded at the detective, and said something about Craig knowing the Pruitt family and all, as if that signified something. Corrine wanted to correct him on her name, but he was already pulling the curtain open, leaving.

Once the deputy was gone the detective jumped into official language, saying *abuse* and *battery* and *foul play*; all the while he was sizing her up like she was merchandise at the

Walmart. She always knew the exact moment when a man started doing that, when he started taking her measure, and it was those moments when she knew—instinctively—that she had an advantage.

"Go get my aunt," she said to the nurse while the detective was still doing his calculations.

When Sally pushed her way past the curtains, Leeland's face lit up as if his fairy godmother had flown in. Sally held his hand while they all waited for the doctor to show up. When he finally did, he went to the sink, washed his hands slowly, and turned to the detective with a look that said, *No one's dying here.* He stepped to the bed but didn't bother to comfort Leeland. He said something about this being a job for Children, Youth, and Families.

"CYFD," he added with a sneer. He took a clipboard from the nurse and flipped pages and signed in several places. Then with the cap of the pen in his mouth, he asked, "Who's the mother here?"

Like he didn't know.

When Corrine nodded, he glared at her, then turned and left, all business in his stiff, shiny street shoes.

Detective Reynolds looked at Corrine and said, "I worked the Pruitt murder-suicide case."

"We know who you are," Sally said.

The next morning Corrine sat in her aunt's truck and watched Leeland head over to the group of kids standing by the old school bell. That morning when she got him up, he kept saying that he wasn't tired, but she knew he was. She'd fought with her aunt on that point.

"If I keep him out of school I'll look like the bad parent, when it's Luke who put that bruise on him." Sally hadn't liked any of it.

It was early, not yet eight, and Corrine had already gotten her aunt delivered to work. Now she had the day and her aunt's truck all to herself—at least until she picked up Leeland at three.

Driving aimlessly—any and all thoughts scattered—she passed by grimy Fat's Burritos. *This*, she thought, *summed up Roswell, New Mexico.* She kept going south on Main, driving too fast, when she made up her mind to have herself a glazed donut with coffee out of a mug at Daylite Donut—it was her vacation and all. But when she got to the fork—keeping right—she saw a minivan and a Suburban parked there in the lot with the pickups. A cluster of women—youngish and bouncy stay-at-home moms—had formed in the Daylite parking lot. *They certainly weren't staying home*, Corrine thought.

She made a U, surely illegal, and slammed the truck through its gears. She headed north past the handsome new Chaves County Sheriff's Department where she had to be with Leeland by four p.m. Four stoplights up, she watched as the New Mexico Military Institute came into view. The cadets were parading, and she rolled down her window to see if she could hear the commands. Being one of them had never crossed her mind; their honor code had been a joke with the Roswell High crowd in the late 1980s.

She took a right on Highway 380 and headed out to the Bottomless Lakes State Park. A lot of babies had been conceived in parked cars out at the lakes, she knew that for a fact. Corrine watched as the cap-rock north of the highway began to grow. Now she could see the outcropping of sheer rock that sealed it. Something was different about that rock. It always had looked to her like it was keeping something safe inside, probably safer than the silos. *There's probably silo babies too*, she caught herself thinking and shuddered.

It was only fourteen miles to the lakes, but going out there had felt like an adventure when she was a teenager. She passed the faded sign for Mini Donkeys that had been there for as long as she could remember. One day when she and Luke were taking a drive out to the lakes, Leeland had read it aloud. It was before they knew he could read. He'd read it hopefully as if he thought Luke might really stop and let him see the little donkeys. There'd never been any donkeys.

A few minutes later she pulled into the overlook and got out of the truck. The wind kicked her back a bit, made her think of spring days in Aunt Sally's backyard, fighting the wind as she tried to tan. All the boys she liked went for the tan girls.

Lea Lake was greenish-blue and smooth, as if the wind couldn't touch it, protected the way it was by the tall cliffs behind it. Boys bragged about climbing those cliffs, said there were caves in the limestone. There was always some guy trying to get some girl out there. And there were the stunts pulled on the lakes. Lazy Lagoon Lake was the prettiest of the nine, she thought, but swimming was allowed only in Lea.

"I can see bottom," one of her boyfriends had shouted after diving in. He'd come out gulping but swearing he'd seen pebbles and dirt. Well, she was certified in scuba now and could come out here and disprove the bottomless myth herself. That's if she had time to waste busting Roswell myths, and she didn't.

You could spend a lot of time around here doing that shit.

Her aunt had written last summer about the hundreds of dead fish floating up to the surface of Lea Lake on one single day in August. "The Russians," Sally had written.

Corrine grabbed at her hair and knotted it with the scrunchie she always wore around her wrist. She got back in the truck. One day she'd show Leeland the ocean, not some toxic sinkholes fourteen miles from a nowhere town.

That afternoon she was back at her aunt's house in time to change into her uniform, and she got to Christian Life Elementary early. She didn't get out of the pickup like the other moms who were standing around in the schoolyard visiting like it was their entire reason to live. Sharing recipes, Corrine told herself, but we knew, and she probably did too, that they were talking about her.

Word was out about the bruise and the trip to the ER. We were a touch shamed by it after all the gossiping we'd done—never letting up for years now with the Pruitt murder-suicide talk. But now it was a kid.

Leeland spotted the truck right off and did his straight-legged, stiff-armed walk over to her. He had never done that walk before this visit. She thought it was because he was shy around her. She had no idea what to do about that. She'd bought him a comic book, and she passed it over to him.

"Don't tell me—not Flash," he said and rubbed his forehead in disbelief. "Flash is faster than time and existence."

"You don't say..." She smiled.

In the reception area of the Chaves County Sheriff's Department there were cameras focused on the doorway. Corrine resisted waving, crossed the room, and leaned on the counter. She watched the clerk, who was apparently mesmerized by the amber dots and dashes on her computer screen. Corrine was not into computers and couldn't believe that her ex would seriously know how to use one. But Leeland had told her about his dad sitting up nights at the computer; it was as if Leeland was proud of his dad for being so smart. "He has AOL," Leeland had said.

The clerk knew she was standing there. Corrine waited, thankful that the girl looked younger than her, hadn't known her in school.

Corrine reached down and took hold of Leeland's thin wrist. Her fingers circled clear around. She held tight, and put her mouth up against the speaker and used her US Navy voice. It was respectful. She'd been taught when she first joined to assume that whoever she addressed was her superior until she knew different. One of her first commanding officers had said, "It's all acting."

And so Corrine said, "Ma'am, I'm here for an interview."

She watched as the clerk traced her finger down through a list of names on the screen and asked, "Corrine Pruitt with the victim?"

Corrine nodded. It wasn't worth correcting every mistake.

"You'll be in interrogation room A with Detective Roseann Powers. Somebody will call you to come back. Sign in, please." The clerk pushed a clipboard through the little tunnel, and when Corrine reached for it, their hands touched.

She saw Luke's signature up near the top. He always signed his full name. She would know his hand, with its big puffy P, anywhere. She signed in and, pushing the board back, said, "Can I ask you..." Corrine kept her voice soft, "did Luke Pruitt see this lady detective or did he see Detective Reynolds?"

The girl checked her back and said, "Detective Powers interviewed him. But don't be thinking of her like some weakling. Detective Reynolds might have special talent with punks, but Detective Powers never walks off a case."

"So, did she arrest Luke?"

"He's the father, right? No way, no arrests on the first report. Fathers get a whole long list of rights."

Corrine said, "I wait, right?" And then, when the girl stood and leaned on the counter to see the boy, Corrine remembered her son and wished she could just stoop down and tell him something about him being the sunshine of her life, that she'd always be around, like the stuff her mother-in-law used to say. But she was no liar.

"Cute cowboy," the girl said. And in a whisper she offered, "Your ex tried to sweet-talk me and told me a sob story about how he'd missed his kid the last two days. And he said he wanted to raise him right, but that the boy had been talking in school, and he couldn't tolerate that."

Corrine said, "That's Luke. A paper tiger."

Leeland said, "I won't talk anymore in school. I already promised."

Corrine put her mouth right at the speaker and said, "Be careful. Luke Pruitt knows how to ooze that Code of the West talk with the best of them." She patted Leeland on the head mostly to keep him quiet, but a love pat is what she liked to think it was.

Just then Detective Powers came out and took them to a room with glass across one wall. Corrine knew it exposed her, but to what all she didn't know.

"How long have you served?" the detective asked.

"Two years."

"And Leeland, here, has been in the custody of his father?"

"Yes," Corrine knew most people judged her for that, but she wasn't sure it was what the detective was going for.

"I still have legal custody. I didn't give him up. We share the legal part. And he has a good stepmother now. I stay in touch with her."

The detective didn't write anything down. She was listening like she needed to remember what Corrine was saying. Then she asked Leeland where he went to school.

"Christian Life," he said.

"Home of the Eagles," the detective said, and the boy nodded.

Corrine said, "Can you tell me what happened with Luke this morning? I'm in the dark here, and I don't want to be caught off guard." She wanted to pat her boy's head again and wondered if she wasn't acting.

The detective looked right into her eyes and blinked before she said, "I can tell you that I had him look at the photos Detective Reynolds took in the ER. I had to advise him that there would be no criminal charges. I left that to the end." Corrine shook her head in disgust.

"I'm referring the case to CYFD as required by law. They'll open a file. But they are slow. Just warning you."

Leeland shifted in his seat.

"They'll investigate as a civil matter. I'll press them to contact you prior to your leaving for Washington." Corrine didn't remember telling her where she was stationed.

"I'll make arrangements for Leeland to be dropped off next Sunday with Reverend Carter Glen. Much better that way. Safer. I informed Mr. Pruitt he can pick Leeland up there."

Leeland said, "Angie can come get me."

Corrine caught Leeland looking across the room to the corner where a white board was standing. The detective must have caught it too because she said, "We'll keep the paddle here. It will be placed into evidence pending the full investigation."

When they all stood, the handcuffs on the detective's belt caught the edge of the table and Leeland said, "Sorry."

Going along to get along—we saw a lot of that in this town. Apologizing too. Leeland was learning fast—no thanks to us.

Luke

1998

Luke drove his pickup like he was leading an uphill charge, heading due west out of Roswell on Pine Lodge Road. Forty-three miles would put them in the Capitan Mountains, and then a turn south and another three mountain miles would get them to the campground. Since the time the sharp-edged Capitans suddenly appeared in the windshield of his Ford F-150, he'd passed one jeep, one genuine pickup, and an ancient, canary-yellow 4Runner, which was nothing more than a pathetic pickup with a cracked fiberglass shell over the bed. He wasn't planning on passing another vehicle now that he had turned onto what was labeled on a weathered road sign as a primitive county road. The campground was usually empty, even in the middle of summer. The Pruitt boys were banking on that.

"It's not a road race," his wife said.

"Weren't you the one was whining for a getaway?" Luke

87

said as he looked over at Angie. She was picking her face. Sickening. But he had his mind on the do-gooder forest morons, protecting thickets of forsaken junipers that sucked up water like it was free. The same idiots who protected fire-ripe, tall grass. One flash from the southwest sky in drought season, which was now, and poof, flames would jump, leave the canyons charred and grim like the fire in the Sacramento Mountains his father had always jabbered about. You could still see those scars.

God, he hated those do-gooders, and he hated Angie. Hated the way she'd held him back from living his life. He wanted her gone.

As they climbed up in elevation, ponderosa pines added shade, and if he'd been willing to take the washboard road a little easier—he was in the lead, not about to eat Stralin's dust—Luke might have heard some mountain sounds, birds maybe.

As it was, all he heard was Leeland claiming he could smell the mountains and Angie, in that thick-as-mud voice of hers, saying, "What's the rush?" She always sounded as if she was yawning or swollen. Luke looked over at her. Enough was enough.

He needed her to shut up so he could get his mind around making his move. He didn't need her, never had, and if he didn't do it now it was going to be like this forever, with her yapping about nothing and everything.

"Just shut up, Angie," he said and shoved the truck through its gears, and the pines began to grow taller, and all that quivering at the top of the trees turned his stomach.

He couldn't look.

When he was a little kid, younger than Leeland was now, his family went up to the high country once. When the road got narrow with deep ruts on both sides, and the sunlight began to flicker through the tall trees, he had gotten sick. And it was the real thing. Barfing and all. His dad had stopped to let him get out and throw up, but then he told him he'd have to hold it from then on like it was something anyone could do, holding back vomit. And so his mom had him put his head in her lap and told him to look up at the tall trees. She'd said they looked like Titans—impossible to knock down—and tried to get him to speculate about how many stories tall they were.

He didn't care about those trees, but he said, "Three stories, I bet."

And then he remembered his dad saying, "There's no fuckin three-story buildings in New Mexico."

If Luke could have gotten away with it, he would have said, *How do you know?* But with his dad, turnabout was not fair play. His dad liked to stab his long brown finger into Luke's little-boy chest and say, "So you're sure you're not telling me something you know to be fuckin' false?" But it wasn't false. Everybody in the Hondo Valley knew the mansion on the Diamond Crown Ranch was three stories tall.

So Luke kept his mouth shut and held the vomit back until he could feel holes burning through his throat.

Why his mom had ever chosen Payton Pruitt, Luke couldn't figure. His dad didn't stand out for anything at all. It had to have been dumb luck. That was the only explanation.

Luke caught sight of another wilderness sign and he slowed to read it—Capitan Mountains Wilderness: Lincoln National Forest. It was an odd-shaped sign on a metal post. *Ugly thing to be putting in a prissy wilderness*, Luke thought. He slowed down to read the smaller print. Luke read aloud between clenched teeth, "Designed as an area for the use and enjoyment of the American people."

Playground for trust fund babies was all he could think, and right here practically in his backyard.

"Are we enjoying ourselves yet?" Luke asked and hit the gas hard. He kept his eyes on the hillsides. In his book, the rocky slopes of the Capitans were meant for grazing sheep, not meant to be turned into some stupid wilderness, the GD culture of the rural West was at stake.

"Those East Coast morons are always surprised when a place like this suddenly catches fire, even now when they've got Smokey protecting us all with his superior knowledge."

Angie said, "You know that they saved that cub from these mountains and nursed him back to life. He's an orphan now, Luke."

He looked her way, blew out the smallest breath of air, and said, "Poof."

He slammed his fist on the steering wheel, hit the brakes, and stopped short. Leeland grabbed the back of his seat and shouted, "Did you see elk, Dad? I'd really love to see one of the huge bulls." On the way out of town Leeland said his teacher had told him that elks stayed together in families, survived that way.

My own GD son—a pussy.

How stupid could the kid be? He hadn't stopped for elk. He'd done it to kick up a dust cloud, a signal for his brother. Luke sat there in the stillness and watched in his rearview mirror while Stralin and his family appeared, taking it slow for their baby daughter, no doubt. And then Luke, just for his own benefit, smiled big and gunned it. He knew where he was going. He had his plans made whether Stralin approved or not, and he didn't need any more wilderness signs. He'd have plowed one of them down if it weren't for the metal.

"Did you bring a bat?" he asked Leeland as he kept his foot on the gas. But Leeland didn't answer; instead he said, "My teacher said elks have their summer coats clear into fall."

"Higher ground. Gonna keep on trying till I reach my highest ground," Angie sang off-key.

My mom could sing.

Angie had bought a few of his mother's record albums at

the yard sale out on the Diamond Crown three years back, including the Stevie Wonder.

"Stupid to pay for what's ours," Luke had said, but he let Angie pay. He'd already taken the *Talking Book* album, the one with Stevie wearing a brown velvet getup on the cover. It'd been his mom's favorite, but she'd had to hide the album from his dad. Luke knew where she hid things. Cornrows could make Payton Pruitt crazy the same way Angie's acne scars made him nuts.

Get through this sissy vacation, tell Stralin, and then he was out.

The old Boy Scout campground was, in fact, deserted. Stralin and Luke, with the help of their three boys, got working first on the tents. Stralin was in good humor, not all distracted like he'd been before he got his bankruptcy papers filed at the courthouse that week. Luke had figured out what was going on with his brother's state of mind. It was bankruptcy that was freezing up Stralin's face whenever Luke had seen him in the last month. He'd recognized it because he was feeling the same way waiting for that stupid Children's Services shit to be over and done with. It'd kept him in GD limbo for over a year now.

"A good name is more desirable than riches," Stralin had said to Luke when they met up at the courthouse that week. "Now I got nothing," Stralin added.

"Between you and me, there's nothing to be ashamed of. Bankruptcy is in the law for a reason," Luke had told his brother and it wasn't a lie, not the bit about the law.

But the shame thing was racking up on them. We couldn't help but notice. You couldn't keep something like bankruptcy quiet and you couldn't blame us for talking stink when Stralin was driving around town in a new pickup. Still, when it came to Stralin, someone was always willing to add, "He'd do to ride the river with." And besides, it was not like their parents gave them a dime the way some ranch families did, leaving their kids an outfit, a herd, something other than talk. And then we heard about the vacation deal the Pruitt boys were taking, and near as we could tell it was a good sign.

It was cool up there in the mountains, and as their camp took shape Luke figured it would be an okay time. He'd clear his mind. Clear the deck. His plan was to move on with Deona Flood and leave behind the East Grand Plains methane fields that Angie was rooted in. Deona had already said she'd work a ranch with him. She said she could cook too, and she knew how to show him respect. Said she'd follow his rules for Leeland. "Iron fist," he'd told her and she'd agreed. Plus she had a daughter of her own and knew what it took.

Get my real life started, finally.

Luke knew his brother. Stralin wouldn't like Deona Flood any better than he liked Angie. It was marrying divorcées that Stralin objected to. He liked things simple. *Keep it simple, stupid.*

Maybe he didn't need to check in with Stralin, didn't need to tell him. Their smart-ass old dad had had a saying about that: *Don't tell all you know, keep some things to yourself. Life is on a need-to-know basis.*

That'll work.

He watched Angie now as she leaned into the bed of the truck. Pretty clear she could damn well fend for herself. She'd breathe her last breath on Hummingbird Lane, her beloved hollyhocks—wood weeds—blocking the front door. She'd be eighty and still training GD honeysuckle to climb up strings she hung at the kitchen window. "But she won't have Leeland around to sprinkle hollyhock seeds like some faggot fairy prince," he said under his breath and felt good about the way he was looking out for his son. And while he was changing things, he'd stop that prancing thing his son did, make him walk like a real boy.

"I don't care about going afoot to the top of the mountain," Stralin tossed out suddenly. He was that way—making announcements after long silences. Luke watched as Stralin checked the top button on his starched shirt. Luke laughed. The guy had to know he was funny. He'd learned to be that way as a kid out on the Diamond Crown. Most times that fool stuff Stralin pulled took the edge off things. Stralin never failed to play that dumb-shit role, just like he never failed to back down. Luke got that, and so he gave his brother a friendly shove.

"That mountain?" Luke pointed. "That's a cakewalk, big brother."

With the three tents up, one for the boys, one for Luke and Angie, and the other for Stralin, his wife, and their baby daughter, the brothers stood back and admired the setup. Then Stralin herded the boys back to the trucks to haul out the cots, the Coleman gear, and the campfire chairs.

"Leave them .22s in the truck," Luke shouted. "Safer."

Stralin nodded and said, "So you brought the family heirlooms, did you?"

Stralin's wife, Trudy, shot Luke a look. She had this way about her where she'd look at him a second or two longer than was necessary. He didn't look away. As usual, she had a camera hanging around her neck, and the minute Stralin set the camp chairs down she took possession of one and sat with the six-month-old in her lap. That baby was the first Pruitt girl in a long line of males. Too bad Linda Pruitt had not waited around long enough to meet a girl baby.

"Put some coffee on," Luke said to Angie, who had just said something about it being nice and peaceful up here right before she took a seat next to Trudy.

God, Angie isn't even cute.

Angie wasn't moving.

Just then one of the three kids asked, "Can we go explore?"

But they were already in a mad dash uphill. Leeland was in the lead. Stralin didn't bother to check with Luke before he said, "Watch yourselves. If you trip, you're gonna catch some high ground."

The boys kept going and Luke shouted, "Keep your eyes peeled for Bambi...it's a wilderness, you know." And then he turned to Angie and said, "Coffee?"

Finally Angie said she'd set the fire, like it was her idea, and Trudy, who was a decent cook, said she'd get cooking. And so the brothers wandered down by the trucks and leaned up against Luke's pickup, visiting.

"It comes down to a controlled descent," Luke explained to Stralin as he pointed with his beer to the stash of rappelling gear he'd left in the back of his pickup. "I'll talk the boys through it."

They'd gone on like that for a while, skirting any subjects closer to home, and then Luke smelled the wood smoke and pointed the way back to camp. The two of them must have heard the truck approaching about the same time, and they turned and watched the flash of milky green through the trees.

"Smokey Bear Ranger is on his way," Luke said. But the two of them kept heading toward the fire, where Luke could see the women were standing still, watchful.

The truck was taking it slow and then the engine stopped, and soon a man in mustard-yellow boots approached. He came up on them with the deliberate swagger of a house cat sure of its next meal. It was that walk that made Luke start right in with the man, staring at him as if it were a staring contest, and he was going to win. Luke held his beer chest level, not in greeting, but as if it were a badge. The man, who wore a cedar-colored uniform, had a paper in his hand, and as he got close to Angie he said, "Camping tips."

Luke was still staring at the man, who had taken off his Forest Service cowboy hat and was dusting it off. He smelled like a ripe cigar. Luke took the paper from his wife and took his eyes off the man long enough to read it through. "Would you look at this, Stralin? Our own Lincoln County Sheriff over there in that brain trust town, Carrizozo, has come up with some brilliant camping tips, and the park ranger here was thoughtful enough to bring them along."

"I'm not a park ranger," the man said as he looked over at the trucks. "I'm a law enforcement officer of the US Forest Service, Smokey Bear District. My boss is the District Ranger."

The officer walked back down to the two pickups and began taking down the license plate numbers in an official-looking notebook that he then stowed securely in his breast pocket. He took his time securing the button on the pocket. And then he patted the badge that covered the pocket and headed back to the campfire.

Stralin took the paper from Luke and read silently. Luke could see that it was all act with the officer, like he was some Sunday shopper, just looking around. But he was taking in everything about them. The man spotted the ax and said, "Keep that ax away from those boys I saw up on the rise. You got flashlights?"

Stralin answered, "Yes, sir," with a big slow nod of his head.

"When you folks are ready to turn in, let your campfire die down and then break up the coals. It's always a good idea to spread them out and soak them with water or cover them up good with sand."

Stralin tried to hand the officer the paper, but the man said, "Keep it."

Luke pointed at the paper and said, "Good tips."

"Had dinner?" Angie asked.

"Appreciate the invite, but I'm on duty," he said. Luke thought the man seemed set on liking her.

"Y'all local?" the officer asked.

God, Luke hated a poser. He snorted some beer through his nose and turned his back on the man as Angie whispered, "Play fair, Luke."

Stralin said in the voice Luke had heard every night at the dinner table when they were kids, "We've got a fresh pot of coffee on."

The officer accepted the offer, and when Angie left to get him a cup Stralin pointed at Luke and said, "That's Luke Pruitt, my kid brother. That's his wife Angie getting the coffee. They're Roswell people. I'm Stralin Pruitt." He never introduced his wife but continued: "Me and my family live and work over at a ranch around Corona, near Ramon." Stralin pointed north and then, holding his arm steady, rotated it east and said, "You gotta know where you're at to know you're there."

Luke had heard Stralin say that a dozen times and figured he practiced it so that it always sounded like he'd just thought it up. Luke wasn't interested in hearing any more good ideas from the forest ranger, and so he just walked off. As he brushed by his wife, who was returning with the coffee, he said, "Way-to-me," as if she were a sheepdog and he was giving her commands. She smiled like she loved him—her scars stretching this way and that, and he handed her his empty beer can.

Before he got any distance at all the officer called out, "Take care now, Mr. Pruitt." Luke didn't answer. He could hear Stralin visiting with the man, showing him that he was a regular guy and not just some bankrupt cowboy.

About two hundred yards off from the camp, Luke spotted the boys. He could see the color of their shirts way up the slope, and he could hear that they were happy. It should have felt good. He was smart enough to know that. But he stood there telling himself that if you let up on a kid like Leeland, the next thing you know he'd be thinking he could win every argument, and so Luke yelled, "Get your sorry butt down here, Leeland, and bring your cousins with you." That was all it took to get the three boys sliding down the slope.

Luke pointed towards camp and turned to go back. From behind him he heard Stralin's youngest boy, the one not so afraid of adults, say, "Leeland lost a tooth."

"You don't say," Luke said and kept walking, the kids behind him.

"Yes, sir. He was eating a donut with Angie," the kid said like it was way beyond funny. "He's got it in his pocket."

"Well, Leeland can wish all he wants for a fairy to show up at this camp, but it's not gonna happen," Luke said.

Stralin's older son said, "Grandmother wanted us to believe in fairies."

Luke stopped, turned around, and said, "Give him the tooth, Leeland. What are you, five or something?"

"I'm seven, Dad," Leeland said as he patted himself down as if he were a comedian. Finally, he found the tooth in the pocket of his shirt, handed it to his cousin, and then took off for the camp.

"Seven-year-olds don't God damn skip."

When they got close to camp, Luke heard his brother say, "No, sir, no one on a ranch is ever caught up."

Well, Luke figured, he hadn't missed anything. He'd heard that one before too.

After dinner, for maybe fifteen minutes, Luke stayed off in the woods, smelling the sticky sweet marshmallows held too close to the fire. He'd never been a Boy Scout, but he knew how to keep a marshmallow from turning into a lump of ash. The scorched smell and the bursts of boy voices hit a raw nerve.

It was his mother hovering near, just watching—full of opinions. She would have sat the ranger down and explained to him how the Endangered Species Act was upsetting the balance. And she would have had the officer grinning. He probably would have stayed for dinner. *No, that's wrong*, Luke thought, doing that would have pissed off his dad—*but if his dad had not been there...*

At bedtime his mom always stood in the doorway of the bedroom he had shared with Stralin, arms straight up braced in the doorjamb as if she had wings, humming, still dressed in her jeans, waiting for his dad to take his two long steps down the hallway, and drop like a sack of shit into bed. Then Luke would hear whatever dog his mom had at the time settle in under the front steps and yip once or twice for her to come out one last time. Stralin would already be asleep. His brother escaped his family the minute he heard his father's second boot hit the floor. The night silence had always scared Luke, but still he'd lay there in the cold little room wishing for it. It was never good to wake up Payton Pruitt after he'd called it a day.

She'd protected those sheepdogs.

Suddenly, there in the forest, he couldn't hear his brother or the boys or the fire popping. There was silence all around him. It was so damn silent he didn't know where he was.

"Mom, you should have let me kill Dad," he said aloud through clenched teeth. It just came up in his gut sometimes, made his breathing quicken, and it was better to just say it.

It was thick darkness in the woods. He kicked the roots he'd been careful of earlier. Kicked hard until he could feel his right big toe at the top of his boot. He kept at it the way he used to as a boy until it smarted. Back then it had always been black and blue.

He wished he had brought his mother's letter with him on the trip. Looking at it helped.

It's his doing, Luke. That was how his mother started the letter. Luke headed uphill thinking that was the way towards the campfire and kept going until he took a full gulp of wood smoke. It caused his eyes to tear.

You'll forever stay in my heart, kiddo, but I can't stay around.

She knew he'd recognize those lyrics. She'd loved that sunshine song.

Had she written the same things to Stralin? Had she told him to beware harm to innocents? That, she'd said, would eat you alive.

But brothers didn't talk about those things, and Luke hadn't taken the damn dog either.

"The dog just took off," is what we heard Luke saying out there at the yard sale on the Diamond Crown. But we all knew that collie was taken in by one of the old Mexican families in the Hondo Valley, and those folks called her Linda's Dog. It was a good name for a dog.

"Fine by me," Luke caught himself saying and stopped long enough to wipe at his face and pick up a few sturdy sticks for the fire.

Angie held out the s'more she'd made for him and patted the camp chair next to her.

He sat. "Ick, you got that sticky Boy Scout treat all over my chair. Am I right?" he said, mostly to keep his mom happy, to keep her away from the fire and to keep his heart from making the thumping sound that had turned his ears hot.

There was a second before anyone knew how to respond, and then Leeland said, "Sticky butt," which made his cousins giggle cautiously.

"Dad," Leeland said, "Uncle Stralin was telling us about John Wayne's 26 Bar Ranch. Maybe we can go there next year on vacation?"

Luke made like he was stuck to his chair and, after standing to check the seat of his pants, said, "You paying?"

Leeland started in talking fast: "Just thinking, sir, that since you and Uncle Stralin have registered the 26 Bar brand like the Duke's is all…" Leeland said.

"Let's see if we survive *this* vacation first," Luke said and watched everyone relax. It was a good-natured thing for him to say, hopeful and all. Luke felt proud of himself then and wished his good old dad had been here to see it all.

Then, against his better judgment, Luke let the smoke from the fire take form, and he saw in that form his mother's fit silhouette. Her ghost was walking away, all saucy in her black dress boots, and sure of herself as she could be.

"Who wants a bedtime story?" Luke asked as he waved off the s'mores mess Angie was pushing on him again. Trudy raised her hand up in the air and the boys all followed, waving and bouncing on their crossed legs like little girls.

"See that flash?" Luke pointed north, high up on the ridge none of them could see now in the dark.

"Here we go," Angie said.

"Here's the story. Way back after the war, the last one where we kicked ass anyway, this Roswell guy named Jim Ragsdale and his woman friend were right here at this very camp." He pointed to the fire. "He and this girl were in the back of his pickup, buck naked."

"Luke," the women sang out, but no one was stopping him now and the boys, hands over their mouths, were giggling.

"For real?" one of them asked.

Luke continued, "Something made the two of them look north." He pointed off to his left. "You see, they didn't have any fire—well, not campfire, let's say—to ruin their vision like we do."

He softened his voice, hunkered down with his elbows on his knees, looked at each of the three boys, and said, "Sitting here like this before this fire, something could be right on us before our pupils get all big trying to adjust." Luke saw his son open his eyes wide.

"Anyhow, there they were in the flatbed in total darkness

when suddenly all hell broke loose. There was this flash brighter than a welder's arc. Something was coming right for their campground and it wasn't any stupid weather balloon."

The little boys refolded their legs and tried not to look in the direction Luke had pointed. Luke tossed some sticks into the fire and it hissed.

"And whatever it was crashed about sixty feet from the pickup."

"Sixty feet," one of the boys repeated in disbelief.

"Ragsdale said he thought it was going to hit right smack in the campground. Said it took off the tops of trees. Topped them. But that was nothing compared to the little people who climbed out of the spacecraft."

"They came out of a real flying saucer?" Leeland asked. "They had eyes and everything?"

Luke nodded. "Arrow-eyed. But the big brass at the Army Air Force Base got ahold of the spacecraft, and they hauled it off. The whole mess scared Ragsdale so bad he kept quiet until just recent. He didn't think people would buy his story, and he didn't want folks telling him it was some fairytale. Forty years he kept it all back."

"Why was he naked?" one of the boys asked, and Luke, thinking it was Leeland, said, "Don't be stupid." But it just made everyone laugh.

Then there was a lot of giggling around the fire with the three boys pushing each other until their world became a little less scary.

Finally Leeland said, "Those aliens had to land so they could see humans close up with their own eyes. I'm thinking they have to report back."

Before anyone could say another word Stralin said, "Tomorrow we rappel. Uncle Luke was trained by the army, so it's gonna be the real deal. I say we turn in."

"Put it gently between the sheets," Angie said, sounding as

if she were already half asleep. He hated that saying, but she always said it was a family saying, and she was sticking with it.

Trudy said, "You boys need to be real careful out there tomorrow."

"It's not all that dangerous," Luke said. "If we wanted a padded room we should have stayed home where everyone's safe. Besides, what difference does another bruise make on a kid?"

Trudy was giving him that look again, but Luke didn't care. He started in on the fire, kicking dirt on it and everyone followed.

With the fire out, the stars seemed to be dropping down on them. Leeland moved close to Angie. She put her arm around his shoulder, and he said, "The officer said it's a great place for stargazing. I bet that man and his girlfriend were doing that."

"Real smart kid, isn't he? A real problem solver," Luke said to Stralin as the two of them followed the three boys to their tent. "But turn him loose outside, and he's helpless. I have to get him on a ranch before he goes totally pussy."

Stralin said, "Mom always said ranch-raised is best."

"And I'm leaving Angie. It's not up for discussion. I'm gonna ranch with a gal I met at work, and she'll get Leeland straight. That's all you need to know."

The two of them just stood there outside the tent while the boys got ready for bed. And then Luke tied the loops on the door flaps with special knots he was proud of knowing, and when Stralin said, "G'night, boys" his two boys said, "Goodnight, Daddy" and Luke decided, *what the hell*, and said, "See you in the sunshine."

We didn't know a thing about Stralin's wife, Trudy, except that her people were from West Texas. But we learned that summer she was a picture-taker because a photo of that family vacation appeared in the local paper. They credited her for that photo. The caption said, "Locals find ways to keep cool in the dog days of summer." We thought they looked happy—an all-American family standing there in front of two clean pickups.

Deputy Greenwood

Morning July 6, 2005

"What do you say we stop first at the Moon Café?" Paula said, and Greenwood turned to give her his full attention.

"Rumor mill has somebody thinking we're offering a cash reward for information on Leeland's whereabouts. Some guy called Dispatch and said he'd be at the Moon if we were interested in paying. Wouldn't give a name."

Their plans had been to go direct to the Hondo School. The school counselor was on the road from Alto to meet them there.

"Sure, the Moon is on the way," Greenwood said even though he could feel the tightness in his chest that he recognized as urgency to get someplace fast. He resisted the urge to rub his chest. *Think this through*, he said to himself.

"Do they know you there at the café, Paula?"

He looked over again as she made a show of looking herself over—looking down at her brown uniform. She tapped her shiny badge.

"Not so much," she said.

A girl from Jersey can look out for herself, he thought, but didn't say.

"I'll go in the back to the kitchen and visit with the twins while you check out the café," he said.

"Light and sweet, right?" she said.

She'd told him that was how you ordered coffee with plenty of cream and real sugar in a New Jersey Dunkin' Donut. "They'll take you for a local if you order that way, and in no time, they'll remember you and how you take your coffee," she'd explained.

The last thing he needed was coffee. He kept his hands on the wheel and started talking himself out of panic. *There's time,* he told himself.

They passed over the cattle guard. The reporter was sitting on the hood of her car holding her tiny phone up to the sky as if making an offering to some western deity. Greenwood pulled up alongside Deputy Conley's truck, and seeing him slumped there he felt sorry for the young man he'd banished to keep watch outside the gate. He thought Conley might have been dozing, but that was okay by him.

"Duff is holding a press conference here at noon," Greenwood said.

"So, I heard," Conley said. "Put some spin on his side of it I suspect."

"You're in charge, not that gal over there. And don't answer any of her questions or Duff's for that matter. Sheriff will be here. Accommodate him, of course, but take charge, and if you run into trouble blame me." He looked around and then added, "Have them set up right under the flag, and if I'm not back in time take some good notes."

Conley looked up at the sky and then snuck a look at Paula.

"You know Investigator Magliaro, don't you?" Greenwood said.

"By reputation," Conley said and used his index finger to tap his forehead and point at her. She did the same. Everyone smiled.

"Cell phone," Paula said as she reached into her breast pocket and took out a card. She passed it across to Greenwood who handed the card off to the young deputy.

A mile down the road Greenwood slowed to a stop and pointed over toward the lean-to.

"See that there?" he said.

"What am I looking at?" she asked and shaded her eyes.

"There's a clubhouse there off about one hundred yards. Long story short, I checked it out this morning. It's a neat little hideout. Pretty sure it's Leeland's."

"Okay, sure, I see it now."

"I'm leaving it off the record."

"Never saw it," she said.

He pointed at the run-down home and said, "Course, at that time a posse of porch watchers saw me head out there. I warned them off, but I suspect the place will be cleaned out by dark."

"Could you send Conley down?" she asked.

"Yeah, after the press corps leaves. Yes."

Paula's phone rang and she identified herself. Greenwood slowed because when you got a good connection in the Hondo Valley you stayed put. Paula put her phone on speaker. It was Rosalie again. The Hondo post office which she had run since he could remember sat on the service road down off Highway 70, and when she was not busy, you'd find her sitting on the porch watching the highway traffic. He thought he heard an eighteen-wheeler in the background of the call.

"If you're heading to the school, don't. The feed salesman, Smoot, is back doing what he does best. He's snooping around. He was tight with Luke Pruitt. Kisses up to the foremen at the big outfits. When his truck pulls up here folks find another

place to take their business. He's up at the school now. He has
no business up there, just looking for Leeland, and no telling
what he'd do to that boy. So I called over at St. Jude's and
Father Frank is going to open up the sanctuary. Trust me, it's
a better meeting place. Park back under the trees."

"Got ya," Paula said. "We'll head there soon. The school
counselor is on his way to the school though."

"He drives that step-up van, doesn't he?" Rosalie was
talking to herself. "I'll take care of it," she said.

"Helpful bunch," Paula said when she ended the call.

The tension in his chest was not letting up. He knew
Rosalie—he had been called out to help when the marine
chaplain came to the Valley to tell Rosalie that her son had
been killed in Afghanistan in friendly fire—and knew that
today she was scared for Leeland. He looked at his watch—
reminded himself to log her call as coming in at nine a.m. The
tightness became pain, and he tried to picture something
peaceful.

The front lot of the Moon Café, which sat right off the
highway, was full. He hadn't intended to park there anyway,
and he pulled up behind a shed at the back of the place.

"Hello, ladies," he said as the screen door banged behind
him. The two very little women who were working at a short
metal table turned their backs on him long enough for him to
read their names embroidered in white stitches on the back of
their matching blue blouses. Melissa and Melinda. These shirts
suddenly reminded him of the blue gym suits girls in his high
school days wore. He'd seen Melissa and Melinda wearing
bowling shirts and chef's jackets—always embroidered. He
wondered if they did their own embroidery work. He'd ask
them someday when things were not so urgent.

"Melissa, Melinda," he said and they both grinned. He
always tried, really tried, to keep them straight—to tell them
apart—but always failed even though one of them had an even

smaller head than her twin sister and could not speak. It was
the names that got him and the stab of misery that knocked
him down every time he saw them. They were nearly the same
age as he was. He'd heard about them the whole time he was
growing up.

There had been so many theories about them. Some
people said it was water on the brain. But his mother had
always corrected people. "Inflammation," she'd say as if
people were idiots to spread rumors about water. "The girls
were fine at birth. Like two perfect pink peaches," she'd
sometimes bother to explain, and she knew what she was
talking about because she had been best friends with the girls'
mother. They'd been pregnant together, and his mother said
that meant something.

"It was ticks got those girls," his mother had told him
when he was older so he would not worry, but he had.

Things could have been so different.

As little children the girls had lived up in Albuquerque at
the Carrie Tingley Hospital, and when they simply did not
grow like other children the rumors flew that they were alien
babies who had been left behind. Then they moved home, and
their mom opened the café in the Valley. Their dad, like his,
was long gone. Right now their mom was out front at the
counter taking orders and filling honest-to-goodness vintage
Fiesta coffee mugs. The place was known for its Hondo Valley
beef burritos and for being the only decent place to pee
between Roswell and Ruidoso.

"Got a minute?" Greenwood asked and saw that it was
Melissa who patted her sister on her tiny, gloved hand.

"Let me talk to the sheriff now," she said.

He vowed he'd remember that it was Melissa who could
speak.

Melinda kept working. She was wrapping and stacking
foil-wrapped burritos in piles of six.

He stepped over to the screen door and Melissa followed. He pointed up toward the Bounty. "What you hearing about the Pruitt family?" he asked.

"Mean mama. Nasty no-good father," she said. "Take my word for it, and Melinda agrees, don't you, sis?" She stopped and looked at her sister, who seemed to be in her own world.

Melissa began to pull her gloves off. They were much too big for her perfect little hands. "That mama gives Melinda bad dreams."

"Have they been around this summer? How about this weekend?"

"Too damn cheap," she shouted and Melinda heard this and stopped what she was doing to point at her sister and nod her tiny head.

"How about Mr. and Mrs. Duff? They stop by much?"

"We see Mr. Fancy Pants on the news. He's too good for the Moon."

"This weekend did any of the Pruitts come around? The kids maybe?"

"No," she said and pushed her glasses back up on the bridge of her nose with her freed left hand. "But Leeland's friend came by here with a truck load of friends right at the crack of dawn on Stampede Sunday. That'd be Joseph Salado. They ordered a Moon Café dozen. Thirteen, don't you know." This last bit was shouted and in response, Melinda clapped her hands.

His mother had called them mirror twins. One was a leftie and one a righty and one had straight hair and the other curly. But they both wore hairnets these days so it was hard to tell.

"I'm sweet on Joseph. He puts butterflies in my stomach." She patted her stomach and then used her little hands to mimic butterflies fluttering.

"Could Leeland have been out in the truck waiting?"

"No way. That is a long road to the Bounty. No way José.

And besides, I looked. That's when I saw they had Yolanda with them."

Greenwood took his notebook out and wrote down the names Joseph Salado and Yolanda, which pleased Melissa.

"Say, can you tell me if anyone in the Pruitt family wears glasses?"

"Leeland, of course." She laughed so hard that she spit. "He's just like Melinda and me." She pointed at her own face and her rather small glasses.

"Thank you," he said. "You ladies keep your eyes open, would you?" He wanted to shake her hand, but she'd pulled the gloves back on.

"Back to work," he said and she repeated it. Then they both spotted Paula coming around the corner with two coffees and Melissa reached out and put her arms around his waist— where she could reach, which was not far—and then tickled him.

Looking at Paula, Melissa said, "Cute girl." And because he did not want to be rude he said, "Yes, she is."

He stepped outside and held the screen door open with his back while Paula handed him the two coffees. She reached in her pocket for a card and passed it to Melissa.

"If you see or hear anything about Leeland give me a call. He could be in danger," she added, which didn't seem like protocol, but it was so damn true.

On the short walk to the truck Paula said, "Change of plans. I just talked to Father Frank and he's learned somehow that Leeland is with the Salado family at the end of White Goat Road. I'm betting you know them."

The disappointment—or was it relief—was so sudden that Greenwood had to steady himself by backing up into the truck. "Run, Leeland, run," he said softly. Then he watched as Paula reached out for him, but only briefly because Melinda—who was the smaller woman—was trotting up to them. She had a bag of burritos that Paula took.

And then Melissa came walking over slowly. She waved everyone over a few feet to stand behind the shed.

"I've got a clue for you," she said in a whisper. "The other Pruitt family stopped here on Stampede Sunday. Way later, after Joseph. The mama came in and bought a Moon dozen and they headed up to the Bounty. They were pulling a horse trailer with a horse inside." She nodded to herself, took her sister's hand, and together they returned to the kitchen.

"There you go," Paula said.

Once in the truck Paula stashed the bag at her feet and said, "So you know the Salado family?"

"Yes. They've been in the Valley for generations," he said but did not start the truck.

"Here's the thing..." she said. "Rosalie called too and told us not to head straight to the Salados. Said to go left from here to throw off the scent."

"The Salado family...do they know we're coming? Because if they know..." He didn't finish his thought because he didn't know how.

He set the coffees in the console cup holders, checked his watch, and took his notebook out long enough to jot down the time. "Get anything out front?" he asked.

"Enough to know better. One guy, splayed across his chair, was our bounty hunter, but he was staying put. We are out ahead of him. Say, why don't I drive, and you can take calls. About time to check in with the commander," she said, and he knew it was because she wanted to get moving, and he'd stalled.

They were doing the loop around the back of the truck when she said, "We date—Pete and I—the commander."

It added up.

He wanted to say "check" but just buckled up and took the phone. The pressure with the shoulder belt crossing his chest was a sudden punch. He'd hunted down killers before, but this was a kid, and he wanted none of it on his hands.

"What does it mean when a boy bows up to his dad?" she asked. She had pulled up to the stop sign on the highway. "Shit, never mind that," she said. "How far out of our way do you think we go?"

"Heck, Paula, let's just get there."

It was only minutes before Greenwood saw the church from the highway, but their turnoff was another mile up. It was impossible to see precisely who all was parked at the pretty little stone church, but there were plenty of trucks and cars there.

Paula pulled the truck up into the Salado yard and then did a neat K-turn in the space just big enough for turning around and parked under a tree. She'd probably been taught this at the academy she'd been to in New York City. Greenwood liked hearing about her training, and he liked the idea of facing out.

"Mr. Salado speak English?" she asked.

"I'd say yes. He's the custodian at the school," Greenwood added. "Kids around here all know him, but don't count on learning what he knows right off the bat. He has a crew of good-looking sons and one of them, according to Melissa, is Leeland's buddy."

A woman stepped out of the house, and before Greenwood could introduce himself or Paula, she said, "How can I help you officers?" An old collie had followed her out and sat vigilantly at her right foot.

"We understand that Leeland Pruitt might be staying with you," Greenwood said.

He and Paula kept approaching her, but the dog wasn't having it. They stopped about ten feet away from her, and no hands were offered in greeting.

"He's with my boys down at the river."

"We'd like to talk to him," Paula said.

The woman turned and went back through the door to what looked like a screened-in porch.

"Come on, Linda's Dog," she said, but the old dog stayed planted.

It was five minutes at least by his watch before an older Mexican man came out with a tall Anglo boy. Greenwood had not expected Leeland to be so tall, but he hadn't expected him to look like such a kid either. He had little-boy arms and a head so closely shaved that Greenwood could see where the barber, he suspected Luke, had nicked the boy repeatedly.

A band of boys in a variety of sizes followed out the door and headed over to a truck parked close to the house. Each one of them leaned up against the truck bed as if they were hosting a meeting, and the dog trotted over and jumped up into the back.

Greenwood heard one of the boys tell the dog that it was okay.

"Leeland?" Paula said and shook his hand.

Greenwood did the same.

The boy is here and he is alive.

"Mr. Salado, we'd like to talk to Leeland."

"We've watched over him pretty good. Gave the boy a vacation," the man said in perfectly fine, soft-spoken English.

"We will just step over to our unit," Greenwood said and put his arm on Leeland's shoulder to direct him back behind the trees, which were full of dark, waxed leaves. This side of the highway was the shady and cool side. The river made all the difference. Greenwood felt a trickle of relief, and he thought maybe a few deep breaths would stop the sound of his heart beating in his ears.

But Leeland was shaking and humming so softly it sounded like the river. When they stopped at Greenwood's truck, Leeland pulled out a white handkerchief from his back pocket and patted his forehead. Greenwood had not seen anyone use a handkerchief since his grandfather died, and that was decades earlier.

"What you been doing, Leeland?" Paula asked and Greenwood saw Leeland pull his shoulders in. They'd agreed on the questions on the ten-minute drive from the café—after he'd gotten off the phone with the commander; after they'd learned that Luke and Deona had each died of a single shot to the head. A pistol shot. And they'd agreed that Paula would do the asking.

Leeland sort of shook his head, but it wasn't attitude he was pulling. He still had the handkerchief out. He was wearing a tee shirt that said *Only the strong survive*. And his sneakers were wet and worn down.

"Mrs. Salado said you and the boys were down playing in the river," Greenwood said because he'd decided he might make more headway with the boy. "So Joseph, he's your friend?"

"Yes, sir. My best friend," Leeland answered, but he was shaking so bad now that Greenwood thought he might cry or break out running.

"Why are you shaking?" he asked, and Paula stepped back.

"Cops," he said.

"Got ya, Leeland, but cops look out for kids," Paula said.

The boy's arms were badly scratched, and what looked like blisters were oozing.

Greenwood checked his watch and said, "Did you drive here, Leeland?"

It was a mistake. He saw it instantly and so he said, "Hey, I spent summers, when I was nine and ten years old, on a wheat farm sitting on a stack of phone books driving my granddad's tractor."

"Yes, sir," Leeland said. "I drove my dad's pickup here. I ran it off the road and scratched it up pretty good. It's bad. I'm taking the blame for it. Mr. Salado put it in the garage." He pointed and Greenwood saw Leeland was not shaking so bad now.

"You got the keys?"

"Yes, sir. Inside. Hold on. I'll get them."

"We'll get to that," Paula said and stepped back up to join them. "Your sister with you here, Leeland?"

Leeland got a look on his face that made Greenwood think the boy thought he was being tricked. It took a bit for him to answer. Finally, he said, "No, she is with my aunt and uncle. They took her home after the Stampede. My dad didn't trust me to go."

Greenwood knew then, and suspected Paula, with all her training, knew what the truth sounded like when it was coming from Leeland Pruitt.

"Your folks know you're here?"

"No. I called the house but no one answers." He took a big breath and said, "I've been thinking about living with the Salados."

"You call anyone else?"

Leeland didn't stop to think before answering and said, "I called my friend Sarah. I asked her to ask her dad, Alfonzo, if he could go find the filly I let loose. Alfonzo is a hand on the Bounty. He looks out for the horses. I knew he could find her. She had a problem with kicking, and my dad tied her tail to her leg so she'd pull her tail out when she kicked."

It was a lot to say.

Paula grimaced and said, "You think there is a better way to break a horse of kicking?"

Leeland nodded.

The odd thing was that Greenwood wouldn't have taken Leeland for a ranch kid except for his honest-to-God politeness, and then this with the horse.

Greenwood took his notebook out and asked Leeland for his home address and his date of birth. "Nearly fifteen?" Greenwood said.

Leeland nodded, eyes down.

"So, you've been here two days?

"Yes, sir."

"And you say you put some pretty good scratches on your dad's pickup."

This time Leeland hesitated. "I couldn't see so good. I lost my glasses back at the house and I couldn't find them."

"Maybe you can go get those keys now. Looks like some burns on your arms—anyplace else?" Greenwood asked, but now he was keeping his eyes on his notes.

"Yes, my back."

"Okay. Someone put some ointment on them?"

Leeland didn't answer.

"How did you get those burns, Leeland?" Paula was doing the asking now.

"My dad. With a torch."

"I'd like to take photos of those burns," she said. "Let's do that inside. My camera is in the truck."

Greenwood followed them and found Mr. Salado with his boys still gathered around the pickup.

Greenwood asked, "Can you show me the Pruitt truck?" The man said nothing but led him off into the garage. The truck was scratched up pretty bad, especially the racing stripe which Duff had failed to mention. Greenwood took down the license plate and looked inside the truck. It was locked up which pleased him.

"I'm going to impound the truck, but it'll take awhile for the tow truck to get here. Good job keeping it locked up."

The man didn't say anything and Greenwood didn't expect him to, but he had to ask what he had to ask. "You know anything about why Leeland showed up here?"

"I know Luke Pruitt," he said.

Greenwood had to nod to get him to say more.

"He is no good, and when Leeland needed a place to cool

off, we took him in. I am not going to allow that boy to be taken back until I know he'll be safe."

"Okay," was all Greenwood said.

Leeland and Paula were standing outside the garage. Leeland had started the shaking again.

"When I first got here I called my dad to tell him about his truck, but no one picked up," he said. Leeland reached out and handed Greenwood the keys.

Greenwood said, "I understand, Leeland. Things are not simple, son, and should not be made to appear so." He paused and then went on, "Here is what we are going to do. Investigator Magliaro and I have to check out some things. But we'll be back. In the meantime I want you, Leeland, to stay in the house with your friends. Lock that front gate. Don't make any more calls and don't any of you be on the phone."

Mr. Salado walked over and checked the garage door. Greenwood hadn't noticed the padlock until Mr. Salado pulled it tight. And so Greenwood fished in his pocket and handed the man the keys.

"Hold onto these, would you? I'm not going to call the tow now. Don't want to be hauling this outta here like some trophy."

As they pulled out Greenwood watched in his rear-view mirror while the five Salado boys pulled up the gate, which was stuck from lack of use, and dragged it closed. He looked over at Paula and was pretty sure she was shaking now. The tension in his chest was gone, but his forehead was wet like Leeland's had been, and the smell of the still-hot burritos had taken over the cab. Paula was on the phone as soon as they got out of sight of the gate.

She said, "Drop me off at St. Jude's. Sounds like there's quite a crowd there. I can get the priest to put up a roadblock where we came onto White Goat Road. Block it off from anyone going in or out." She put her phone and one of her cards on the console and said, "You hold onto the phone. Churches have phones."

"Okay," he said. He was putting two and two together. "It is possible the boy left the ranch when he got the chance. He could have tore out of there leaving Deona reading her book. Just maybe. And then someone else who knew Luke and Deona were alone at the Bounty could have gone up there and killed them. What's stopping someone from doing that?"

"Plausible," she said. "Salado?" she asked as he turned off White Goat Road onto the little private lane that would take them to the church the back way. The road was rutted but he didn't mind the time it would take.

"I don't think it'd be Salado but maybe this Alfonzo. His wife thought the kids were being abused."

> Everyone is looking for a "sure enough" kid horse for their grandkids. Haven't we all, at one time or another? What these people don't realize is that there just aren't that many "sure enough" kids' horses around. First thing they fail to grasp is the years of service these horses have already put in doing ranch work. Most of them having already paid their dues, they're too tired to try anything anymore; it just takes too much energy! You can dude almost any horse, but you cannot turn any kid loose on any horse!
>
> Linda Pruitt, *Ranching Weekly*

Deona

1999

"Tell me about it," Luke said to her when she complained about the cold. The house the Byrd brothers provided them out on the Sweetspread Ranch was slump-block—known for holding the cold in winter, and the heat in summer. She had hoped for something more homey, and she hadn't banked on being cold.

The Sweetspread Ranch was a sizeable place in the area of the Sweetspread Draw in a country of holes, gullies, and ravines. Luke had told her that only the draws had names. "Someone back then decided to name them and put them on maps. You know a draw when you see it. It has zero level ground." Luke said all that to her patiently at two a.m. in the break room at Leprino Foods, back when they were still in their horseplay days. They'd been the subject of graphic stories that made the rounds and pleased Deona, because having Angie find out what they were up to, on the job even, was Luke's plan. Word leaking out would make it easier for him to move on. Deona got that.

In those days we were having our own fun talking up the way Luke Pruitt had moved on to his third wife. This gal, Deona, was a mean one—ten years older than him if a day—and had a slew of marriages behind her. Standing in the Roswell Post office just visiting, some of us got her past all tangled up. There'd be lots of confusion, and then someone was sure to laugh it off and add, "Well, in these parts you don't lose your woman, you just lose your turn." And then Luke Pruitt sounded to us like an ordinary guy, just getting by like the rest of us. We'd stroll out of the post office and climb into our vehicles—still chuckling. There was always work to be done.

When her new husband interviewed for the job at the Sweetspread Ranch, he was told that the three Byrd brothers—living on neighboring places—ran the ranch. Everyone around Roswell knew that this ranch was famous for its tiger-striped heifers and loose rock. It took Deona one day on the place to figure out that it was not the brothers, but their mother, who held the purse strings.

The Byrd family dynasty dated back to the 1890s when a local banker loaned the patriarch five hundred dollars to buy thirteen hundred head of sheep. "Old Byrd's descendants kept adding to the place," the sun-damaged matriarch had proclaimed when she came by unannounced to show Deona how to load the washer and what not to flush down the toilets.

"Keep after the clutter," Mrs. Byrd said as she crossed the front room taking a mental inventory. That woman was a sly one—used to getting what she wanted. Well, so was Deona, but she didn't do clutter. And then when the woman was standing at the front door with the screen door open, letting in God knew how much dust, she said the most peculiar thing. She said, "It's all over so fast."

Deona knew that ranching was going to keep her busy, but after the methane gas in East Grand Plains, this house smelled sweet to her and, being miles off the highway, there was no one to mess with her most days. It was long past time for Luke to get back to ranching, and she'd decided she'd take credit for getting that done.

But we knew, even Luke knew, that family was family, blood was thicker than water, and the Pruitts were not Byrds. Still, there was honest work to be done on the Sweetspread. *Stepping-stones* we'd have said to Luke and his third wife, if we'd had the chance to be neighborly. *Play it clever. That matriarch is like a pussycat tossed out into the wild. Feral,* we probably should have told the Pruitts.

Luke got busy right from day one, but it didn't surprise Deona when he took time off to go with her to enroll the kids— her daughter Karmen and his son Leeland—at Berrendo Elementary. She planned to let him do the talking. He always wanted it that way. The four of them were paraded around the school by a series of teachers. They'd been talked down to, and that was why Luke had gone off at the guidance counselor in the cafeteria. It was the big cat—a stubby-tailed bobcat with yellow eyes and big black pupils—painted on the wall of the cafeteria—that ticked him off, that and the male guidance counselor.

She'd seen it coming.

"That's no berrendo, you know," Luke said with the wide-mouth Pruitt smile. Deona knew he saved that look for ridicule.

The counselor put his hand on Leeland's shoulder. "It's our team mascot," the man said, and Leeland said, "Cool. Like Big Al." And then, the tour over, they were taken to the principal's office where they were seated like a panel before her desk.

Tapping the end of her fountain pen on her big front teeth, the principal said, "We have a reduced-price lunch. Perhaps you'll qualify for that program."

"Their mother will pack their lunches," Luke said and Leeland sighed, all disappointed-like. "We don't need handouts."

"Well, forms are in your paperwork if you should change your minds." Then the woman pancaked her hands on her desk and said, "It's a privilege to be part of your children's journey. It will be our pleasure to watch Leeland and Karmen grow and succeed."

She didn't mean it.

"Let me give our curriculum specialist a call," the principal said. The specialist came in promptly as if she'd been itching for something to do. She stood behind the principal and repeated a little speech. She kept saying, "Let me point out," before she made a point. When she got to Leeland she said, "Let me point out that as a third grader Leeland will be investigating the number line and fine-tuning his division skills. And he will be applying what he learns to real-life situations."

"Real life, Leeland," Deona said because she noticed that Luke was off someplace in his mind, and because they'd told Leeland to keep his mouth shut. Somebody had to say something after all that.

"'Yes, ma'am,' is all you say. That's the beginning and end of your conversations," Luke had told his son in the truck before they went inside to register.

Right at three the next afternoon, Deona parked the truck in the dirt parking lot across the road from the school and marched down the hall to Leeland's classroom. There was a little window in the door with crisscrossed wire in it, making it look to her like a prison cell. She had to laugh because it went with the haircut Luke had given Leeland the night before. "You look like a prisoner," she'd said.

"Welcome to Berrendo," the tallest of the three women

who had snuck up on her said.

"We're room mothers," the short one said. She wore black pantyhose with ballerina slipper flats. She did a little sweep with her well-cared-for hand indicating she meant the three of them. It was kind of a pivot she did, on one toe.

"I signed up to be one of those," Deona said.

"Maybe next year they can use you," the tall one said way too quickly for Deona to believe it hadn't all been planned out.

"Of course, we do class parties and can use help sometimes with cleanup. And we work with students who need help," the short gal said. All three nodded, even the silent one with the banana-yellow hair.

It was the tall, antelope-looking woman who asked right off the bat, "Is Leeland your son?"

"That pussy? No way." It came out so fast that Deona was saying it while one of the women was saying, "Cute kid." And then Deona saw in their faces that this was going to be spread around.

"They were gunning for me," Deona told Luke at the supper table that night, right after she told the kids to go their rooms.

"Meaning what?" Luke asked.

"Meaning those three came marching down the hallway acting like a little posse looking for a chance to blame me for whatever Leeland was or wasn't doing."

"Pick the kids up outside, like I told you, D. Those mothers don't have nothing better to do all day than hen party. Get the kids and get home. You've got work to do back here at the ranch."

That "back at the ranch" bit was their private joke ever since they'd up and married days after his divorce from Angie came though, and he'd taken the foreman job at the Sweetspread. Deona smiled all sweet at him because she really did feel like she'd won the prize; his teeth were white and straight, and she was sure he was going to keep his Clint Eastwood hair. She said, "Just trying to be on good terms with school people," but he'd stopped listening and was staring at the dirty plate in front of him.

Early the next morning, Deona sat tall and stiff as a stone statue on the cold leather seat. She was the third vehicle in line for drop-offs at Berrendo Elementary School.

"Seven-fifteen," Leeland said from the back seat of the extended cab. He was hovering over the back of her seat and reading off the clock on the dash of their family pickup.

Deona checked the rearview mirror. An SUV so big she couldn't see around it or over it had climbed right up on her butt, so close that the driver looked like she was about to dive into the bed of Luke's spit-and-polish pickup.

"Hold your horses," Deona said as she glared at the mirror. Just then Leeland spun around to stare at the woman behind them. And then Deona's daughter joined in, bouncing and shouting, "Whoa, Belle," as if there was a big old cow on the loose.

Still watching the mirror, Deona said, "Shut up and sit on your butts." And then she swung her right arm around and poked Leeland in his chest with the one fingernail she kept long. Halfway into a wave the woman driving the SUV must have realized it was the new family up ahead of her, and she switched to touching up her hair. She did that thing that Deona had never been able to do with her permed hair; she flipped it with her index finger so that it sprung away from her face and bounced all at the same time. No doubt about it, the woman was a member of the flossy posse who'd shown up outside Leeland's classroom the day before. Deona had decided after talking to Luke that the principal had called the mothers in from the schoolyard to keep an eye on her and report back.

Deona hadn't liked that nodding thing they'd done.

Sitting here trapped in the silly procession of mothers was one giant waste of her time. She rubbed her eyes and avoided the mirror. Thing was, those mothers had, no doubt about it, been slinging mud about her last night, making up stories about her as if they'd sniffed things out by just standing there in the hallway. They could have invited her to coffee. She wouldn't have gone, but they could have invited her.

She picked up her paperback from the passenger seat—she always had one going—and held it high enough for the woman behind her to see she was reading, and thought to herself, *What would be the point of being on good terms with the posse?*

The noise came up on them from behind. It was a street sweeper barreling up Pine Lodge Road, spraying water to lay the spring dust.

"Hold on. Would you look at that?" Leeland shouted and began bouncing on the back seat and rocking the truck like some sort of moron.

"Stop it, you pussy," Deona shouted as she slammed her book on the dash. She checked the mirror. No way could that hoity-toity behind her have heard that, but still Deona knew she shouldn't have said it, not when she'd said what she'd said the day before, not when she hadn't admitted it to Luke at the supper table.

We heard about that hallway conversation as it was being spread around that night in organized calls, likely using the school telephone snow chain. We felt kind of sorry for her, being a newcomer and all that. Especially with us supposedly being the welcoming types. Truth of the matter, we knew that threesome of women—knew the one with the blond hair was called Straw behind her back. We got a kick out of watching them showing up at coffee shops midday like they were on the show circuit.

"Wouldn't I love to drive that truck," Leeland said softly,

speaking now to his stepsister, who said, "Me too."

The line of cars and trucks behind Deona had now run out into the street, everyone with their engines running so that the roar of it all ran up through the bottom of her Keds. After seeing those slipper things she'd decided she wasn't going to wear her boots to school again. But now her feet were cold and she suddenly remembered that the scarecrows her uncle had put out in the open fields always had old white Keds on. What did it matter anyway? She wasn't getting out of the truck.

Leeland was still watching the street sweeper; they all were. The water spray was making colors out of the dust, but it was doing nothing to clear the air.

"Ah, the smell of money," Leeland said.

Deona turned to look at the boy as he went on saying, "In these parts ranching is all about water." Too late, she recognized the boy was imitating his dad, who'd said that about water maybe one hundred times in the last month.

She had to admit the boy could be funny. "Think you're pretty smart, don't you?" she said, because no way, no how was he going to drive a wedge between her and Luke. She'd made her mind up about who she was siding with.

She'd only made the boy giggle, which made her daughter, Karmen, laugh. The pickup ahead of them moved up, and Leeland called out as if life was a lark, "Here we go."

> Activity really picks up at this time of year. Everyone is busy finishing up mechanic work, shoeing horses, and getting ready to gather sheep. Others of us are keeping an eye on our mothers-to-be. Those favorite cows and even the not-so-favorite ones are getting closer by the day. My adrenaline really gets to flowing during calving season. Each day brings another life into this old world and no two are ever alike. Even if they are all the same color, their personalities are very different. It's really exciting.
>
> Linda Pruitt, *Ranching Weekly*

Luke

1999

Luke crossed the room, knowing the exact spots to avoid where the floorboards were loose—*not his house, not his problem.* He checked the prod to see it was on; it was a premium hotshot, meant for herding stupid, stubborn, or scared animals. It had come with the job, and he'd remembered to charge it overnight. It had two exposed metal electrodes at the tip. He tossed it back and forth from hand to hand considering the plus and minus of using it on his boy.

"Get up, faggot," Luke said as he squeezed the trigger and used the tip of the prod to shock his kid awake.

Leeland shot straight up and was on his feet in less than two seconds.

"Bet you'll think twice next time you decide to sleep in on a workday," Luke said. "And oh, by the way, every day is a workday on a ranch. Get used to it."

Luke turned around and headed for the door, found the

light switch and flipped it on, and turned back around so his kid could see him flash his open-mouthed John Wayne smile. Luke had been practicing it for years now by looking in a mirror. The point was looking all-American.

Leeland pulled his arm up to shade his eyes.

God, that boy could piss him off. *Shit*, Luke thought as he made his way back to the kitchen, his dad had never shown him the courtesy of a wake-up—you got up or you got beat up. Western justice had been the code in the Pruitt home on the Diamond Crown Ranch, where Payton Pruitt was famous for doing mean shit.

I could have killed him.

Leeland appeared in the kitchen, wearing Wranglers. Corrine had sent new Levis just to piss him off. He'd told Deona to get rid of them. Deona had pressed Leeland's shirt because he'd told her to.

"Thank your mother," Luke had ordered when he woke the boy up after nine p.m. the night before to come get the shirt.

Now, Leeland just stood there in the kitchen and looked at him like he was some sort of monster. And so Luke did his stare-down thing he'd learned from his dad.

The kid smelled sweet, like he had splashed something from a bottle on his baby face before coming into the kitchen. From Angie, no doubt. Well, now was as good a time as any to cut off Leeland's visits to Hummingbird Lane.

The house was stone quiet. Slump-block held the quiet. The two of them began to move around the kitchen in silence. Deona and Karmen were still sleeping, and Luke had reminded his son the night before that the girls slept in on weekends.

"Did Grandma sleep in?" Leeland had asked, wide-eyed, like the smart-ass he'd become. That was going to stop.

But still, he'd answered the boy: "No, she was always

writing. Sneaking off to write stupid stuff that got spread all over from Roswell to Ruidoso, so that I had no fuckin' privacy. Everyone knew our business."

The two of them got their own breakfast and ate standing. Leeland had cereal and Luke toast. He was on his third cup of coffee. He watched Leeland rub his arm where the prod had got him. And when he did it again, Luke picked the hotshot up off the kitchen table and pointed it at him. He really hadn't intended to do that or to touch him with it now or earlier there in the bedroom. He didn't know why he did some things. It didn't matter anyway. Leeland's long-sleeved shirt kept the evidence, if there was any, hidden.

Luke pushed the kid playfully and whispered, "Oh, pardon me." Then he fixed his eyes on his son, squinted, and began the warning. "Here's the situation. My boss's uncle, Ham Byrd, is gonna be there at the branding. You mention aliens and I'll knock you silly."

He rapped his knuckles on the pine table and said, "Knock, knock."

"Yes, sir," Leeland said.

Luke stepped up to the sink and put his hand out, signaling for Leeland to hand over his cereal bowl.

"I'd like to see Ham Byrd produce one single piece of proof of aliens. If he really thinks E.T. landed on his place he ought to sweet-talk the governor into getting a goddamn body exhumed. Some big deal legend he's got buried out there. Folks are suckers, and now Ham Byrd gets filthy rich taking curiosity-seekers around his ranch. And they see shit for fifteen dollars a pop."

"I won't say anything, Dad. It's rumor, right. Not like it's the truth. Not like Boy Scout Mountain, where there were witnesses to those visitors from outer space."

Luke ignored him and poured coffee into his big to-go cup. And then he motioned for Leeland to pack up the things they'd left out on the table the night before.

Leeland said, "I'll go pee."

"Do not tell me you haven't peed. Guess you'll have to hold it," Luke said.

"I have to, Dad. Plus I have to brush my teeth. Mom said."

Luke turned out the kitchen light and said, "Deona? I don't think she gives a rat's ass if you brush your teeth, you little liar. She's your mom now. Don't forget and don't flush."

It was not quite six a.m. when Luke backed up the truck. "From this minute on we are on Byrd time," Luke said and patted the dashboard.

We'd already noticed, just from them being around town and all, that the father and son looked a lot alike. They both had good milk-fed teeth. Luke had become a square-built man. He'd been a lean kid, not fleshy, which was Stralin's fate. Luke and his son were well-groomed. Their dust-colored hair was always neat, and they never left it to crawl down the back of their sunburnt necks the way some cowboys do nowadays.

In the truck driving to the pens, Luke went on with his rules. "Keep quiet about the brand Stralin and me registered. No one needs to know about that, hear me? You breathe a word about 26 Bar, and I'll make you wish you hadn't."

"Yes, sir," Leeland said.

Family life was such a crock of shit.

"You ride for the brand, right? The Lazy K, a scatter brand? One of the Byrd boys, at recess, he told me," Leeland said.

Luke slammed his hand on the wheel and said, "Talking to the Byrd boys in the schoolyard? Told you not to. Let me give you a speed read of it. The Byrds don't care about you. We're not family." Luke hit the cattle guard going forty and regretted it. It had rattled his teeth. "Get it?" he yelled over the roar of his tires.

The highway was pretty empty that early. He watched the

headlights of an eighteen-wheeler heading north, while he sat and let the tires cool. But then he crossed. It still was not full sunup when they reached the corrals. Luke parked the pickup off behind the low-down barn, and then without a word to each other, he and Leeland headed up to where a crowd of men and kids stood around chewing the fat. Leeland kind of bounced his way up there, spinning around like a toe-dancing fairy, in boots.

Luke spotted each of the Byrd brothers in the crowd. The one he considered his boss nodded at them with his chin. All three of the brothers had long bodies and brows that hung over their eyes as if years of southern New Mexico sun had selected out that trait especially for the Byrd dynasty. It was a handsome look, Luke thought, but not for their sisters. He'd known one of those Byrd girls in high school, and she hadn't given him the time of day. But she sure hadn't looked like Corrine looked back in the day in a pair of cut-offs with her April tan.

The first item of business was visiting. It was the way things got done, and Luke had the visiting performance down. It was all give and take. He reached over and rubbed the back of Leeland's neck like someone who was proud of his kid. Then somebody tossed Leeland an apple.

"Thank you, sir," Leeland said to the man who had already moved on to someone else with his bag of apples. Luke nodded as if it felt good to have such a great kid. He'd seen his mother do this.

"Got a good day," one of the men said to Luke. They all agreed on that point. Finally, Luke's boss handed him the reins to a tall, handsome horse Luke had ridden before—a gelding. He pretended he did not know the horse was named Sugar.

Luke packed his gear in the saddlebags, put his freshly washed duster on the back of the saddle, and pulled himself up onto the horse. Leeland had a mouth full of apple and was already yakity-yakking with grown men. He was going at it like old wind-up teeth set loose. Luke reached inside his jacket and grabbed the hotshot and tossed it to Leeland. "Know how to work that?" he said over his shoulder. It passed as a fatherly thing to say. "It's for protection if you need it."

Luke pulled the horse's head up tight, chin up, and then said to the two Byrd brothers who were saddled up, "It's Leeland's first branding season, but he'll be a good hand. You'll see."

This job would work, he thought. It wasn't a hard place. He'd seen worse. He dug into the horse's sides, firm like, with the metal taps of his rawhide boots. He leaned back into the duster. Then as if it had been planned in advance like a dance routine, Luke and two of the brothers stepped out in sync with one another. The sun was up and it was going to be warm. Leeland wasn't going to mess up, and if he did he'd pay for it. Luke rode away from the boy.

The three men headed to the big corrals and met up with a team of four other men and two cattle dogs. Luke estimated there were near about two hundred cows and calves, all staring at the men. The dogs were down, forepaws out, lying watchful and proud, just waiting to catch some cow up to mischief. The men began working to get the cows and their calves, which were two months old at the most, mothered up. It could be tricky. The dogs went up on all fours repeatedly and then got into the mix and back out of it without being hurt. The Byrds occasionally shouted a command at the dogs.

Other dogs, furry terriers Luke had zero use for, trotted around the corral and messed with the biggest cows. It always seemed stupid to Luke that you had to do this matching-up thing right before you split them up and pushed the calves off into a separate pen right under the mother cows' noses.

The two Byrd brothers were all serious now. They were checking brands. They cut some of the cows out, and a young hand herded those strays up and away from the corral with their bawling calves following behind. There was a God-awful racket, and every one of the cows was a part of it. Luke's mother had always worked the branding at the Diamond Crown, and no way would she have allowed the calves to get so skittish. These calves seemed in a frenzy to get to the corner near the feed barn to pee, and the minute one calf finished another took the spot.

There was cow shit everywhere; some of it hot and steaming, but no one ever complained about that smell. It was the smell of straw that Luke liked, but later it would be no match for the smell of skin smoldering.

Everyone was yelling, and even the men with puny voices—there were always some of those on ranches—shouted and yelled. That was one of the things Luke had missed most about ranching. Anytime he had done some well-deserved shouting out on the cheese factory floor, someone came looking for him and wrote him up.

He hadn't seen how it started, but one of the Byrd brothers moved across the corral quick-like to rein in a hired hand. The guy must have done something to stir up the cows over in the far corner, and now about ten calves—it was darn impossible to count them—were kicking up sawdust with their fist-sized hoofs as if they were in some damn competition. It was the sawdust that Luke was thinking about. It was a stupid lazy thing to lay down in a corral. "Don't breathe that dust," he could remember his mom warning them whenever they came across some of it at a show barn or at some outfit where people liked the clean look of it.

"Eat out your lungs if it doesn't burn your barn down," Luke suddenly remembered his dad telling his big boss, Nathan, when they'd all been touring a barn off on a bit of acreage the owner of the Diamond Crown was considering buying. His dad had not given his mom a bit of credit for that information, but Payton Pruitt had caught his son eyeing him. Later that night when Luke was stripped naked for his shower his dad had pushed his way into the bathroom and hissed, "You helpless little brat. Chicken Little. The sky is falling, the sky is falling." And he kept at it, making Luke want to cry, not from fear but from despair. Instead, he held his breath until his mom came in and found him turning blue. And he was holding his breath now.

The Byrd brother said to the hand, "Did I see you throw a rock at that cow?"

Luke watched them work it out and then saw the two men split up. Things settled down in that corner.

When the herd was finally in good shape, even if many of the cows were frothy-mouthed, he and his boss decided it was time to cut out the mother cows. On horseback it was not all that hard to push the calves into the crowding pens. "Keep after 'em," is what his boss kept saying to no one in particular, but it irked Luke. And it irked him when he rode back down and spotted Leeland sitting on the corral fence with the other little kids. Leeland made ten and not a one of them was paying attention. Fun and games.

Luke would have preferred doing the branding on a weekday. Better to keep it professional. It was not some bean-burrito Mexican fiesta, he'd told Deona. But Luke's boss, Finch Byrd, had explained patiently that they made it a family-bonding thing, and the kids looked forward to it. He told Luke they always lined up the little kids on the fence and called them Crows.

But it wasn't like Luke had ever expected Leeland to be one of them.

He couldn't worry with it now, and he couldn't fix it. The game was on with the calves being pushed through the Byrds' fancy squeeze chute. They kept theirs painted. The days of roping and dragging one hundred calves to the fire were over—Luke knew that, and he knew it'd been mostly Hollywood.

When he was a kid there had always been someone out on the Diamond Crown come to watch the branding who was expecting fancy rodeo work. Some dad who knew shit about ranching was always bellyaching that his kid needed to learn how it "used to be done" with ropes and a big old fire to heat the irons. And when video cameras became the rage, one dad showed up wanting to get his little girl on film dragging a calf. And he wanted everyone to smile for the camera.

Luke came up all quiet-like behind Leeland, pulled in the reins on Sugar, and said, "Leeland, your job is down there in that last crowding pen. You've gotta push those calves into the squeeze. You can't just waltz in there and expect them to line up for the squeeze. Be tough with them. Now get down off that fence."

He'd said it in the boy's ear, all quiet-like. But it wasn't long before we all had our opinion about what Luke Pruitt had said to his boy that morning.

Leeland moved, fast.

The stench of the seared hides and burning hair began to fill the air. It made a lot of grown men wipe at their eyes, but it never had bothered Luke much. He knew not to have a big breakfast before branding—his mother had taught him that— and for a minute he was thankful Leeland had not eaten much. It'd be a damn scene if his kid tossed his breakfast in the pen.

"Get up close and stay there," one of the hands yelled at Leeland. "Don't give them a chance to kick you."

"Luke, why don't you take over castrating the little bulls," Ham Byrd shouted and Luke dismounted, tied the horse up, and got his gloves out.

Since when was Ham his boss?

It felt like he was being corrected for something, but he was fast at castrating and figured the Byrds knew that about him. He'd done it plenty and knew how to work the instruments so that there was only a little blood. But he didn't move just yet because he was watching Leeland.

The next calf pushed into the pen was on the small side and it looked scared witless. His eyes were caked and red. Luke watched as it went right at Leeland. The kid went for the fence. He climbed it and hung on like some sort of rodeo clown. He never even bothered with the hotshot.

Luke moved just as fast. He got a hold of his son's collar and pushed him back into the crowding pen with the little calf. Other calves had already been pushed on in. But we all heard that it was the slick, little scared calf that hauled off and kicked Leeland in the rib cage. A bunch of folks—not all kids—seen that animal back up, getting ready to stomp him good because, as if a chorus, everyone gathered breath and then began shouting and pointing at Leeland, who was down.

Luke didn't move, not even an eyebrow.

It was Kragen Byrd, still a grade-school kid himself, who jumped into the pen and pulled Leeland out. The work in the squeeze chute had not stopped, but it got quiet with the two boys in the pen. All that got broken in the melee were two of Kragen's fingers. Luke harped on those broken fingers; blaming Leeland for that part of the accident and for the caked manure he got on his shirt. Kragen kept saying it wasn't really Leeland's fault, but Luke wasn't taking a kid's word for it.

"Need to wrap your son's ribs. Precaution," old lady Byrd called to Luke as she came waltzing over with her first aid kit. His mom had had the same exact kit.

Ranch work ethics kept the talk to a minimum out there at the chute, while there was work to be done, but by night we put the blame on Luke.

For a while that night Luke just sat in his recliner in the living room, even though he was sure he heard Leeland crying. Then he heard Leeland humming to himself. Deona was reading and taking no notice, and so he finally got up and went to the doorway and stood there trying to make sure he could hear the kid breathing. He took up the whole doorway even in his stocking feet. Then something changed in the room, and it got dead still. The boy was not asleep. Luke flickered the light and then said, "I've got my reasons and I don't have to give them to you. Like I told you, Little Duke, if you don't do what you're told, you're gonna get hurt bad. That is the nature of the beast."

Luke listened to the silence. Then he said, "G'night" and thought he heard the boy say something that sounded like *yes, sir*.

Angie

1999

"Slow down, Leeland. Let me catch up," Angie said as she reached across the boy to check that his door was closed tight. Then she drove out of the crosswalk as he went on about an assignment, and she could see he was shook up bad. Still, he waved at a little girl who had followed him out of the building.

"Cassandra," he said to Angie. "She's my best friend. She knows all about the planets." He rubbed his hand across his forehead like an old woman and said, "I forgot the lilies poem in my desk. I have to memorize it, and Dad and Deona need to sign it. Now I've gone and done it," he said but slowly. "I only got the first part: 'I have been thinking about living like the lilies that blow in the fields.'"

"That's nice, Leeland."

"It's about hummingbirds," he said. "I think my mother likes hummingbirds. I can't really remember."

Off work early, it was Angie's weekend to have Leeland.

Ever since Luke moved out to the Sweetspread he had tried to tell her that her weekends were over.

Just this week she'd said to him, "Talk to the judge. I've got court granted rights." Then she hung up on him. She hated scaring Corrine, but she was thinking she'd better call her and explain things. She'd do it next week, right after supper one night. After-supper talk is what her mother always called those kinds of calls.

And so today she arrived at Leeland's new school right before the bell rang. Now that the buses were loaded up, the steady line of pickup trucks, a few minivans, SUVs, and Jeeps was pulling out of the lot onto Pine Lodge Road. Angie let a Ford Bronco cut in. She couldn't help noticing that painted on the back it said, "Family Forever." It was an amateur paint job.

Coming out here to pick up Leeland on Pine Lodge Road would forever make her think of the vacation they'd taken last summer to the Capitans, right before Luke had come home and announced he'd found someone new. She'd been so silly happy heading out on this road on their one and only family vacation, and it'd been good. God, she'd been such a fool not to see it coming. The way he did it made her think she'd never meant a thing to him. Him choosing Deona Flood over her was a hard thing to stomach.

And then Angie smiled big. For her it had worked out. She slapped the steering wheel like someone who'd just had a fantastic idea. Leeland did a double-take. She had remarried too—a neighbor she'd known since she was a kid. Married him as soon as her divorce was legal. She'd gotten the better deal, except for the bad feeling she had about Leeland. He was still looking at her.

"It's my hair that's different," she said.

"Yeah," he said. "I knew it was something."

He was the sweetest thing.

"I just gave up on the bottle. Wes likes natural." She

pushed her long, grey braid back over her shoulder.

"Me too," Leeland said.

The line of vehicles moved at a crawl as some of the moms and one of the buses was waiting to take a left turn onto Highway 285. She put the truck in park and said, "Okay, Leeland, so this poem thing..." They were eating exhaust, but it was too hot to roll up the windows.

"I'm gonna be in trouble," he said. "I'll lose all my TV privileges if I don't get the paper signed and the whole poem memorized. Basketball too." Eyes closed, he was holding his head in his hands.

Angie put the truck in gear. She didn't want Leeland to get the next part of his one single life wrong. Back when she was still married to Luke, this wouldn't have happened. There would have been no meltdown. Luke hadn't much cared about Leeland's schoolwork. The difference had to be Deona. She was a meddler and hard-hearted. "She's as authoritative as God herself," Angie's friend at the Roswell Ace Hardware had told her at the checkout.

Leeland mumbled through his hands, "It's my first ranch. I'm learning a lot of hard things."

The woman in the Bronco took a sharp right and peeled out.

"Hold on a minute, Leeland, while I get on the highway, okay?"

Angie took a cautious right. She'd lived within miles of 285 her whole life, but she always said she wasn't much for highway driving. It was merging that got to her. She stayed in the right lane and let two pickups pass her. Court-ordered or not, she was not needing a ticket with Leeland in the car. When she was safely moving with the getting-home traffic, she told him that he needed to pay no more attention to that poem business.

"I'll call school Monday. Let's have us a good supper

tonight and some fun. Wes is getting home early, and we're putting ribs on the grill."

That got a sweet smile out of the boy.

"The calves miss you, Leeland."

"I know," he said. "It's awful quiet on the ranch, and at night, Angie, it's so dark the whole ranch disappears. Like sleeping in a gravel pit. You can't even see Venus, and Cassandra told me it's big." He waited a good long minute and added, "Asteroids are just rocks, but they can become meteors. For real."

It was a long drive back through town with stop-and-go Friday traffic. As they passed the Military Institute, Leeland seemed to take an interest in the cadets. Angie thought, just maybe, that was an option for Leeland. He could live there. Thinking that lightened her up, and before she knew it she was turning into the Sonic.

"How about a burger?" she asked. About the best she could do for him was spoil him.

They sat there all quiet while he ate, and she made up her mind to do some checking on the institute. Back in the day, all the big-time ranchers sent their boys there, even as from far away as Hatch and Silver City, but now they even took girls. Everyone in town always bragged that Conrad Hilton had been a cadet. It was then, lost in her thoughts, that Leeland had fallen asleep right there in the truck with his head up against the window.

When she turned off the Old Dexter Highway and headed to Hummingbird Lane, he sat up straight and said, "I smell home."

She said, "All these years and I cannot smell dairy cow. But oil...pee-uw!"

That got him laughing. It was an old joke in the Pecos Valley. Then he said, "I'll do my chores. Dad said I better."

"Sure, Leeland, but it's not your dad's place any more...

well, it never was his place."

She pulled into the hard-pack drive and stopped to point at the mailbox. "Jones," she said. "Wes went out and bought those letters to let the postman know whose place it is now."

Wes Jones had lived down the street from her forever, and so when Luke learned that Angie was marrying Wes, he started calling him *Neighbor Boy*. It wasn't a kind thing to do.

Angie started up again and passed under the low-hanging branches of the huge old cottonwood. She'd already heard hatchlings up there and it wasn't yet May. Thank God Luke Pruitt wouldn't be pulling any more switches off her tree.

"I love to swing," Leeland said when he spotted the new glider off to the side of the house, near the barn.

"Wedding present," she said.

"And blue is your favorite color," he said.

Angie kept him fed real good that weekend and would have let him sleep way late, but he seemed trained now to rise early. And she let him wear the Aerosmith T-shirt he loved and had left behind. It was an easy weekend. Eight-year-old boys were no trouble.

On Sunday when the sun took its late afternoon slant, and Wes finished up shooting baskets with Leeland, Angie saw the kid begin to shrink up. That's when he started begging to stay one more night. There was no other way to describe it.

"Call my dad, please. Please," he said stringing the *please* out like the three-year-old boy she'd first met.

Yes, it was begging.

"I can't do that, Leeland. You know your dad won't allow it." It was lame, she knew, not to stand up to Luke. It hadn't stopped her before. But things were different.

"One more day. That's all, one more day so I can get my poem."

It took her and Wes both swearing to call the school first thing Monday to calm him down.

"You can still trust Angie," Wes kept saying. But then he got down close to Leeland and said, man-to-man, "Listen to me. You're a smart kid. But you've got to remember never to backtalk your dad. Even when you know you're right and he's wrong." She and Wes had agreed on this the night before when Wes had asked her if she thought Leeland had more responsibility than other ranch kids. She really didn't know, she just knew Luke.

And then finally, when Leeland had a clean, long-sleeved shirt on and there was nothing else they could do, Angie told him to check his backpack and make sure he had everything.

"Look, Angie," he shouted. He could go all happy so easily. He opened his sketchpad and turned to a drawing done in black ink. "I've been practicing the Wing-A logo. Aerosmith!" he said. "I drew that freehand. White is for wisdom and black is for energy and power."

She would keep him if she could.

Leeland tucked the pad away in a pocket of his backpack and shook Wes's hand, thanked him for a nice time.

On the drive back through Roswell to the turnoff for the Sweetspread Angie tried to get him to talk, first by talking about silly stuff and then music. "Next time we can CD shop," she said.

"Sure. I've saved up some. I could buy one for Karmen. She makes up lies to get me in trouble. She spies on me."

"Okay then, we'll shop," Angie said.

"Dad's getting extra for coyote subsidy," Leeland offered.

She nodded.

"He has to take the lower jaws to Game and Fish," Leeland said.

"Pee-uw," she said and they both shook their heads like they got one another.

"It's okay because it's to protect the herd. But Mr. Byrd, he doesn't allow Dad to run any personal livestock other than a saddle horse or two. 'Can't skim the cream on this place' is what he told Dad. Dad is real mad about that and says Stralin has it different on his ranch."

"Rules are rules," she said. "And remember what Wes told you. Easier that way, kiddo."

That got a smile.

"I won't forget to call school," she said.

Angie had never met any of the people at Berrendo Elementary. It was pretty far north of Roswell. But it was clear that the two women in the office knew exactly who she was, as if they'd been expecting her. She got the feeling they were wanting to tell her stuff but couldn't. People were always telling her stuff, and so she knew the look. They told her to go down the hall to the school counselor's office.

There was a row of pint-sized chairs outside his office, and two boys who looked like sixth graders were sitting there, separated by two empty chairs. One of the boys was clean-cut and had an all-American look. His little chest, however, was all sunken in. He smiled at Angie. It was the smile of a flirt. The other boy had a bit of a lopsided face. He puffed up as she walked by. Of the two, he was more the rebel in his cargo pants, but neither of them looked like boys who'd cause any real trouble.

The counselor stepped out into the hall, extended his hand, and said, "Leeland Pruitt's stepmom?"

"Call me Angie," she said.

Before the counselor closed the office door the little flirt said, "We know Leeland."

"Don't you two move," the man said.

After explaining to the counselor what had so horribly upset Leeland, she sat silent. The man had flipped through papers he'd pulled out as she talked, so she decided to get to the point. "Abuse is what's going on out there on the Byrd place. It's way off the highway like a wilderness. Twelve miles,

I think. Luke told Leeland he'd knock the piss out of him if he ever got a call from school. Luke has a drawer full of scare tactics." She waited for the man to roll his eyes, but he only looked up and did a little nod.

He got up and opened his office door and said, "Jacob, Reed...let's try harder today. Go back to your classroom." He sat back down and said, "Someone in the family needs to make a call to CYFD." He pushed the phone across his desk to where she could reach it. "Get down to brass tacks. They need to know about his family life, not just school."

And so Angie Pruitt Jones reported the suspected abuse that day to CYFD, told them her full name and relationship to Leeland. They already had a file on Leeland. She knew that for a fact, even though she gathered that they had not taken any action.

But it wasn't a local Chaves County person who took the call that day, and at first Angie thought maybe that was good, to have an outsider. But the Albuquerque person didn't talk like someone who knew anything about southeast New Mexico or ranch kids, and that kind of scared her. Still, the Albuquerque woman was polite and let Angie tell the whole story.

"He's a good kid. Bright and tries real hard," she said and the counselor nodded. "Luke and Deona are calling him some terrible names and that's just what's heard in public."

Asked if the ranch owners were absentee, Angie admitted she didn't know, but the counselor motioned for her to cover the mouthpiece. He said, "No, they run a tight operation. They are big wheels in Roswell, part of the wool council cartel."

Angie repeated it for the woman who then said something about needing to analyze. "We'll send out a child protective-custody worker to gather information."

But when Angie asked, "When?" the woman said, "It depends." And Angie didn't feel at all hopeful.

After giving the woman her contact information and the counselor's name and number, she hung up, pulled her braid over her shoulder, and began to tighten it. It was a habit of hers that calmed her. When she had her wits about her she said, "And then there's still the poem. Leeland was supposed to have it memorized by today."

"I wouldn't worry about that, Angie."

"Well, I am worried for Leeland," she said. "I think you should be worried too. You do not know Luke Pruitt like I do."

"What I mean is that Leeland's teacher is not going to report anything to Mr. Pruitt. I promise you that. His teacher is looking out for him. All of us at Berrendo are."

"You sure?" she asked and flipped her braid back.

"I'm positive. Zero chance of any teacher at Berrendo doing that to Leeland."

Because eleven- and twelve-year-old boys love to trade in gossip, word got out that Leeland's stepmother, not Deona but his first stepmom, was at Berrendo that day. They told other kids and some of the kids told their moms that Angie had left by way of the back schoolyard, through the green tumbleweeds, and that was a pretty weird thing for a parent to do. There was no fence then—it was before Columbine.

We speculated that Angie would be taking the boy for the summer. Well, it was what we hoped, but it was stupid to be hopeful that way, and we all knew it.

> *Another deer hunting season has come and gone and we hear the same story again: the hunters tell us the deer population is way down and it's hard to get to the public land. But in just a day or two, the intelligence of God's creatures begins to show. First the does and fawns come into the fields, followed by the bucks. It seems as if they know they are safe here, that deer season is over and it's time for another type of hunt. When they stand broadside and watch you as you watch them, you get a lot of respect for them.*
>
> Linda Pruitt, *Ranching Weekly*

Corrine

1999

"Pick up," Corrine hissed into the phone as she sat waiting for someone to come back on the line.

She buried the handset in the curve of her shoulder as if she were frozen in a shrug. And she was frozen; the office was frozen. "It's an island, so it's damp," her commanding officer told her daily, as if he needed to apologize for the weather. She hovered over the phone. Like everything else in her part of the navy it was old, but not old enough to be retro. *The best thing about this phone*, she thought, *was that if you really got into it with someone you could lift it and then slam it down for attitude.* That really wasn't possible for her, she knew, being in the navy at the rock bottom of the chain of command.

The phone hummed like it was barely alive, and she wasn't sure she was still connected. But she couldn't afford to start over here, not with her boss due in any minute.

She'd done everything she could to get in to work early:

she'd dropped her boyfriend, Douglas, at work long before the weak, filtered Pacific Northwest sun began breaking through the low cloud cover. That meant there'd be zero blue sky all day long. She'd never thought she'd miss anything about Roswell, but blue sky was it, and her son—of course her son.

She'd begged a sentry to let her into the parking lot a full hour before the designated time to clock in. "It's going to be chilly in that metal building," he'd warned, but he opened the gate for her. And it was cold—a damp cold.

She'd come prepared with notes about things that needed to get told and a list of calls she'd gotten about Leeland and the treatment he was getting. The first call she'd gotten was from Leeland's elementary school counselor telling her they'd be calling the Children, Youth, and Families Department. She'd asked her aunt when elementary schools decided they needed guidance counselors and Sally had said, "When the Russians came looking for the aliens." But then Sally had added, all serious, "You do know, Corrine, the only reason that counselor made that call to CYFD was to cover his butt. CYA. Bet there's a fair bit of that in the US Navy too."

"It won't help one single thing to put blame on the counselor for doing his job," Corrine said. "At least he was doing something other than just talking about it at the supper table."

"We're all in it now," Sally had said.

There'd been the calls from Angie, lots of those, and from her cousin Patty Ann too. Patty Ann could be obnoxious. Corrine always said Patty Ann was the reason she'd known the word obnoxious when she was five.

We had our opinions about Corrine's cousin. We thought maybe she was going too far—itching for a fight she wasn't likely to win with Luke Pruitt. That spring she was always showing up at the elementary school, especially at lunchtime, to see if Leeland had brought a lunch. Patty Ann had her shortcomings, but families took care of their own in southeast New Mexico, and she was family. We all got that; we were just staying clear of a fight.

"Good morning, short-timer," Corrine's boss said as he walked through the door.

He dropped a mess of papers on her desk, which was going to be her desk for only three more weeks. She gave him the most respectful nod she could imagine, which was nothing unusual, not for him. He was smart, and he made it clear he thought she was smart too. Still, she added a look of calm efficiency. It worked. He kept moving and let the door to his office close behind him.

If it hadn't been time to point fingers she would have hung up and gotten busy because the others were filing in and stashing away their personal stuff so that they could get to the impersonal business of work.

Say a prayer for the hard-working people.

Sometimes Corrine didn't know where her thoughts came from. But she had to point fingers now at Luke and the new Mrs. Pruitt and their broken excuse for a family; otherwise folks would be accusing her of being off on her private planet while Leeland was being neglected, or worse. It sounded worse.

I left my son in a shitty deal.

Corrine had about given up when some woman named Amy came on the line. Quickly Corrine said, "I'm Leeland Pruitt's mother."

"You're calling Roswell, you know."

Corrine said, "Yes, I know who I'm calling."

Corrine's desk faced up to a matching desk, and Grace, the woman who was sitting there, looked up and made an "O" with her little mouth. Corrine tried to imitate the wide-eyed look of an alien to get her to look away and it worked. Corrine wasn't going to miss Grace when her promotion came through.

Amy said, "Can you tell me when you last saw your son?"

This was not going well. Corrine knew judgment when she heard it. She did the single best thing the navy had taught her to do; she put on the respect act.

"Yes, ma'am. I made a trip out last month. I have the dates," Corrine said and once again saw Leeland standing in the six-foot-deep ditch right off the highway. He'd been waiting a long time for her to come get him, so he said. He'd climbed down in the ditch to keep the spring wind from beating him up.

We all heard the story about the boy being left out there on 285. Anyone could have snatched him. We didn't take it up with Luke Pruitt—not a one of us—not that we didn't expect more of ourselves.

Corrine remembered that at first she hadn't been able to spot Leeland, and she'd felt that panic thing that the navy was trying to beat out of her.

"I went out to pick him up at the Sweetspread Ranch where his dad moved him when he married Deona. And Luke, his dad, had left him alone on the highway in a sandstorm. My cousin Patty Ann drove me out there that day. You can interview her if you need proof."

Patty Ann had been more than willing that day to load up her car with her four kids and haul them all out the twenty-six miles to get Leeland. Patty Ann was a busybody who called herself a 'busy bee.' She knew how to get in someone's face. Corrine thought about this Amy woman trying to get information from Patty Ann. Her cousin always spoke a beat before anyone had finished up with what they were saying. It took some getting used to.

Amy said, "We will get contact information if we need it."

But seeing him left that way on a highway, waiting there in the ditch—his back to the sandstorm—well, it changed things for Corrine. She remembered going a little mad that day, but she wasn't going to admit it to Amy.

We could have stepped in and told the Children's Services people that Leeland was only doing what he'd learned from the livestock. Left out in bad weather, horses and cattle turn their backs to the oncoming storm. A ranch kid would know that. We didn't intend to get into the Pruitts' business, but it hits your heart when you see a kid do something like that.

The woman on the phone said, "I understand you have concerns. Tell me, what is your custody status?"

"We share custody. We have this agreement."

"We will need a copy of the divorce papers," Amy said. "Okay now, I'll have to have Central Intake call you back to get the particulars. You have a number?"

"I'm in Washington state," Corrine said.

"That's no problem."

The phone was humming again. Corrine gave Amy her number. It was better this way since she wouldn't have to log in another personal call. She didn't need the navy docking her pay for this shit. Now she had no choice but to wait.

She got some work done and did it by ignoring the looks she was getting. Grace put on the face that said, *I'm not judging you. Talk to me.* But that wasn't going to happen.

The call back came in at 10:30 from a Tina.

"Yes, I am the birth mother. Like I told Amy, Luke and I share custody and we had a parenting plan. Everything has changed now. There's a new stepmother. I think she's simpleminded." Corrine hesitated and then said, "And they have him out on a ranch that looks like a rock pile. It's a long road out there from the highway." Corrine said that part in a rush, because she hadn't driven the road—just heard about it. And the navy had taught her that too—hearsay and all that.

Corrine watched as every set of eyes in the now-crowded office raised and then lowered. Mostly, Corrine saw fear in their faces. Columbine had done that to these people who had all joined up expecting to face down fear, and then found the real danger was at their kids' schools. Ever since April 20th it was all anyone talked about. Well, Corrine hadn't had so much to say.

"The counselor at Leeland's school called and he told me they've made a report to CYFD about my son, Leeland. He's eight." She stopped, took a breath, and added, "It has to be pretty bad for a school to file a report."

Corrine stopped. It felt like terror. And it made her brain freeze up on her. She couldn't remember what she'd already told Amy. There was nothing to do but go on. She checked her list.

"I'm calling because nothing has been done. There's already a CYFD file. I filed child abuse charges against the father in 1997. That was over two years ago."

She waited and then said, "You've heard of Detective Roseann Powers and Detective Craig Reynolds? In the Roswell police department...? Look at their reports."

The woman said, "This is Albuquerque. I'm taking it all down. Remember, this is no longer local."

"This is not working for me," Corrine said, and lifted the phone and dropped it in the center of her desk. It made a nice little falling apart sound, and the woman said, "Hello?"

"It was all swept under the rug. Now, the father, Luke Pruitt, and his third wife, who Leeland is stuck with, are calling him faggot and pussy boy in public and all. They tell Leeland not to talk about the abuse and they threaten him. I'm not sure they even feed him." She waited and the phone amplified her breathing.

" 'What goes on in this house, stays in this house,' that's what he tells Leeland and I'm afraid of what he'll do. You have to understand that Leeland's a ranch kid. That is important because it's summer." Corrine pulled the phone closer to her and turned her back on Grace.

"I'll push this up to Enhanced Intake as a priority two," Tina said.

Tina and Amy. It couldn't get more lame.

Corrine felt her mind flood. She'd been warned off of Luke Pruitt by all sorts of people at Roswell High, and her aunt had pitched a fit. But she'd gone on ahead and married him because he was cute, and he said he'd take her with him when he left Roswell. But knowing that she had walked away from her own good kid, that part was eating her up.

She cleared her mind long enough to give Tina directions to the house off the highway on the Byrd place. She heard the woman say an investigation would follow. There'd be a social worker assigned. Specially trained and all that.

"Just so you know," Corrine said, "Luke will try to make you think he owns the ranch. He doesn't. He doesn't own anything except a ten-ton truck. He always has a truck. And there are no neighbors looking out for Leeland."

Tina said, "Let me ask you something. Have you considered summer camp for Leeland?"

Corrine snickered. "He's a working hand on that ranch."

Corrine had gone to summer fun at Military Heights Elementary from first to sixth grade. Aunt Sally had made it clear that she would go and would like it. Corrine had spent lots of time those summers on the metal teeter-totter which had always felt nice when you were in the air and cruel when you hit bottom, and you had to trust the person on the other end. Social skills, Corrine figured, like the way she had to trust Tina now. She felt herself hit hardpan, and she turned and looked at Grace.

"We're staffed twenty-four hours," the woman said by way of finishing up with her. And then, "Thank you for your consent to investigate the matter."

"Is that what was holding this up?" Corrine said.

"I can't say. This matter has just come to my attention. I

can promise you a call back after our social worker visits your son. I'm thinking I'll send out Art Morales. He knows Roswell."

"Well, I never got any call back before."

"Give us a chance to do better this time."

Corrine turned back around, pulled the phone back to the spot where it belonged, and said, "Okay, but if you are twenty-four/seven, can you call me at home next time?"

"We can do that...surely, we can do that."

Corrine saw Grace nod.

It was summer—dusty and dry in southeast New Mexico, and we had it on good authority that Leeland wasn't allowed off the ranch. All's we knew for sure was that nobody had seen him since school let out in May. Now, who we did see was the CYFD guy. Most mornings he was hanging out at the Daylite Donut at the little table for one. Word got around that he arrived right when they opened, which was six a.m. "Watch out or he'll get in your business," ranchers having coffee would warn each other. The man must have liked working there out in the open with his files spread out on the table. Maybe he liked being there to hear things or maybe he thought if things were urgent people would speak up.

For weeks while she waited, Corrine talked to her aunt and Angie and Patty Ann too, when she could stand it.

"Luke has Leeland twenty-six miles out of town," was the way Angie always started her conversations. "He won't let me take Leeland on my weekends."

Angie told Corrine that the last time she'd gotten Luke on the phone he'd said, "Leeland is a working hand. Get it? He doesn't have time to be hanging out with you and Neighbor Boy."

"That's what he calls my husband," Angie said and Corrine knew it was real genuine hurt she was hearing in Angie's voice.

It was Patty Ann who jumped into threats to get Deona

arrested: "It's that horse-toothed woman Luke married who is turning his mean into criminal." It was after those rants that Corrine got so despondent that she took Grace up on lunch.

Sitting in the too-cute seafood place—Dock on the Bay was what Corrine called it even though she knew that the name was simply Whidbey's—she let Grace ask her, "What exactly do you want this children's agency to do? You want them to take Leeland out of Luke's care and do what then?"

"I want them to keep an eye on Leeland is all," Corrine said.

"No one is going to do that for you, and you know that," Grace said. "What you want is for them to scare Luke and Deona straight."

"Okay, maybe. Yeah, until I can figure out how to get him back."

"Serious? Because you can't start that and not mean it," Grace said.

"Serious," Corrine said. "Douglas says he'll adopt Leeland if we get married."

"Wow, he asked?"

Corrine nodded. She felt sixteen again.

"Being careful..." Grace said and Corrine nodded again and thought she might tell Grace about the Bottomless Lakes.

"Okay, here's what you tell them. Tell them to keep Luke scared and on his toes until you can take Leeland," Grace said.

And because it felt like wisdom that Grace had bestowed on her, Corrine did that little "O" thing with her mouth.

It was Amy and Tina on the line together who called Corrine back, but it wasn't until after the Fourth of July and New Mexico kids went back to school in early August. Corrine had given up hope that anything could be done for summer.

"Let me give you the basics," Tina said. "Art went out to their place. He likes to do surprise visits, but that didn't work. It seems Mr. Pruitt locks that wire fence; the one on the highway, and Art had to go back into town and make a few calls before he could set a time to visit. So, it gave Mr. Pruitt a warning, and we'll have to factor that into our assessment."

"I told you about that gate being locked," Corrine said. "Besides the ranch house is twelve miles off the highway in a pit. There's no surprising Luke Pruitt out there."

"Yes, you told us about the gate, but we wanted to try it on a workday and all that. Anyway, Art went back and took Leeland way out into the yard and they talked. We always have to get the child off alone where they feel safe."

"That puts the kid in a tight spot," Corrine said.

"It's the best we can do on a first home visit. All we got from the boy was that sometimes they call him names and that he works hard doing ranch work. Said they had him picking rocks."

"Where was Luke?"

"He and his wife were at the screen door watching, so Art put Leeland's back to them."

"Oh yeah, that's going to trick him," Corrine said.

"We gave Leeland a lot of good information on how to reach us and what we could do for him. And we questioned him pretty hard. And we met with the wife separately. She denied everything. And then Mr. Pruitt was waiting at the gate and Art spent a good amount of time with him. Art advised him that he could be arrested for leaving an eight-year-old kid out on a highway."

"Did any of it scare Luke?"

Tina hesitated. "That would be pretty hard for Art to assess."

Real quick-like, Amy added, "Mr. Pruitt swore he never called Leeland stupid. He said he didn't care if Leeland hated him, because he was seeing to it that his boy was going to be a good citizen."

Corrine kept quiet because too much was crowding her

head, too many scenes.

Tina said, "Mr. Pruitt said that it was his duty as the father to get Leeland in gear because his grades had been falling all year."

"A third grader?" Corrine said.

"We know, Corrine. Next step is for Art to get back with the school. Art stopped there at Berrendo after the meeting, but it was locked up tight, and he didn't want to hold up his feedback to us any longer. As soon as he gets with the Berrendo counselor he will complete his safety assessment summary."

"Then what?" Corrine asked.

"Then we will determine if services are recommended."

"It's going to fall through the cracks," she said, but she didn't say it so Tina and Amy would hear. She was the one who hated Luke, and she was the one who had to fix it.

I'm not sure if you read the latest from our opposition. I'm referring to the protests made at the National Cattlemen's Convention. Some of them blame the upsurge of violence on eating meat! Surely to goodness they cannot believe the American public is dumb enough to buy into that garbage! We are not a nation of ignorant people.... Some folks are trying desperately to find a reason (any reason) for the violence. Something, anything, that will shoulder the blame.

Linda Pruitt, *Ranching Weekly*

Luke

1999

Leeland snapped the last of the pressed silver snaps on his sheepskin vest before he climbed into the cab—*snap*. Luke watched the boy getting his excuses ready and said, "Save it."

"Brrr," Leeland said.

Luke had decided to leave the heater off to let the boy feel the cold. He hit the gas hard and the truck skidded in the puddles the last snow had left.

"Wow," Leeland said.

If this were my spread, Luke thought, *I'd put down pea gravel to soak up the melt.* But his snow tires took the road just fine. He heard—well he and Leeland had to have heard—the jets overhead. Leeland had only been on the Cross T since school in Roswell had let out, but the jets were a daily event. Leeland's eyes looked like they were going to explode.

"Stealths?" Leeland said.

"Doing what they damn well please. Tornados, probably.

Germans," Luke said just as the three jets came in low in an arrow formation. Leeland slid down in the seat to get a better view and shouted, "I can see landing gear." And then softly Leeland said, "Dad, they're sure to scare the colt."

"A little scare never hurt anything," Luke said as he took his foot off the gas and glided over the cattle guard, making the metal sing. The jets disappeared.

Still, the day felt just fine. He'd moved up in the ranch world was how he saw it. He'd found himself some independence way out here with a fourth-generation rancher. "Once the grandsons of the patrón are grandfathers, the blood is thin," was Stralin's wisdom and Luke was banking on that. If he'd known that the Byrds out there on the Sweetspread were looking for a farm rancher, not a rancher, he'd have never bothered with them. The Cross T was more like it.

And that was pretty much the way we had heard it. Luke Pruitt was just not a good fit out on the Byrd place and the parting was mutual. Nothing unusual in all that, we thought when we heard he'd up and left with the wife and kids.

Luke looked over at Leeland in the passenger seat and asked himself why the hell he'd brought the crying-wolf kid with him to the post office.

Even though they'd moved on—to Weed, New Mexico of all places on earth—Luke could not stop seeing Leeland out there in the yard at the Byrd place yapping with that do-gooder state employee as if he were some innocent little kid.

I was an innocent little kid once.

He had half a mind to leave him now, doors locked, in the cab. But he couldn't risk it, not even in Weed, population sixty-three villagers.

"The face of a clear conscience will take you far in life," is what Luke's mother had said whenever he'd turned up late—before he had time to come up with a story.

Luke said, "I don't have to tell you to keep your mouth

clean," and then he hung his mouth open for a nanosecond, thinking that he'd only come close to saying what he'd meant to say. He shot Leeland a stern look and could see that the boy had caught the error. Leeland nodded with a tilt of his chin— no smile, no "yes, sir,"—code for *I'm smarter than you, so I'm going to ignore what you just said.*

"Keep your nose clean," was something his stupid bankruptcy lawyer kept writing in his letters, that and "KISS." And Luke had zero idea what that meant. The attorney, "Second" is what Luke had nicknamed him, had a II behind his name. Luke liked the balance it set between the two of them.

"In a personal bankruptcy, what you want to avoid like poison is a lien. KEEP YOUR NOSE CLEAN. Got it?" Second had put that in writing using the caps key. Luke didn't like it.

Luke would teach Leeland a lesson for that slip, just not here at the Weed Post Office. *Established 1885* it said right over the door of the mostly brick building. And then in small print carved right into the building it read, *A place where winter means something.*

"Living off the grid, are you?" an old-timer said to Leeland as the boy jumped down from the truck. Leeland didn't say a word but dashed ahead to hold open the door. The old guy said, "You family to Maude Pruitt?" The man was nearly bent double.

Luke gave the man a shrug, and the man said, "Lots of Pruitts in these mountains. They helped pioneer it. Maude's place had the beauty of an orchard."

"Sure enough," Luke said by way of ending the oral history lecture. The man pointed the top of his head at the wall of brass post office boxes—each one with a proud eagle pressed into the brass. Luke headed to the counter with Leeland on his heels. But before he got there he leaned over, hands at knees, and said to his son, "See where talking lies to some ignorant guy from CYFD got you—Weed."

Luke straightened up and said to the fleshy woman who had appeared behind the counter the exact words he had practiced, "I'm working the Bates place. Need a PO Box."

The old man came back around the corner, patted Leeland on the arm, and said, "Son, come here while your dad there is doing business."

With the cloud of heat coming at them from the vents in the floor, the room took on his kid's sweet smell. It was the vest. Angie had given it to him, and in the heat he smelled like warmed honey.

Luke nodded for the boy to go. What else could he do with the postmistress beaming her good-cheer approval?

"We can do that," she said, and for a moment Luke had no idea what she was blabbing about. Women outnumbered men here, or so his new boss had told him. Why Mr. Bates had told him that, Luke had no idea. She pulled open a drawer, took out two forms, and passed them to him.

Luke heard the old guy start up, "I'm a goat rancher." Then in a for-real wistful voice the man said, "A fox was walking through the forest when he saw a crow sitting on a tree branch with a fine piece of cheese in her beak..." And then changing back to his old-guy voice he said, "Lots of time to ponder lessons when you're a shepherd. Caw! Caw!"

Leeland jumped back.

"You see, the fox flattered that silly proud crow. Dropped that fine piece of cheese." The man paused and then said, "Hear you're working the Cross T. Seven thousand feet high, that place—a real wonderland."

Without even turning back around Luke waved Leeland over and took ahold of his collar.

"I took care of the mail forwarding form at my old post office," Luke said with his *pays to be polite* voice and put his hand flat on the forms.

"Well, that's fine now, Mr. Pruitt, but we'll need that

information too. Cross-check. Can't be too careful. Y2K." She made a buzzing sound like a hornet and then stared at the papers until Luke removed his hand and took the pen she offered.

He wrote in his folks' old Diamond Crown address—years old now—on the forwarding mail form. No way, no how was Corrine tracking him here so that she could sic CYFD on him again, and nothing from CYFD was getting forwarded to him. He wasn't stupid.

"Y2K is overblown," the old man said to the young woman who'd come in and stood next to him when there was plenty of room behind. She was smiling at Leeland, and Luke could see she too was itching to do some talking. She was clutching a small package wrapped in foil and bound with yards of curled red ribbon. The room began to smell like rum.

"Yes, ma'am, can't be too careful," Luke said to the postmistress and handed her the completed forms. She took them but held her stubby-fingered hand out and shook it at Leeland and said, "Frost bite. Nearly disabled me." And then she said to Luke, "Bates got you out at the place on Mule Canyon Road?"

He nodded, thinking that the young woman and the old man might not have heard her, but the old fool went on, "Quiet place like that, why I'm sure you can get a good night's rest there."

The bells on the back of the door rang out and Luke realized that two new old guys were giving the door a good shake to announce their arrival—all good cheer here.

"Close the door, boys," the clerk said, and Luke watched her sneak a look at the forms. If she started writing in his address on Mule Canyon Road, he'd have to do something, but she put the forms in a beat-up manila folder.

"See our library over here, son?" one of the new arrivals asked.

"Go," Luke said, and then to the postmistress, who'd put both of her fat arms down gently on the counter like a dog lowering itself down for a long rest, he said, "Keys?"

"We better tell Deona about these books," Leeland said from across the room.

"We pass 'em on," the bent man said.

Then the three old men pulled up chairs around a small round table. One had come prepared with his seat cushion. Once settled, one of them said to Leeland, "Have you read *Old Yeller*?"

Luke turned his back on the group. He heard Leeland say that he had not read it.

"American tragedy," the same man said, and the young woman said, "Don't scare the boy." And then she offered Luke a whiff of the fruitcake before presenting it to the clerk as if it were a newborn child.

The bent man said, "It's about a yellow cur dog that gets rabies. Between you and me, Y2K won't scare you once you've seen a dog taken by rabies."

By then Luke had a little index card with a box number and two keys. He gave the clerk cash, thanked her, and said to the old guys, "Work waiting."

"Good for you, young man," the bent man said. "Bates always says he hires to retire. Most don't stick."

Off the grid, yeah right, Luke said to himself, slamming the door of his truck. He could already imagine that woman steaming open the envelope Stralin said he'd send with all the mail that had come in; Stralin had the key to his box in Roswell. Right then Luke decided he'd tell his brother to tape the envelope up good. Jeez, and now he'd have to tell him to put in Diamond Crown Ranch as the return address. Stralin wasn't going to like that. He'd told Luke to play it close to the vest. "Way out there in the mountains is a good place to start over."

The boy took his time getting in the truck, and Luke yanked his arm. "Don't be stupid. Get in. One of those guys will follow you out with more information we don't need." He put the truck in reverse. "Hold these," he said to Leeland and handed him the card and the keys.

As they passed the café, Leeland said, "Are we having lunch, Dad?" The place was all dressed up fancy for Christmas that was coming in three days whether Luke liked it or not. Suddenly, he and the boy saw the lights on the big, decorated pine off to their left flicker and then light up again and flicker. They'd passed over the power cord that the town geniuses had dragged from the café to the tree. The decorated, three-story-tall tree stood right in front of the graveyard. That was Christmas for the town.

"Wow, big tree," Leeland said.

At the crossroads Luke did a K-turn. No one was in sight either way on the little highway—right went to Mayhill and their new place, left to Sacramento and the church camp his mom had gone to back in the 1960s. One day, not today with Leeland all wide-eyed, he'd drive out there. Sniff around. See if his mom had carved her initials in some tree. Truth was, he had planned on lunch. Nothing much at home to eat and with Deona and Karmen off gallivanting with her Flood relatives, Luke figured he deserved a café meal.

"Sure, let's have lunch. Otherwise we starve. But those booths have ears," he warned.

"I hear you, Dad. And I've read that book. Old Yeller saves a kid from a bear. It's incredible, but I just didn't want to let on."

"The face of a clear conscience," Luke heard his mother say as if she was there in the front seat of the truck with them, and he felt sorry for her then—her being a killer and all.

They crossed back over the cord, and Luke heard the little sound his front and then back wheels made as they rolled over it. They watched the lights on the tree flicker. As Luke pulled into the café lot he said, "Christmas lunch. Your grandmother used to take Stralin and me to lunch in Ruidoso at Christmas. We ate steaks."

And in a voice his mom would have used he said, "By the way, Y2K is a bunch of shit, especially in this one-socket town. Here's what we're going to do. On New Year's Eve we're going to come down here and short out that cord. These folks need some good scaring."

"Incredible," his kid said.

"Hear those Stealths this morning?" the waitress said as she put down two menus and smiled. "Ironic, isn't it?" she said to Luke and nudged him with her hip.

"Price of freedom," a man too young to be doing nothing much on a workday said from across the room. His accent was German. Luke thought maybe the guy was trying to shut down the waitress. Then he remembered the town stats and realized his boss had been warning him.

"Get yourself a gift from under the tree," the waitress said to Leeland. "Boy gifts are in green." She moved even closer to Luke so that Leeland could slip out of the booth. Luke nodded toward the decorated piñon tree and said to Leeland, "Get your sister something." And then to the gal, he said, "All you could find was a piñon?"

"They smell the best," she said. "Ready to order?"

With his eye on the menu, he said, "We'll get back to you."

In that moment he decided two things: He wouldn't bring Deona in here—better to keep this gal wondering—and second, he'd have Stralin bring him the mail in person.

Leeland came back to the table with two wrapped boxes, one red and one green. Then as if it was a secret between them Luke leaned forward and said to him, "We didn't have a GD book in our house when I was growing up."

Leeland said, "Deona wouldn't like that."

"Whatever," Luke said. "Didn't matter because my mother knew that *Old Yeller* book by heart. She'd stand in our doorway and start out, 'Long, long ago in the town of Salt Licks, Texas, a dingy yellow dog came for an unasked stay.'"

"Like a bedtime story, Dad?"

"Whatever. Stralin always cried when she got to the part about the dog saving the little kid from the angry mother bear and forget it when the big kid had to kill the dog. Like a flood."

"Rabies?" Leeland said, big-eyed now.

"Yeah, a sick dog can turn on you pretty quick and the boy had to protect his family. But that's a far cry from an American tragedy."

Leeland sat back and rubbed his forehead before saying, "I know a poem by heart, Dad."

"You don't say. Stay put," Luke said and went up to the register where the waitress was wiping the menus with a wet rag. He ordered two well-done burgers and asked if the pay phone outside was working.

"Why wouldn't it?" she said.

She gave him two dollars in quarters when he passed her the ones. "Where's his mother?" she asked. She was a local Weed girl; *Inbred*, he thought.

"She's in the US Navy," he said loud enough for the German to hear and felt something like pride wash over him. He didn't need this small-town shit.

He called Stralin, and because it was noon and Stralin's wife put a noon meal on the table each and every day, Luke caught him at home.

"This post office thing is fucking not going to work," Luke said and held the toe of his boot to the crack in the phone booth door.

"Luke, Mom taught us not to talk that way, and she was my mother too."

"Is that what she told you in her letter? Maybe we better

get matched up on those letters."

Stralin went quiet. If his family was still breathing, Luke couldn't hear them.

"Any other good advice you want to pass onto your no-good brother?"

"Sure, Luke. Mom said to remember that it wasn't all bad. And it wasn't."

Luke could feel his pulse in his neck. *The altitude,* he thought. The GD altitude. His mother could go all calm like she was hibernating when she was pissed. Never did know how she did that. It wasn't a God thing.

She was wrong. It was all bad.

"Okay, here's the problem," Luke said. "A small town is going to be trouble for me."

"So, that's simple. Stay out of town," Stralin said.

"Okay. But then you need to bring me the mail. Let's meet up—with our families, after Christmas. Before the kids start back to school."

"Mom would like that," Stralin said. "And Trudy wants to see your place."

"It's nothing. Trust me. Want to get steaks?"

Stralin said, "That's not going to happen. But I hear that barbeque place on the highway in Cloudcroft can feed a big bunch."

It was Tourist Trap, USA. But Luke didn't know when his brother had become so talkative, and so he said, "Sure, let's do that."

Of course, we were sad to hear Leeland was yanked out of Berrendo where he had friends and teachers and that woman Patty Ann who were looking out for him. But we liked to trade in wishful thinking, and the next ranch was always the better ranch. We heard that some woman had pressed Art Morales after he gave her that "Hi there" look at the donut shop. Morales said he'd put in a recommendation for Children's

Services to do a welfare check when they located the family. Sounded to us like sharing and fishing both, and a good place to leave it. Honestly, we weren't thinking much about Luke Pruitt on those days before Christmas 1999. There were more serious things on our minds.

Deputy Greenwood

Midday July 6, 2005

Greenwood's Lincoln County vehicle was built for rough roads, but the ruts on the lane to St. Jude's cut at odd angles, and now he found himself stopped between ruts.

Paula was taking the bumps in stride. He saw her looking out across the way at what once had been a polo field where the artist Peter Hurd taught ranch hands and local cowboys to play polo. They'd both grown quiet, but then he said, "Back in the day a team called the Snake Killers played there."

Paula shook her head in little disbelieving bursts and began with a story he could have never guessed.

"On 9/11..." she said and paused to look over at him. "I was working in Brooklyn and was called in early and told not to bother with roll call. My precinct included all of Prospect Park, which is quite a place, with meadows to make the Hondo Valley weep." She chuckled at herself, and he started through the rut.

Greenwood knew full well she was trying to take his mind

off the kid he'd just left behind.

"When you're in that park there's not a hint of the Manhattan skyline and goats are left there to roam and keep the weeds down. Anyway, on a daybreak shift a park service officer spotted a body under the waterfall at the ravine. I was a newbie detective so I was sent over with a uniformed officer to investigate. We got to the park gates around eight a.m. It was a stunner of a fall day in New York, but of course everyone knows that now about 9/11.

"We were at the ravine by 8:30. I had never been there before and even with a body and all I admit to being charmed by the water rushing over the falls. But there was a group of school kids around the backside of the falls. They were boys just starting the ninth grade—about fourteen or fifteen years old. I learned that later. They graduated high school this last June. They were far enough away not to have seen the body but would soon enough."

Greenwood had stopped at another rut and decided to cut it at a right angle, but Paula was oblivious to his driving or the ruts.

"I needed to call in the body and get the crime scene people there pronto." She raised her eyebrows at him and they both knew she was thinking about Pete.

It struck Greenwood that this was a disappointment to him, and he felt a hot flash of anger at her for rubbing it in.

"I left the officer with the park service guy and had to climb over some chandeliered rocks to get to the schoolboys. I kept thinking how I'd have to come back to the park with my dog and explore. But then I felt something deep in the earth as if the rocks were being hammered. At the time I blamed it on the waterfall.

"The teacher did this little welcoming wave. He looked up and swept his arms across the morning sky and the forest of trees that surrounded us and said, 'Listen. There are two hundred and fifty species of birds in this park.' A couple of the boys laughed, but he didn't seem to mind. I got him off to the side and explained the body, explained that I'd be setting up a crime scene investigation.

"The teacher didn't want to leave the waterfall—not really. I could understand that, and I could tell he wanted to tell me more about the birds."

"Sounds peaceful," Greenwood said because he hated being angry.

Paula nodded and then said, "But he agreed to move the boys, and I stood there watching them regroup while I called in the body, or at least tried to. I couldn't get through to my precinct. I thought I had to have a bad connection on my radio, but then one of the boys shouted out that his dad was on the phone. The boy held his cell phone up to show everyone and then said, 'That was my dad. He works in the World Trade Center and his building is on fire. He's evacuating, and he can't get my mom on his phone.'

"I didn't feel the second plane hit, but by then I was standing in a grassy area. I caught myself counting the boys.

" 'Keep everyone together,' I shouted to the teacher and started back over to the body. When I was in shouting range I told the officer to take over and stay with the body. By the time I got back to the boys, another one of them had admitted to having a cell phone in his backpack, and he was calling his mom. We all just stood there and listened to him talk.

" 'She's home,' he said, 'but it's real bad. She wants me home.' The teacher kept putting the binoculars, which he was wearing around his neck, up to his face to study the sky. But something in me took over.

"I said, 'Okay guys, I want you to form a circle and hold hands.' I put the teacher in the middle of them and I went on with instructions. 'Look to your right and then your left. Those are your buddies. Until you are home safe you go nowhere without knowing where your two buddies are. Now let's count off.' I pointed to the boy whose dad was evacuating the tower and said, 'You are number one and to your right is number two. Now call your number out.' Sixteen boys called out a number.

"Then still standing in that circle I had them pass the two phones around, but after a few minutes the calls all rang busy. The ash didn't start falling on us until a little past ten. The teacher pointed his binoculars skyward and said, 'All the birds are leaving.'

"At eleven I made the decision to take the boys to a church I knew on Seventh Avenue just up President Street from the park. I knew that the pastor would have the doors open. Sure enough, they were. Sirens were going off in all directions and he was kind enough to take the boys to his office where there was a phone.

"Between those boys there were at least thirty-two parents, and because these kids came from a part of Brooklyn with easy public transportation into Lower Manhattan, many had parents who commuted into the city. Twenty of those parents were in Manhattan on 9/11 and twelve of them died when the towers fell. The boy who got that first call—his dad got out safe."

As Greenwood slowed in front of the church, he realized he knew more about Paula just then than he had learned in two years of working with her. He turned the truck off and nodded at the step-up van parked at the door. Paula read the words that were engraved in stone above the doors to the church. "Hope for the hopeless," she said as if it was a conclusion to her 9/11 story.

"I always begged my mom to let me be a Catholic," Greenwood said. "You all got so much more theology."

That got the only laugh he'd heard all day.

"I'm not Catholic. I'm a not-so-observant Jew." She

reached over and punched him in the shoulder.

Now he was the one to raise his eyebrows. "Magliaro just sounded Italian and I jumped to Catholic."

She was still smiling and said, "Makes sense. My husband was both those things."

And before he could start in with any apologies, she went on. "He died that day in a stairwell, marching up. I'll always be proud of him. That's something..."

And now Greenwood couldn't speak let alone apologize. He felt as if there was a knot where his heart had been.

With her hand on the door handle, she said, "Here's the thing, Greenwood. For the last four years I've felt grief and guilt all mixed up together. Guilt for babysitting while he was responding. But today I feel only plain old grief. It was a good thing to stay with those boys."

She reached under her seat and grabbed the bag of burritos. "Maybe someone's hungry," she said and climbed out of the truck.

Plain old grief, he thought.

Greenwood got back to the Bounty a few minutes before noon and saw Deputy Conley's truck sitting up ahead, smack in the middle of the cattle guard. It was as good a way as any to make sure that no one got onto the ranch. Off to the right side of the road several vehicles were parked behind a flatbed truck with a load of sweet-smelling, premium alfalfa. High horse quality, Greenwood suspected. And on the left side in the shade of the wavering United States flag stood Duff on a stage made of pallets normally used to stack hay. He was dressed up in pressed black jeans and wore black, tooled-leather cowboy boots—hand-tooled, Greenwood was guessing. Duff was testing the speaker system. A group of maybe ten reporters were gathered in front of the stage and were being entertained by a scrawny cowboy who was telling tales, waving his arms, and pointing at the alfalfa for emphasis.

Greenwood pulled up nose-to-nose with Conley's truck. They both stepped out of their trucks and Conley gave Greenwood a friendly, almost playful, salute. "Here for the dog and pony show?" he said.

"I take it that's Smoot over there," Greenwood said as he counted the reporters, ten total.

"Yes, sir. And he's none too happy that I won't let him take his load in. I explained that this is an active crime scene. Not my problem that he can't turn it around. A feed man is responsible for the load he carries," Conley said proudly.

Both deputies looked up at the darkening sky.

Conley said, "Dispatch says that the sheriff is due in any minute and Duff is waiting, but I don't see the storm waiting."

Greenwood nodded. Smoot was heading their way. Conley cupped his hand around his mouth and said in Greenwood's ear, "The medical examiner wants to take the ambulances out ASAP but doesn't want to parade past the press. I'm supposed to radio him the all-clear."

"I'll get the show started," Greenwood said and headed over to Duff. He brushed by the feed salesman, who was watching his pointed, narrow boots as he stepped across the cattle guard. Smoot was heading into a complaint and Greenwood said, "Not now."

Greenwood nodded at Duff, who swept the hand that was holding the microphone up and around as if he were about to begin an auction, and finally said to the small crowd, "Welcome to the Bounty Canyon Ranch. As you know, we've experienced a double homicide. My manager and his wife were found murdered—left in a shallow grave behind the barn. I was away from the compound at the time of the murders but was first on the scene. That was yesterday afternoon. Of course I put in a call to the Lincoln County Sheriff."

Duff had mastered his pauses and took one now. Greenwood wasn't much for watching the news but knew when a newsman was taking credit for a scoop. None of the reporters were writing anything down yet in their notebooks. They seemed to be waiting for the story as if it were going to be dished out and served.

"I will get to your questions..." Duff smiled and added, "even though I am a man more accustomed to asking the questions. But while we wait for the sheriff, I would like to take us all back to an earlier time—to 1999 and the end of the millennium and the last great cattle drive along the same trail ridden by Billy the Kid and the cattle baron John Chisum. It was a six-day drive. We braved the cold for seventy-five miles from Roswell to Lincoln. We wanted to do something for history and have a good time doing it."

He paused again as if waiting for applause. The reporter who Greenwood had met early that morning shot her hand up and said, "Do you have a suspect?"

Duff ignored her and said, "This is a way of life we love. The trail ride helped us preserve part of our heritage."

Duff shielded his eyes as he looked down the road even though there was zero sun-glare now.

"Let's get on with the questions. I've made a formal statement and copies are here in that box." He pointed to a box on the stage.

As Greenwood stepped across the cattle guard he heard the same gal ask another question. It was a challenging tone of voice she was using now, but then she'd been held up here since daybreak waiting for her story. She said, "Topic A is a double homicide, isn't it? And two missing teenagers. Can you tell us where those kids are now?"

Another reporter asked his question before Duff had a chance to respond: "Do you take any blame for the murders on your ranch?"

"I'll take notes," Conley said.

Greenwood said, "Say, as soon as this deal ends, can you

call the hand, Alfonzo, and get his statement?" Greenwood pulled out his notebook and read Conley Alfonzo's home number. "He's the one who drove out of here early with the pink horse trailer. And ask him if he had anything to do with putting a tarp back on the club house."

The deputy gave Greenwood his practiced look that said, *Okay, but I don't understand.*

As Greenwood started up his truck he heard Duff say, "Luke Pruitt was an able-bodied man. He could take care of himself and all he wanted was the best for his kids." Greenwood couldn't decide if Duff was putting himself in the storyline or taking himself out. It didn't matter.

Greenwood shouted to Conley, "As soon as I can I'll send you some relief," and then he hit the gas.

He saw the little pink horse trailer again in his mind's eye. The thing had reminded him of a baby bassinet like the ones Melissa and Melinda's mom had put on the porch of the Moon Café and filled with plants once the girls had outgrown them. Wandering Jew was the plant. He shook his head, ashamed to be side-tracked by houseplants just now and then ahead, up behind Duff's home, a vertical lightning bolt found ground, or so it seemed from this angle. Greenwood never did hear any thunder. "Heat lightning," he said aloud to no one. He'd always loved weather and never tired of hearing old folks opine on dry storms and deep freezes.

Hoyt met him at the Pruitt residence. "Commander said to tell you to head to Guesthouse One, up on Buckeroo Lane." Hoyt smiled with his whole face.

"Sure thing," Greenwood said and then he asked Hoyt if he could relieve Conley as soon as he could leave the residence. A state trooper was not his to order around, but Hoyt was not standing on any sort of official protocol—that was clear.

A woman dashed toward Greenwood from the white tent, which was flapping like a kite itching to take off.

She came to light in front of him and said, "ME wants to see you, sir."

Greenwood got out of his truck, checked the now black sky, and followed her.

"Here it comes," the ME said in a German accent so thick Greenwood didn't understand what he was saying until the rain began. The man had a mouthful of saltine mush and he held out a half sleeve of the crackers. Greenwood was not ready to eat. They were standing inside the door of the tent when they saw the two ravens that circled the house and then took off flying low. Greenwood could hear their wings, even over the sound of the rain on the canvas.

"We Germans believe that ravens are the ghosts of damned souls," the man said. "A single shot in the head to both victims. No fight. No flight. Each died instantly before they were dragged by their feet down the steps and across the gravel, the woman in her stocking feet. Unless you have questions, I'm pulling out of here. This rain will clear up the air and the ambulance chasers."

The man trotted over to his Honda and then, as he opened the door, he shouted back at Greenwood, "Of course, Noah released a raven from the ark to test the flood."

Greenwood drove up to the guesthouses and because there was not going to be a break in the rain anytime soon, he did his own dash up to the porch of Guesthouse One. The commander was inside and a uniformed trooper was posted at the door. Both men had cameras around their necks. The commander waved Greenwood into the kitchen. It was a country kitchen all duded up for visitors.

"Nothing here," he said to Greenwood. "Where's Paula?"

"I left her at St. Jude's. She's putting up a roadblock to the house where we found Leeland."

The man, who Greenwood now knew was named Pete, nodded at the evidence bags he had placed on the tiled kitchen counter and said, "Take a look. This kid laid down a trail. Bloody clothes and bloody pull-up boots left in a pile in his closet."

Greenwood held up the bags to get a better look. He saw all he needed to see.

"You didn't need this evidence did you, Greenwood?" Pete asked, but he didn't wait for an answer before he handed Greenwood a small evidence bag with one piece of paper that had been torn from a spiral notebook. Greenwood laid it flat on the counter to read the note. In block letters, it said, "Sorry. Coppers let it happen. Took a kid to do the dirty work."

"Crime scenes don't lie," the commander said as he narrowed his eyes at Greenwood. And Greenwood knew that Pete was sorry for him. Then Pete called for the trooper to come in and collect the evidence bags. "Meet you in the car," he said to the trooper, who kept his eyes straight ahead.

"What's next?" Pete asked Greenwood. "You brief the sheriff?"

"Probably," Greenwood said slowly. "Actually, I'll get the DA on the phone. He'll be wanting a confession. But first I go get Paula."

As they stepped out on the porch Greenwood's mind slipped into focus and he asked the commander, "Did you get a record of calls on the phone at the Pruitt house? Any calls from the boy?"

"Yes, two calls from Leeland. I'll get you a transcript."

And then the commander did the oddest thing. He put his two hands on Greenwood's shoulders in a manner of not quite an embrace. It was more like the way a football coach grabs a kid before sending him out to play defense, but then Greenwood had never played football. And then he slowly leaned out from under the roofline to test for rain. It had stopped raining, but still he made a run for the car.

> *If you're lucky, like us, your shearing is over and the ewes are all back and settled in their pastures. Weather was good for us this year, and now we turn our attention to other things. Not quite! It is real evident that one or two bucks got out just a tad early.... These early babies usually do all right. A wet winter storm or the eagles are the main cause of trouble. Neither of them are something you can do anything about.*
>
> Linda Pruitt, *Ranching Weekly*

Corrine

2000

The last year had been proof to Corrine that life could be, might be, good. In twelve months' time, she had called New Mexico Children's Services on Luke after she'd hunted him down in Weed, New Mexico—which might just as well have been outer space; she'd married Douglas Jones—one heck of a sweet guy; and, during all the turmoil of the traditional Luke Pruitt finger-pointing, she'd managed to gain custody of Leeland. That last part meant sucking a one-page Modification Agreement to their divorce out of her ex. It had not been easy. Some mail-order attorney had given Luke the words to disown his own kid without actually saying that one word. She'd never asked him to disown Leeland—or maybe she had.

When she'd explained this to Douglas he stayed calm and said, "Well, that takes the cake."

She was so done with Luke Pruitt.

There would be no contact between the father and the son

for any reason and the boy could change his name from Pruitt. Of course, the agreement had been drawn up by Luke and his attorney before Luke got the all-clear from CYFD on their investigation, the one she'd started with a phone call. *Unsubstantiated* was the word Children's Services chose when they closed the file on the matter one year after the investigator had shown up at the Sweetspread Ranch. Maybe it was that matter hanging over his head that turned Luke into a man who'd disown his own kid. So Corrine wasn't taking any chances with Luke Pruitt. She saw him for who he was: that man was crazy like a fox.

And now she was on a road trip with her guys. Her dream team is what she'd called them the night before at dinner, when they'd ordered her a root beer float while she was in the ladies' room. She and Douglas were driving her Aunt Sally's 1989 pickup—burning gas at sixteen miles per gallon—and they'd trade it once they got to Whidbey Island, but they'd needed it to take what Sally had called Corrine's hope chest. It was a mess of stuff, and carefully secured in the truck bed in the middle of all that stuff was a flat of Sally's milkweed.

"It'll transplant gratefully up there in the land of wet pavement. And Leeland will too. You'll see," Sally had said as she presented the flat to Douglas like an offering. "Sure, the monarchs migrate that far," she insisted when Corrine pointed out the miles they'd be traveling to Washington state. "Those butterflies breed along the way and it's the young who complete the journey. Up to three thousand miles. No exaggeration."

"Like the Russians," Corrine said because she loved her aunt.

God, Corrine had thought as they pulled out of town heading north on 285, *let this be the last time I leave this place.*

Now, we had our own predictions. We thought they'd be gone a good long time before we saw them again. Not that we didn't feel terribly sorry for Sally and Angie, too, who'd brought Leeland's extra clothes over to Sally's—all too small. We had it on good authority that there'd been a lot of crying at that sendoff. But we understood that to mean that they'd all been happy for that family of three.

Leeland had been humming that morning as they left Roswell, passing by the fancy courthouse, the military institute, the Walmart decorated with alien art, and Berrendo Elementary. Corrine had learned by the end of that first day out that Leeland hummed in the silence between conversations. As they passed by turnoffs for the Sweetspread he'd begun to swat at a fly that had been bugging him since they left town. She knew that Leeland knew his dad prided himself on his ability to catch a fly in his big, bare hand, had his own technique of getting behind the fly. Corrine sensed that Leeland had caught himself right as he almost mentioned his dad. It was the way the boy took a big gulp for no reason at all.

The kid was already beginning to forgive his dad. Well, okay. What choice do kids have other than to forgive?

"Roll down your window, Douglas," she said as she rolled hers down, and together they waved the pest out.

"He was only hoping for a bite of my Daylite Donut," Leeland said. He was on his third glazed donut. He liked them with sprinkles.

It was mid-July, with hours and hours of daylight on their second day out as they bisected Colorado and finally crossed into Wyoming. The road surface—concrete, Corrine would have guessed—glowed silver, as if the road itself had been laid down on foil. She knew that it was still hours from dusk. The speed was posted at seventy-five and Corrine kept it there. The concrete was beginning to magnify the sun's glare, and she could feel a bit of fresh pain behind the bridge of her nose.

"Almost there?" Douglas, who sat across from her, asked sweetly. He'd been watching her for miles now.

Maybe one day, she thought, she'd learn not to wait for a smart-ass comment to come from this man. She didn't have that down yet. Maybe one day she'd forget the way Luke mocked her, but she figured she'd have to forgive Luke first, and for her, that was unlikely.

She'd always been Leeland's mom but now, finally now, it felt official, and Douglas, an aviation tech without one ounce of cute cowboy in him, was going to work out the adoption.

"We'll make it happen," is what he'd told her.

She looked across at him. He didn't fit in a pickup. They'd have to fix that soon. She checked her mirror and saw Leeland curled up in the corner of the back seat.

"He's nodded off again," she said to Douglas.

"He's a whirling dervish of info," Douglas said and Corrine only closed her eyes, briefly, in agreement. It was a little prayer thing she had learned to do when she'd met Douglas.

"He told me that years divisible by one hundred are not leap years."

"You don't say," Corrine said, and then quickly said, "Wait..."

"Unless it's divisible by four hundred," Douglas said and shook his head.

"There you go," she said.

The road was straight ahead. Out of nowhere, Corrine remembered hearing Angie tell Leeland in that muddy voice of hers, "You can say goodbye to flat and brown." She'd gotten the flat part wrong. Angie, that already grey-haired woman, meant well. Saying goodbye, she'd cried like a baby. If only Luke had stayed married to her...and then the memory left her.

Corrine waved the palm of her left hand in front of her face and said, "Hasn't the sun been in that very same spot an hour now?" She closed her eyes, opened them, and said, "I'm praying for a hill."

"I see one now," Leeland said.

"Welcome back, Leeland. You always did have a good imagination," she said.

"Let me take over," Douglas said. "Leeland can keep me company in the front. You sleep, Corrine, and the next thing you know we'll be in Bozeman having a bison burger."

"Family style?" Leeland asked and Corrine knew it was because they'd ordered that way the night before in Colorado Springs. There'd been a moment, when the waitress suggested it was easier to order that way, that Leeland had gotten a spacey look as if he was trying to figure something out on a map.

Corrine settled in the back seat, and Douglas steered the truck off the shoulder back onto the highway. Maybe she'd stay awake a while and listen to Leeland and Douglas talk. Leeland had already started in on another story, this one about his grandmother Pruitt.

"I can remember her still," Leeland had begun. "Mom says I look like her," he was explaining now. "Well, every spring she had the job of saving the early baby sheep from the eagles. The eagles, they didn't know any better, and if you weren't careful they'd carry off one of those innocent little lambs."

Corrine heard Douglas say, "Your grandmother kept watch, did she?"

"Yes," Leeland said, "because an eagle can fly at fifty miles an hour, and when they are diving, they go at one hundred miles. They can lift up to four pounds. It's pretty incredible."

Corrine had always liked Linda Pruitt, even if she had lied her way into the suicide when maybe she should have hung in. The way Corrine had it figured it was never about suicide anyway. It was murder, justifiable. Figuring it out had made Corrine feel sick. The suicide was Linda's way of keeping the worst of it out of the papers and out of a courtroom. The way Linda played it out, innocence and guilt would not be for public consumption.

That woman was tired of being scared.

"I'm not scared of you," Corrine had said to Luke when she finally tracked down a number for him in Weed at the Cross T. She'd caught him at the ranch office. Luke's boss had answered the phone and put Luke on. It was a stroke of luck. But Corrine hadn't known if she'd believed it herself then—or now—even with each mile she put behind her.

Damn, she was tired of thinking about him. She lay out flat on the backseat, folded her arms over her chest, and squeezed her eyes closed. "Boys, I'm gonna take a little nap."

She couldn't quite drift off. It occurred to her that maybe before they took the bridge over to the island she'd get Douglas to stop at the giant REI, and she'd get Leeland some water-proof sneakers—Keens is what she'd get her boy. She reminded herself he needed some new underwear too. Douglas would help on that end.

When she got her eyes open she saw two ravens circling. They just kept at it.

She was on a hillside flat on her back with her head down as if she'd just come to rest there—as if something had kept her from sliding head first into the ravine. She could see her feet resting above her. Her shoes were gone, and she spent some moments trying to convince herself she'd taken them off. But she hadn't, and she hadn't heard their tires hit the gravel, or felt the pickup take off from the earth and roll. She hadn't heard a thing, and now it was only silence with the sleek, black birds soundlessly cutting through the sky right above her.

And then Douglas was with her and said, "Oh no," and put his fingers to her neck. They were wet and sticky and warm. She tried not to groan. Leeland was there too—thank you, God. He was making the sound a lost baby goat makes. She couldn't remember what the word was for that sound.

Then Leeland said, "Mom, I know a poem." Or was that

earlier today and she was just remembering it? Yes, it was earlier in the truck, and she'd said, "Not now."

So now she said, "Now." But she made no sound.

The boy said something about the tongues of cattle and something about hummingbirds that rise and float away whenever there is fuss.

Douglas patted the boy on his back gently, and the two of them started to float away as if it had all been a dream, both of them human ghosts in stocking feet. Had she forgotten to buy her son shoes? She held her lips very still and said, "Keens." It came out sounding like "Honey," and she was grateful for that because sometimes her boy smelled like honey. Hadn't she called him honey when he was a baby? She couldn't remember.

Douglas said, "Oh, Honey." He had his arm around her boy, and their tears had soaked their innocent faces. Corrine spotted herself in her son's wet brown eyes and closed her own.

Bleat. There you go. That's it, she told herself.

The truth is no one witnessed the accident that day. Not that there was one single thing anyone could have done. There were no bystanders and no one was passing by except for the grey fox that crossed the median that evening just at dusk. A pompous little creature. Cunning is what we would have called him if we'd, any of us, seen him.

The rollover just happened. Calls were made from Wyoming and word spread all over Roswell and into the Hondo Valley and even off in Weed. Corrine was dead and that was that. It felt rotten to once again mix grief for the Pruitts with relief, but it was our first impression that Leeland had gotten out just in time—had left us all behind.

We knew we were trying to believe only what we hoped.

> *Very few things surprise me or shock me. You meet people from every walk of life and most of them are fair, honest, and willing to help others if there is a need. If I could have one wish it would be that everyone get an opportunity to live this life for a while. I wish they could understand our sense of pride and independence, our loyalty and our sense of humor, referred to as 'dry,' by some folks. There are things we do take seriously: life, death, clean air. But if we don't keep our humor during these times, we would just not survive, plain and simple.*
>
> Linda Pruitt, *Ranching Weekly*

Luke

2000

Luke Pruitt, ramrod straight behind the wheel of his pickup, was in the drive-thru line at the Roswell McDonald's—one hundred and twenty miles from Weed—when he heard the thump of bass coming out of the black VW Beetle that had come up behind. The car looked like a piece of Indian pottery. In fancy lettering on the top of the windshield, it said To Serve Man.

I can put this pickup in reverse and run right over the top of that GD bug.

In his mirror, Luke studied the punk kid staring at him, and then the kid turned down his music and yelled out of his window, "Keep the faith man." It was a high-pitched nasal voice.

Luke had been up since five practicing what needed to get done at Corrine's funeral. He had to get finished here in Roswell and get back up the mountain while he still had some daylight to get work done—least so his boss could see him working.

Bates always had his eye on him. It was as if the rancher were hovering overhead in a UFO, watching his every move. Plus the man was grey-skinned with a head plenty too big for his body. Luke knew he wasn't the only one in Weed who thought Bates was part alien.

But Luke had no intention of leaving Roswell today without his son, so he didn't have time for a punk who shared his personal wisdom on his windshield.

The pickup in front of him suddenly lurched forward, and Luke hit the gas, yanked his steering wheel to the right, and pulled his pickup into an open parking space. He dared the punk kid to follow him, but the little black car was rocking again with music.

Luke climbed out of his truck and walked close enough to the back of the VW to have put his foot on the bumper and rock the thing. There were two bumper stickers. One said, "Abbey Road." The other had the call number for a radio station he had never heard of and said, "Where Roswell goes to Rock."

Forget the disk jockey, he told himself, because all he could think now was that he needed a cigarette. He could blame Deona for that. He turned around and went back to his truck and, leaning up against the hood, he smoked what he let himself not count as his fourth cigarette of the day. It was only eight o'clock. It had been dark when he headed out on 24. He had stopped for his second smoke when he crossed the Rio Peñasco. While standing there he'd come to decide that owning a place on the Rio Peñasco would be far enough away from the Cloudcroft Forest Service know-it-alls so that he'd never have to put up with their shit again. He'd line his piece of the river with Lombardy poplars—their roots binding the riverbanks. A rancher could do okay out there with even a small outfit—he knew how to do better than okay.

Dying isn't the worst thing, Luke heard his mother butt in as he stood there finishing up the cigarette, looking at the river. And just when he had been feeling optimistic. He was sure it was her voice he'd heard. It gave him the willies.

Luke stamped out his cigarette and rolled his shoulder muscles to loosen them up. At least his hand had stopped the shaking thing it had started doing when he needed a cigarette, but still he felt like he'd been stuffed full of explosives. *Everything is in order*, he told himself and walked into the McDonald's with the aloofness of a cowboy following a successful roundup.

He got a big coffee and the Big Breakfast with hotcakes and took a seat near the front window. A copy of the *Roswell Daily Record* sat discarded and waiting for him on the table. He knew that if he opened it and turned to the obits, he'd see all the details for Corrine's funeral. There was not a damn thing wrong with turning up at your ex-wife's funeral. What if they hadn't divorced? It made his heart double-beat.

"Have you given this marriage your best effort?" his mom had asked when Luke told her about splitting up with Corrine. But she asked that only once because he'd pointed out the irony to her. "Sharp as a pencil, are you now?" she'd said to him and gone off to get some sort of work finished up. It was one particular day. He remembered so many days—her sitting at her typewriter—getting that peaceful look on her face.

For ten minutes Luke sat perched at the high round table, smelling the coffee that still steamed, and tried to put a stop to his mind spinning around like a carousel. The smell of the coffee and the pancakes doctored up with syrup triggered the memory of another day at the Diamond Crown. It was as if he had a catalog of days and had just dialed up a day in, say, 1983 and went into a time-lapse. Smells meant something when two teenage boys and one big man lived together in a metal trailer home with a mother who started each day with a spray of some perfume she'd bought at the drug store in Carrizozo. She was always trying out something new.

Coming out of the fog, he went over his game plan. He was here in Roswell to call the shots with his son. He'd heard that Corrine's new husband was only twenty-five years old. *Leave it to Corrine,* he caught himself thinking before he got back to his planning. *Fair and simple,* he told himself. *I'm the only biological parent Leeland has left.*

Luke pulled the lid off his coffee cup and drank what was left in big gulps. *Americans,* he thought, *drinking coffee out of sippy cups.*

He'd make Leeland into a dutiful son before it was all over. And he'd provide—he was the father. Luke pushed the newspaper under the tray. He nodded at himself and, with his thoughts settled, started listening in on the two men to his left. One was an old guy with yellow teeth. He was wearing a cap with the insignia for the 509th Bombardment Group. If you grew up in this part of New Mexico, you knew the 509th was formed with one mission: Drop the atomic bomb. Luke had seen the patch with its white mushroom cloud and blue wings a zillion times. It always pissed him off as much as it amused him.

Poof.

People could be so stupid.

Across the table from the old man was a cadet, in uniform, from the military institute. The kid had removed his cap, and it sat on the table between the two of them. The older man had his hands on top of the boys, and they were praying with their eyes closed.

The old man said, "When the kindness and love of God our Savior appeared, he saved us, because of his mercy." When they opened their eyes, the war hero looked at Luke and said, "Morning devotional. Join us?"

"That's okay," Luke said and looked around.

There were three other tables of men like this, praying. The old guy smiled at him. Luke looked away, but the man said, "In the big scheme of things, life is as short as the steam that came off your coffee."

One more word...

A trash can with the open mouth of an alien sat on the other side of the restaurant. Luke made his way there with his tray of trash and the newspaper and noticed the little tent cards on several of the tables: Earthrise Service. 7:30 a.m. Well, he had not known.

He parked right at the front of the police station. He spotted a picnic table off to the side of the building. It looked like a perfectly good place to smoke. Stralin had offered to drive down for the funeral from the ranch he was working now. "All's I'm saying is that we know how it feels to lose a mother," Stralin had said.

"He's not an orphan," Luke replied as he decided he wouldn't need his brother coming to Roswell to muck things up.

Stralin had gone all quiet on the phone like he was napping and then finally said, "Behavior adjustment, brother, if you want Leeland back. You show up with a chip on your shoulder, and it'll be trouble of your own making. When you are dealing with the law, you can't act like you've been treated unfairly."

Going along to get along, that was his brother in a nutshell. But it had been a sermon.

And then Stralin added, "Trudy and I would take Leeland for a while. Give him time. Let him adjust."

Luke walked into the Roswell Police Station with a cool confidence. The fluorescent lights were popping. Those things always bugged his eyes. The on-duty officer asked Luke to follow him back to the conference room. Without turning around he said, "Custodial interference is something we see a fair bit of these days."

The conference room was totally bare except for a table and four folding chairs. There was nothing but paint on the walls. The officer said, "I've been the DARE officer for going on eight years now. Maybe I know your boy. What school was he at?"

When Luke gave him his *I'm drawing a blank look,* the man said, "Drug Abuse Resistance Training."

"Berrendo," Luke said and pointed his chin at the man. They both sat, and Luke patted the paperwork he'd brought into the station.

"Okay now. What is it you'd like us to do for you, Mr. Pruitt?"

Luke started in on what he'd practiced, and after he'd gotten all of it said he stopped, and then added, "My brother can speak for me and the folks at the Diamond Crown Ranch can too."

He could see that was a mistake. He saw recognition in the man's eyes, and then the questions started.

"Now, as I understand it, your son was with his mother—your ex—and his stepfather when this ex was killed...and this stepfather is in the military."

Luke nodded.

"Car accident, you say?"

"Yes," Luke said and pressed his hands on the top of his thighs.

"When was this?"

Luke blew out a big breath. "Two weeks, give take."

"Okay. And your son is with this man now. In his custody...should we say?"

Luke nodded again.

"Does the stepfather have any reason not to release the boy to you?"

"I'm the natural father," Luke said. "Until recently he lived with me." Then he pointed at the spiral notebook the officer was scribbling in and said, "Got all that?"

The officer was a fast writer. It felt to Luke like a mini-trial, as if the officer was trying to sniff out motives.

"I didn't come here looking for a fight," Luke said.

"We have to be clear first, Mr. Pruitt, on the facts. Have you spoken to Leeland? Told him you want him back?" He waited and then added, "Plan to take him back to the Cross T, do you?"

"Yes," Luke said, but he was so done here.

The officer took a long time to get that last bit recorded and then he said, "There is the law to consider. Let me take this to the Assistant DA. Won't take but a bit, he's just across the parking lot. You can wait here."

Luke looked around the square room. His right hand was shaking bad.

"I'll wait outside," he said.

Luke didn't have long to wait before he saw the officer coming back across the lot. He nodded at Luke. "No question, Mr. Pruitt. You have legal rights to the boy as the biological father. Let's have you follow me over to the church in your vehicle. Wait in your truck while I report in."

Luke followed the officer to the metal-sided church where they both pulled up right at the front door. "All going according to plan," he said aloud and then added aloud, "Doing the right thing." He would have forgiven his dad, Luke thought then, if he had only once done the GD right thing.

It was his brother who had called him to let him know that Corrine had been killed in an accident on the road. Stralin said that Corrine's new husband had been behind the wheel, but that Leeland was fine. In the silence, while Luke was trying to get his mind around what he was hearing, Stralin cleared his throat and said, "Luke, forgiveness is giving up every last shred of hope for a different past."

"Did you hear me blaming that kid she married?" Luke said.

"I didn't mean Douglas," Stralin said. "I mean Leeland. You have to forgive him for going with his mother. That'd be a good start. That and taking him back with no strings attached."

The church receptionist told the officer that she'd get a note to the youth pastor that they were here to get Leeland.

"We didn't come here to interrupt the funeral," the officer said. "That's not our intention."

"It's no funeral. It's a memorial. No body. No burial," she said. "So why don't you move your patrol unit over behind the building so we don't go starting any rumors. Follow me, Mr. Pruitt. I'll put you in the youth pastor's office, and then I'll flag him down in the auditorium."

There was no other way to do things than the way she wanted them done, and so Luke followed her to the youth pastor's office. She had a sense of urgency in her steps that Luke kind of liked.

The pastor's office was full of so much stuff that Luke didn't know where to look. There were posters on three walls. He stood back and studied the six-foot Captain America poster. It was under glass. Luke didn't know if kids even knew who Captain America was. He was still trying to figure out what a superhero was doing here in a church when the officer came in and took a seat on a small sofa. Luke walked over to the side of the pastor's desk. A computer was sitting right in the center, proud and tall like a graphite sentry. Luke moved closer to make sure of what he was seeing and said, "Power Mac." He wanted one of those bad. His boss in Weed had bought one for his secretary to help run his empire, and Luke had never seen her use it for anything other than a place to paste sunny yellow Post-It notes.

"I call it Sawtooth," the pastor said from the doorway and

then crossed the room to slap Luke on the back, friendly-like. Luke didn't know how the thin-lipped man had managed to get anything said with that mouth. It looked sealed. The officer stood and shook the pastor's hand, and the pastor handed Luke a xeroxed paper and said, "Here's the program. On the back there's the poem Leeland wanted the congregation to read aloud."

After they all got seated the officer asked Luke to explain to the pastor why they were there.

"I've been denied access to my son. I don't want him to be removed from the state by some twenty-five-year-old who has no rights to him. I've cleared it with the police that I've got legal rights to him." Luke looked at the officer, who just blinked some sort of official agreement with what had been said.

"We'll wait for the service to be over," the officer finally said because the pastor just sat there, lips sealed.

We were keeping our eye on Leeland there in the dry, hot auditorium. Leeland was dressed like a kid all ready for his class picture. We saw right off when he walked in that he was wearing brand new Justin Stampedes. Then late in the service, we saw something change in the boy's demeanor. It was like he'd been kicked. The boy was seated between his mother's aunt and the young man who had married his mother. The aunt suddenly looked like a trapped cat—claws ready. It was clear that someone had passed the word that Luke Pruitt was in the building, come to get Leeland. You could see word spreading. Luke's second ex was seated behind Leeland, and she squeezed Leeland's shoulder. She wore her now grey hair in a bun at the back of her neck and had wound a white chiffon scarf around that bun, making it look like a cottontail had perched behind Leeland.

It was darn cruel to interrupt a service that way, and we let it happen.

We watched as some woman in a white naval uniform stood up and moved to the back of the room. She stood there by the double doors as if she had the authority to do so. She'd come in with Corrine's new husband and had introduced herself as Grace. It looked like she had come here to save the boy, and we put our faith in her right then, thinking it was a good thing someone was willing to protect the boy.

After the last prayer, it was Corrine's Aunt Sally who was the first person to get down the hall to the offices. Luke could have guessed that she'd be on the move. The head pastor was right on her heels. She was yelling that Luke had no right to be in the church. It was the youth pastor who got the people sorted out and into separate offices. Meanwhile, someone must have got Sally settled down because it was suddenly quiet in the office wing. It seemed forever to Luke that they left him there with the head pastor, who had nothing at all to say to him and who sat staring at the youth pastor's computer like it had some answers for him.

Finally Luke heard Corrine's cousin out in the hallway talking with a young girl she called Cassandra. The head pastor jumped up and left the Captain America office to speak to the two of them, and then he took them somewhere. Luke wasn't sure where they were taken, where anyone was. Finally the police officer opened the door and ushered Leeland into the office. The officer said he would stay while the two of them talked things over. But the officer said first he had questions he had to ask.

"Do you want to go live with your dad again?"

Leeland kept his eyes down so long that Luke stood up and went across the room as if drawn to the boy and hugged him. He was such a scrawny kid.

"Yes," Leeland said, "But I'd like to spend time with my family first."

"Sure, we can arrange that, can't we, Mr. Pruitt?"

Luke's heart was beating like a ticking bomb, and his hands were shaking, but something made him happy.

"I mean Angie, Dad. And Aunt Sally, and Douglas came all this way to bring me back."

"Sure," Luke said. "I want you back, is all."

After the officer finally told them to shake on the final agreement, he opened the office door. The young girl who Luke knew had to be Cassandra was standing there. She burned a hole right through him with her metallic green eyes and then said, "Leeland's run out of luck. He should never have come back." She was a mess of tears.

"Hey, Cassandra," the officer said.

"She's one of my DARE kids," he said to Luke.

Luke had no idea what to say to the girl. She was about the size of Karmen, who was an inch or two shorter than Leeland, but she looked dangerous.

"He'll live on the streets before he goes back to his dad," she said as the officer lifted his arm like a big wing and pulled her under it. Then he pivoted and motioned for Leeland to follow the two of them down the hallway.

From down the hall, the officer said over his shoulder, "We're good. You pick him up at Sally's a week from Sunday, after church. All done here."

We weren't so stupid to think the Pruitt sideshow was over. Lots of us were still milling around in the auditorium, waiting like our hands were cuffed and there was nothing we could do. We didn't know if it was shame or fear that had washed over us.

"Seriously? I don't get to see Leeland?" a young kid in the crowd said.

The gravity of it all seemed to have silenced the rest of us, and then Douglas, the stepdad, came back into the auditorium and the woman in uniform went to him and took his arm. He was crying like a little child. The woman looked at the congregation and said loud and clear, "Disgraceful."

> As I sit at my desk this morning, a slow gentle rain is falling. What a peaceful time it is. Here in southeastern New Mexico, we have been blessed with enormous rain. It has always amazed me how the Good Lord always comes through, even when man has given up. I wonder if it's His way of keeping cowboys humble.
>
> Linda Pruitt, *Ranching Weekly*

Luke

2000

Standing there in the church auditorium with our hangdog faces, we passed around the story of how Luke had showed up at the Roswell social security office a few days after he heard about Corrine dying. Maybe, we thought, that was the "disgrace" the woman in the uniform was talking about. But like blame, there was plenty of disgrace to spread around.

Damn, if we had ever really wished to help Luke, we should have told the story of the Pruitt family—how Linda Pruitt had to kill Payton Pruitt. Should have told it out loud on the front page. Linda Pruitt had no other choice. Sure, we did lots of talking, but we never got around to telling that story and just maybe, if we had, we would have saved Luke Pruitt from whatever it was he was out to prove with his nine-year-old kid.

"That Luke Pruitt is one cold, proud SOB," someone said as we worked our way to the exits, women fanning themselves with their programs. Story was that a week back Luke had been spotted in the social security office, rocked back on two legs of the waiting room folding chair with his arms crossed high up across his chest. Only men cross their arms that way, self-satisfied men who think they've got you on something, holding you in judgment as if they were robed judges. And then just as fast as that silly story came together, we were done with keeping an open mind and a shut mouth.

Luke had gone to the social security office to sign up for Leeland's survivor's benefits—a child of nine would be claiming benefits for nine years and we put that windfall at fifty thousand, give or take. And that man would be taking it. We didn't have to see the evidence to know that Leeland would be signing over those monthly checks to his dad, never to see a red cent for his care or future. It was easy to draw that conclusion, and we were passing that story around.

It was Leeland now, motherless, not Luke, who needed our watchful eyes. We'd missed the point of the murder-suicide out there on the Diamond Crown those five years earlier. Linda hadn't been out for blood and not even a drop of revenge. That had never been the point. It was Leeland—the still innocent four-year-old—not Luke, she was looking out for when she started making plans. And we'd have heard as much in church if any of us had been listening back in those days when Linda and Payton were put to rest.

Grandchildren are the crown of the aged.

And so, no one much noticed today when Luke left Roswell and turned west onto Highway 380, heading for the Hondo Valley where he'd been raised by his mean-as-shit father and his damaged mother, because it was Leeland we were tracking now. We were raising the alarm and ringing some bells. We were going to call the dogs on Luke Pruitt.

Luke had been heading west for thirty minutes, riding more than driving, when he turned off the highway to the main entrance to the Diamond Crown Ranch. He slowed in front of the gate, a lacy wrought iron masterpiece. The gate was new. A gate was always the first thing a new owner put up and this one boasted a crown smack in the middle of all that iron. Luke pulled up close enough to see it was locked. Didn't matter, there was always a gap when a cattle guard was involved.

I'm just a stupid kid, was not so much a thought as it was Luke's impression of himself as he climbed out of his truck, sucked in his gut, and trespassed onto the Diamond Crown.

Being raised someplace should mean something.

He kicked dirt and told himself again that part about being a stupid kid, but he knew it for a wish. From where he stood just inside the gate, he could see that the pond was choked with weeds. The new owner of the ranch was too green to realize that the bright yellow flowering American Lotus floating peacefully—unrooted—was a weed and in no time the fish would all be dead—drowned. The rancher would be left with muck.

Waste.

It was late afternoon; the July air was cool in the shade. He'd forgotten his cigarettes in the truck, but he didn't think about them now, and if his hand shook he didn't see that.

Across the pond, one pastured horse stood watching, and Luke decided that's what he'd been missing at the Cross T—a good-looking horse all his own. The horse locked his legs, gave up worrying about the stranger, and took a snooze. Nothing rippled in the pond; it would be like that from now on—infestation and all.

Thinking he heard his mother's voice, he called up another day from his catalogue of memories: finding his mom out here with Leeland, coming up on them unexpected, the two of them reciting some baby thing over and over again:

Ladybug. Ladybug
Fly away home
Your house is on fire
And your children are gone
All except for that little
Leeland, for he crept
Under a frying pan

"What a thing to teach a kid," he'd said to his mother.

"Little bits of wisdom go a long way, son," she'd said, and
he knew it wasn't her voice he'd heard just now but the
unkindness of ravens that were taunting the horse, mimicking
some human voice they'd learned—maybe his mother's. He
remembered those oval-eyed ravens. He knew that they had
long memories just like him.

He deserved killing. Exodus 2:11-12.

Now he was reciting aloud what his mother had copied out
for him in the letter she left him: "One day when Moses had
grown up, he went out to his people and looked on their
burdens; he saw an Egyptian beating a Hebrew, one of his
people. He looked this way and that, and seeing no one he
killed the Egyptian and hid him in the sand."

"Always trying to protect the innocent, Mom?" he shouted
across the mucked-up pond and watched the ravens beat it out
of there.

A sense of being lost and a rush of images came over him:
a cattle chute, his mom's typewriter, pudgy Stralin breathing
through his mouth as they ran from their father—he'd been
such a crybaby—and Corrine's tan legs as he drove her out to
the lakes. But then the images stopped like a snapped
filmstrip, leaving him dazed. He hated it when he thought of
Corrine. He hadn't cared when she walked out on him, and he
hadn't cared when she'd left for the navy. But he hadn't
wanted her dead. It felt like a conspiracy, as if his mom's death

and Corrine's were arranged to do him in.

Someplace in his heart, he reckoned he should have shown that verse to his brother and that maybe his mother had meant that verse for their dad's stone. He squatted down and waited for his head to clear. The ravens swooped back in, circled the pond, and disappeared off toward the three-story mansion where the rancher lived one or two months of the year.

Waste.

"He's motherless now," Stralin had said about Leeland on that first call after Corrine died, as if it was some sort of hard-boiled factoid.

"Here's a little bit of wisdom for you, Big Brother. At least Corrine didn't kill herself like our mother," Luke said.

He wanted a cigarette. He stood and kicked raw dirt into the pond. Then he bent over in the dirt, looking for a sizable rock but there were none. The Diamond Crown was not that sort of place, and so he made his way back over the cattle guard. He leaned up against his truck through two cigarettes while he made his plans. He'd start Leeland in on putting stays—put those shiny new boots of his to decent use.

What America wears to work.

There was plenty of summer left for the boy to learn what work was, and damn if he was going to provide his son with fancy boots—a cushy life. When he was Leeland's age he'd been popping out one-seed junipers and dragging their still-green limbs into windrows. And that had been in the dirt flats in the heat of day—a place where flies ate on the weeping eyes of calves. His mom never did put that bit of ranch reality in her folksy little "life is grand" column, even though she'd seen such things, knew them for true.

Luke climbed in his truck and headed home to the Cross T. He had a long ride ahead of him. He'd cut through the Mescalero Indian Reservation, open range. It was a death trap with loose cattle on the road, and the random elk willing to take on a Ford 150 for the sport of it.

The Mescalero, sure enough, had got their inheritance. Chosen people.

He felt like spitting out the window, but his mother had taught him not to.

Still, he'd be home well after dark. The Cox Canyon Baptist Church foundation that had been left there to rot would tell him when to turn off the highway in the pitch-dark July night. He wouldn't miss it.

But he did miss it, because there was no bloody moon, and had to drive five miles past before he found a turnaround. But he didn't mind so much. He liked being calm in his head, like now when he was repeating the exact words his mother had used in her letter: *I've read that on the original pressing of Stevie Wonder's Sunshine album he inscribed this in Braille: "Here is my music, it's all I have to tell you how I feel, know that your love keeps my love strong." I was writing for you, Luke.*

It was an afternoon in late August when he came in, after bringing in the backhoe, after telling Leeland that it was his job to scrub it down, when he'd been disgusted to see his neighbor, Lark, standing in his yard yakking it up with Deona and Karmen. Back in early spring he'd first spotted Lark standing in the middle of her never-cleared pasture, and it was then that he had an inkling that she would be trouble for him. It was just something he saw in her stance. It didn't take a genius to figure out that a woman who'd named herself "Lark" was someone to avoid. He'd heard her real name was plain old Linda. She'd kept mostly clear of him in the months he'd worked the Cross T. So today he slowed up and took his time crossing the yard.

Miss Captain America come to visit.

"Lark brought over some fresh milk," Deona said and gave Luke her loose marbles look.

He knew that Deona was afraid he'd say it, and so he did, "I don't drink milk."

And then to Karmen, who had been fixing to pick up the cat that had followed their neighbor into the yard, he said, "Go inside with that milk." And when she didn't move he said, "Now."

He felt an urge to boot the cat, and when he looked up at Lark she said, "Come here, Puss in Boots. Mr. Pruitt doesn't take to cats. Am I right?" And then after a pause that gave him time to stare at her weatherworn face, she added, "He protects my place."

Fairy stories.

We'd heard about this gal for years now. She'd named her little ranch White Rabbit. She was the one who had planted the white wooden crosses all over her one thousand acres, which every fool knew was nothing in New Mexico. And we knew Bates had never been able to buy her out and had stopped trying. Folks sometimes took their families out that way on a Sunday drive to see those crosses.

She pointed at Karmen, who was walking toward the back door of the house with the heavy jug as if she was on ice, and said, "For the kids. Kids like fresh milk."

"You got kids?" Luke asked, knowing full well she was a woman living without a man.

"Nah, I didn't bother with that. Too many go wanting. I keep a nice front yard, grow columbine in honeysuckle shade. You can come see it, bring your kids. Not one weed, and I have never once used a drop of poison."

"Learn that at UNM?" he asked. It was where all the hippie communists went to college. When people talked about her, and they did talk, some said that when the Jefferson Airplane touched down at UNM in 1968, she got off. His mom had owned one of the Jefferson Airplane albums. She'd kept it hidden with her Stevie Wonder albums. *Crown of Creation* was the name of it, and the cover had a glowing mushroom cloud with the band hovering inside it. He had the urge to ask Lark about it.

Psychedelic.

"Word runs downhill, doesn't it?" Lark said and moved closer to him. She smelled like warm bread.

But he wasn't going to encourage her with another question.

Once she'd struck up a conversation with him at the post office in Weed after she'd introduced herself as his "neighbor lady." She'd gotten too close to him then too and said, "Your mom would have been about my age. Linda was the most popular name for baby girls in 1950." And when he had nothing to add to that she said, "That mother of yours had wit and wisdom fit for my refrigerator, that I can tell you!"

Luke looked down at her sandaled feet. She was a woman who came looking where she had no business, where she had no right.

And then she said, "See you've got your boy back. Putting him to work like a full-grown hand, are you?"

"You better believe it," he said and started for his back door. He needed a smoke, and he needed her gone. Deona held her ground.

To his back Lark said, "Keep him working out there in those fields in the heat of the day and Bates will not be liking it. Even grown men get some shade and rest midday."

Luke heard Leeland running up the road right behind him, and he put his arm out to stop the kid.

"Say hello," Deona shouted way too loud. She was like that when she got nervous. She just started in doing stupid stuff.

Leeland's hands were bloody. Luke gave his son the look.

As Lark walked over and put her hand out to shake

Leeland's hand, she said, "I brought you fresh milk."

"He's dirty," Luke said and Leeland shoved his hands into his pockets. But then the kid started in as if talking was the thing keeping him alive.

"You the lady who puts up all those white crosses?"

Luke was sure no one knew that many dead people.

"Sure do," she said in a gentle voice Luke figured she saved for kids. "We can put one up for your mom if you want."

Leeland froze.

"Get inside," Luke said because he was tired of the woman's games. "Deona is his mom now."

"Then I'm sure Deona will tend to those blistered hands, won't she?"

Leeland started inside but said, "Ma'am, I like your cat."

That's how we heard it because Lark was a town crier with a healthy dose of righteous indignation. Maybe it was the hippie in her. She put in calls that very night. She told some folks that maybe she had gone too far with Luke. But she intended to keep her eye on him for sure and besides, everyone knew she was on friendly terms with the sheriff. He'd make a trip out for Lark even if he and the deputies in his department called her place The Airplane.

Luke got up in the middle of the night and poured the milk down the drain. It had smelled sweet, as if she'd laced it with sugar. And he wondered if she didn't wash her hair in milk—it was the color of thin milk after all—*and kind of freaky*, he thought.

What does she know about straightening a kid out? Don't mess with me, lady.

The next day he left her jug at her gate. And he wasted no time repainting the two-foot-square plywood sign on his gate—the sign that rattled in the wind. He hadn't bothered with the polite No Trespassing. He just added Stay Out at the bottom of the sign.

God, it wore him out—keeping ahead of the busybodies.

Keep your nose clean.

Keep it simple.

But even New Mexico Baptists—good people of faith and good wishes—talked, and so we heard all about Luke and Deona bringing their two kids to Sunday school in Mayhill as the fall term was beginning, and how all four of them stayed the entire hour in the back of the room in the education complex in the doublewide behind the white frame church. It had freaked out the other kids to have a whole family sitting there like extraterrestrials, watching eagle-eyed.

Story went that the Pruitts had shown up starched and ironed in plaids and denim. And when Miss Alice, the Sunday school teacher, suggested that the parents could leave the kids and go to the adult Sunday school class, Luke Pruitt said, "We are here to observe." The boy had not said one single word the entire hour he sat there, hands folded in his lap. Miss Alice told friends she felt the urge to fling open the doors to the classroom and shout to her students, *run away!*

All of that got around fast. And it got reported that Leeland's hair had been cut short like a prisoner's. It'd been a shame to cut off that boy's curls, is what some of our softer sorts said.

> *Just the other day, after riding my four-wheeler all over the pasture, I finally located a small herd of goats. As soon as they heard me they ran over looking for the corn that I didn't have. Then it seemed as if they turned on me. "No corn? No going back!" At that they pushed up against a mesquite. Rocks, sticks, and begging couldn't get them out, so I just left them there. You know what? A few hours later they were at the gate, begging to be let in and fed. Patience, what a word. Think of all the work I could have saved myself in the past if I just hadn't thought that man was so superior to animals. Silly me.*
>
> Linda Pruitt, *Ranching Weekly*

Luke

2000

It was late that fall before Cloudcroft School hosted Back to School Night for grades five to twelve. The community looked forward to such things and all that week, folks were heard saying, "See you at Back to School." Principal Willingham had made a point of calling all the parents to give them a special invite. It had taken the better part of one day. Deona had taken that call.

In the late afternoon on a school day, the traffic on Highway 82 was busy in both directions, with everyone heading home. Cloudcroft Village residents liked to say that you didn't need to use your turn signals in the Village because everyone knew where you were going.

The school sat directly on 82. Tonight a few cars were mixed in with all the pickups in the parking lot. Even the spots under the basketball goals were taken, so Luke circled round and parked down on the east end with the nose of his truck pointed at the school mascot. It was still light enough for Luke and Deona to mock the grinning bear that had been carved out of the stump of what had to have once been a tall pine. Up on its hind legs, the creature held its clawless paws out as if it were a docile circus bear.

People are stupid up here in this tourist-trap town, Texans especially, Luke thought. They actually, God's truth, left food out for the bears right down the street where all the town trash was dumped. Luke always took a quick peek when he came into town from the east to see if he could spot one of those lazy bears, who were in no way pressed by hunger, prowling around the trash. Not that he wanted to see a bear, he'd told himself. No, just so he could prove human stupidity.

Luke pointed at the mascot and said to Deona, "Welcome to the home of the dancing bears."

The Pruitts were a little ahead of schedule, and so they sat in the truck and waited. They had planned not to give themselves any extra time to visit in the hallways with people they didn't care to get to know. They had Leeland's schedule, and he'd carefully written room numbers down for them. The school had sent all the kids home with a map of the school.

When Leeland handed it to his dad that afternoon, all Luke said was, "What kind of moron gets lost in a school?"

Luke sat behind the wheel of his debt-free Ford pickup, smelling the scent of dropped pine needles. He closed his eyes and told Deona to wake him at ten till. He tried to keep his mind off places it didn't need to go. But it went where it wanted. His mom had always liked Cloudcroft. Once she'd brought him and some of his schoolmates to a 4-H meeting here. His friends had thought she was the prettiest mom.

But then another image appeared. He could see himself reaching across Deona, snapping the door handle forward and pushing her out. It'd be a pretty easy stunt when the truck wasn't even moving. He didn't know what made him think of some things.

His dad had done it while he was driving and managed to keep the truck on the road. One minute his mom was in the truck and then next she was out there in the dirt. He and Stralin cried without making a sound.

Corrine...flying free.

He couldn't stop seeing that day. It was the day his brother stopped calling their father *Daddy*. That night in their bedroom Stralin had said anybody could be a father, but it took better to be a daddy. Well, Luke had never called him that. He shifted in his seat, and suddenly he didn't care about being early.

"Get out," he said to Deona.

Hat, no hat? He stood there by his door, unable to decide. And then finally the beaver-felt Stetson won out.

Luke was ready for the first period teacher. She'd given Leeland his first-ever "F." He'd gotten minuses when he was first at Berrendo, but an "F" was a new thing. Luke knew all about it. He'd told the teacher on the phone that he'd take care of the problem with swats and punishment. And he had. He'd sentenced Leeland to his bedroom, minus everything except the mattress and a sheet. If the kid wised up he'd start earning his stuff back. Luke figured that'd teach Leeland about survival techniques. Weed always got cold enough to teach a kid a lesson. The kid still had time before winter to do the right things.

But that matter was not something he wanted to put out there for all these proud-as-punch parents at Back to School Night, and so when he and Deona came through the door to the classroom, he gave the teacher a nod that said it all. People were standing around visiting like it was a sport with set rules. Luke watched as one of the men shook hands with each man that came past him, and then the greeter said to the last man through the door, "Good to see you, Rick. I was afraid I'd be the ugliest guy here."

Luke told Deona to get busy and find Leeland's desk, and then told her to sit and keep quiet. He took a seat in the back on a folding chair, took off his hat, crossed one knee over the other, cowboy style, and rested the Stetson there.

"Get on with it, Teach," he said under his breath. All his life he couldn't much stand being inside, and this was going to go on a long time. With his big toothy smile he looked up at the teacher and said, "That's the bell, miss."

The teacher moved to the front of the classroom, stood straight and tall, and waited.

Then she said, "Can you hear my voice?" She waited a few seconds and going softer she said, "Can you hear my voice?" And finally, when she had most of them on the edge of their seats straining to hear, she said, "Let's first talk about *Robinson Crusoe* and what the children, your children, learned when they read this classic and took their first test."

Oh, let's, Luke thought. He saw Deona turn in her seat to check with him. He gave her a two-fingered wave, which others could take as a sweet little greeting if they wanted. *Here it comes*, he thought, *life lessons*.

"All they had to do was watch *Survivor* on TV," said one of the mothers who had fancied herself up with lipstick and earrings for the night in school.

"That guy, Robinson Crusoe, was like reality TV," another mother said and added, "Only the strong survive."

"No, seriously," the first woman clarified, "I read it too so me and my daughter could talk about it. We figured if you are stuck someplace all alone, then you better make the best of it."

"Yes," said the teacher eagerly. "Yes, Crusoe was stuck there a very long time, and so he began to write his story as a record of human experience and anguish."

The discussion bounced around the room. The teacher was no Oprah. And then a woman, who seemed very timid, said to the teacher, "I liked the bear story at the end but not the part about teasing the bear. Friday didn't have to kill the bear. That was a lesson for our kids."

The teacher held up her copy of the book and waited until she had a window of silence and flipped to a place near the back of the book. She said, "Yes, you are so right. Friday turned that encounter into a spectacle. Let me read..."

Luke couldn't believe they were going to have story hour. He took his hat, the El Patron, and settled it on his head, forward, as if he planned on a siesta.

Stop it, he heard his mom say, but shit, she'd checked out, hadn't she? Still, he sat up straight.

"Here we are," the teacher said, "I'll start mid-sentence, '...if you do not meddle with him, he will not meddle with you...'" She paused and then went on, "'If you are really afraid, your best way is to look another way and keep going on, for sometimes if you stop and stand still, and look steadfastly at him, he takes it for an affront; but if you throw or toss anything at him, though it were but a stick as big as your finger, he thinks himself abused, and sets all other business aside to pursue his revenge.'"

Luke watched, head down, through his eyelashes.

Revenge. Mom never gave Dad time to figure out that part of the whole murder deal.

The teacher stopped, closed the book, and said, "That alone could lead to quite an essay. Thank you," she said as she nodded to the now proud mother who had brought up the bear.

The teacher took her time and eyed them all as if they were about to hear something amazing, and then said, "Defoe wrote this book for adults. That pleased your children. He included three elements that have made it a classic novel: survival, religious awakening, and examination of character traits such as pride and humility. If I assigned no other reading all year, we'd still have plenty to discuss."

She continued, "Of course, the children must first read the book, all of it, not just some SparkNotes pamphlet. You might miss the bear if you just read a condensed version."

Luke took his hat off and put it on the floor at his feet. She was meddling with him, directly. But she had gotten some prissy laughter with that stuff about the SparkNotes. And Luke wondered if the teacher had set it up for the timid woman to mention the bear.

"My point is serious," she said. "We have a lot to learn this year. Complex vocabulary like scheme, ravenous, ambush, despair, fortress, cowardice, survivor, barbaric, stranded." She was reading from an index card. "The students will learn how to make connections, how to investigate issues. I'll be working very hard, but your job is to encourage them, engage with them. Ask them questions and get them talking aloud. Thinking for themselves."

Underhanded.

He didn't like being ambushed.

"And yes, read along with them." She was smiling again and gave a nod to the woman who had started all of this.

And then she moved on quickly. Luke could tell she'd lost more time than she had planned on messing with that bear. She hefted a stack of five books over her head and said, "These are the other books we will read this year." She stepped to the front of each of the five rows and handed a parent one of the books as she pronounced the title.

"Please take a look and pass it back," she said. "And please, please, please, come in and see me or call with your concerns. Any issues you have, I'm here for your children."

The bell rang. Luke put his hat on and gave Deona, who had turned around as she passed the book back, a nod towards the door. By the time they met up, Deona had the schedule out and scrunched up her eyes trying to figure which way to turn.

"Computers next," she said.

"Like I care," Luke said and took her by the elbow.

Shouting a "Hi" at each new arrival, the computer teacher, Ms. Madrid, pointed to open spots in front of the computers. The things were all turned off, the screens dark grey. Luke steered Deona to the back row where there were no computers, just two long tables. As the room filled, the parents began praising the hardware using old sage sayings like the ones you'd hear over at the Roswell livestock auction. Same old bullshit with hardware substituted for livestock, like they knew anything about either.

The bell rang and the teacher began by asking who had a computer at home. Several hands shot up. He wasn't going to participate in the tell-all.

"What I'm doing with your fifth graders is first a full semester of keyboarding, and then we'll turn to word processing," Ms. Madrid said.

"Why doesn't she just say typing?" Luke said to Deona. "My mother typed up a weekly column. She never did any word processing."

But the teacher had already moved on to another topic, and all he heard was something about wanting the kids to learn how to use a computer and wanting them to enjoy it too.

Then she gave her fair warning, saying, "But they have to get their work done."

Luke took his hat off—he saw his dad's name embroidered on the satin lining—and held it in his left hand like it was a pointer. He raised his right hand in the universal signal: *Pick me, pick me.*

These teachers had conspired.

And she did. She pointed at him.

Pointing the hat at the teacher, Luke said, "Your class is not worth taking because my son Leeland is going to own his own business someday, and he'll be able to hire a secretary."

This teacher was small—and she was new—but she didn't

take all that long to answer. She made it clear that she could see ahead into the future. She said, "Leeland will need to know how to run a computer."

Then she softened her voice and said, "Besides, Leeland always has something wonderful he wants to share, and computers will be there to help him. And glasses would help him too. I've requested that he be tested."

One of the mothers turned around and smiled at Luke.

"I'm here early if he or any of your children have work to make up, and I'll stay late. But I know that it's a hardship for the bus kids, so I have makeup days."

She filled up the rest of the time with handing out a syllabus and apologizing for not being able to turn on the computers. And then, even before the bell rang, a firefighter in full Kevlar regalia stepped into the doorway and grinned. He was helmeted but was wearing only one boot. He was holding the other yellow and black boot up to his chest as if it were his pride and joy. He stood in the doorway ready to receive contributions.

"Miss Madrid, sorry to interrupt," he said and Luke thought he remembered the man from the fire line crew near the church camp in Sacramento last spring. It had taken most every building and all the big trees in the grassy yard.

She grinned back and then said to the parents, "Please, fill the boot."

Luke never did hear the bell signaling the end of the second period, but everyone got up and began digging in purses and pockets. Luke came up with something and waited his turn. He had something he wanted to say; something about the wrongheaded so-called environmental logic that had killed logging in these mountains and was going to kill off the ranchers too.

He heard the man in front of him say to the fireman, "Behind you, brother." That was the in thing to say these days, but Luke had waited and was going to get his own say. He stepped forward and took ahold of the uniformed man's shoulder, and said loud enough for the teacher to hear: "The biggest threat to the Mexican Owl is the extreme fire danger in the overgrown forests."

"Yes, sir," the fireman said. "Tonight we are salting away funds for the next emergency our community faces."

Then Luke turned and nodded to the teacher like the gentleman he sometimes believed he was.

But he wasn't a gentleman. We knew it for a fact, and sadly, Miss Alice, at the Mayhill Baptist Church, had learned it for herself. She'd seen him taunt Leeland. We heard how she'd attempted to persuade Luke—five times in all—that he needed to let the boy participate in the Bible competitions. "He could win state," she'd told Deona when she came to pick up the children after the Bible drills.

"He's worked so hard," Alice said to Luke when she called him one evening and caught him at home. "He's worked seven months, and holding him back because of some small imperfection at home is not what a parent who loves their child does." Stuff like that got around.

"And just how does allowing a bad boy to compete in a state competition glorify God?" Luke had asked and Alice knew it for a taunt. She'd heard revenge in Luke's voice. The shame of it was that even with all the Bible verses stored in her head, there was not one blessed thing Alice could say to this man. And so, she'd said nothing.

Deputy Greenwood

Early Afternoon July 6, 2005

"Enjoyed working with you. You've got some good people out here," the commander said as he ran out to the car. The keys that hung from his belt were jangling, and Greenwood had to wonder what all those keys were for. The commander shouted something that sounded like, "Just leave the place unlocked," as he climbed into the passenger seat of the waiting New Mexico State Trooper car and, in the same loud voice, said, "That's the way they left it for us."

"Got ya," Greenwood said, hoping the man would recognize the little theft he'd made from Paula.

Silly man, Greenwood thought, and then decided to take a moment before he got on with it. He studied the three empty hummingbird feeders hanging in a row from the eaves of Guesthouse One. It seemed cruel to only fill the things when there were guests. The feeders were too fancy anyway, made of glass and decorated with red flowers, which was unnecessary here in southeast New Mexico, where the little creatures had already traveled thousands of miles up from southern Mexico for sweet water and did not need fancy. Greenwood's mother had always said they'd come originally for the red-tipped ocotillo. Now he caught himself scanning the landscape for one of those twig plants while he wondered how many species of hummingbirds made it up to New Mexico. Maybe he'd write and ask his mother about that. She'd left for Mexico with the love of her life in 2001, saying, "Keep your eyes open for the right gal."

He was tired and didn't know if he was tired of looking or tired of being lonely.

He pulled Paula's phone out of his breast pocket and called Fay.

"Waiting for the press to scatter," he told her, knowing it was a half-truth, and she knew it too because he then asked her to pass a message to the sheriff. "Tell him I will be alerting the DA that I will be arresting Leeland Pruitt. Paula and I will bring him over there to you—to the courthouse."

"Damn it all to hell," was her simple reply. Then after a full breath, she said, "DA's been having his girl call me every fifteen minutes. I mean it's not like he can't walk around the corner and check in with me personally, not that I want to see his pretty face. Apparently there is some white-headed woman sitting in his office. Just waiting. Named Lark."

"I've heard of her," Greenwood said, and then the tiny little phone buzzed and vibrated, making him think irrationally that a ruby-throated hummingbird had settled in his hand, its grain-of-sand heart thumping madly.

Low battery the screen said before going black.

From the porch he could see the kitchen window of the ranch house, the place where he had stood earlier that day. He saw a person there watching him—Mrs. Duff, he thought. He stepped back inside the guesthouse and crossed the living room to the bar that separated the kitchen from the living area. He spotted the wall phone and pulled out one of the four bar stools. Seeing that the seats were made from small kid-size saddles amused him. He settled himself into the stool, but couldn't help saying, "Back in the saddle again."

Damn, he thought, *Dale Evans and Roy Rogers would have been right at home here.* He took out his notebook and made a few notes, checking the time on his watch each time he wrote anything down. It was straight up one p.m. when he dialed the DA's office in the Lincoln County Courthouse in Carrizozo.

A receptionist picked up and said she'd go find him. "Call you back?" she said.

He had no idea what the phone number for the guesthouse was, so he said he'd wait, and he let the receiver dangle on its curled cord. He checked Paula's phone again. It was dead as a rock and he decided he didn't need one.

"DA Quintana here. Are you going to pick up that kid or not? In case you forgot, deputy, I've got a job to do. Pick him up and get him over here."

Greenwood picked the phone up again and, measuring his words, said, "He's a boy of fourteen. A youthful offender." His heart was pounding so hard that he set the phone on the counter gently and put his head in a cradle of his arms.

Quintana carried on: "I need a confession and I need the crime scene reports just in case I need to up the ante."

"The commander is headed your way with the reports." He didn't have anything else to say, and so he kept his mouth shut long enough for the silence to unnerve the DA.

"You understand this is a double murder case," Quintana said, goading Greenwood the way he did criminal suspects.

Not gonna work, Greenwood thought. "This is no murder mystery, sir," he said after a few more seconds of silence.

"And it's no detective story either. Keep my girl informed so I know your whereabouts."

"Yes, sir." Greenwood hung up. There would be no end to

the chest pounding today.

He stood, crossed the room in three big steps, and for good measure, hit the screen door with both hands flat. He'd never learned to curse much, but when he snagged his pant leg on the nail on the porch and heard the fabric rip, he let loose with, "What the hell?" He pried the board with the exposed nail loose and used the pitching arm he'd once had to let it fly across the yard into the bushes. *Let Sam Duff go looking for what was missing*, he thought. *Or maybe the missus*, because Greenwood saw her again at her kitchen window, and he said aloud, "Love your neighbor, as yourself." He'd grown up a good Baptist and knew his Bible verses, but he wasn't much buying them today.

Greenwood gunned the pickup and the department-issued flashlight he'd stashed on the back seat that morning crashed to the floor. He had no intention of stopping for any reason until he picked up Paula, but it didn't work out that way.

Across the cattle guard, he saw that Conley was holding back the feed salesman while Sam Duff stood arms folded across his older-man chest in his impression of impatience. *Still gaming the story*, Greenwood thought.

The reporters had all pulled out, and two small Mexican men were hauling the makeshift stage off into the bed of a 1960s Datsun pickup. Greenwood knew the men because they parked a Datsun in the Walmart lot in the summer and sold watermelons and wood in the fall. They were always ready to pack up and take the odd job. Hoyt was parked off to the side, waiting to relieve Conley. As far as Greenwood could see everything was in order, and so he coasted across the cattle guard, prepared only to wave. But Conley held up his hand, indicating he needed a moment with him, and Greenwood cursed again.

"First things first," Conley said as he trotted over to Greenwood's window. "I reached Alfonzo at his home. That was him this morning hauling off a horse trailer. Leeland called Alfonzo's daughter last night and asked her to ask him to go find a filly that belongs to Duff. The kid was afraid the horse couldn't survive, being a pastured horse and all."

"The boy," Greenwood corrected him, but nicely.

"Sir?" Conley said.

"And this mess?" Greenwood asked.

"Sir?" Conley was working to keep up.

Greenwood nodded at Smoot, and Conley must have gotten it because he started in with an explanation. "Seems a hard pounding rain, like we just had, on cut alfalfa is likely to lead to a spontaneous combustion fire. The bales build heat."

Conley rolled his eye and Duff, the unsung hero, headed to his truck without acknowledging Greenwood even briefly. *A man with heavy matters on his mind*, Greenwood thought.

"If these here bales catch fire, it is on the county's ticket," the feed salesman yelled as he ran toward the two of them, his skinny bowed legs and pointed boots making him look like a house mouse. "Probably too late to save the load. It's on you."

The mouse of a man was pointing at Conley, who rolled his eyes and said, "Boom."

Greenwood looked straight ahead, his eyes on the road, and shouted, "Get your hay wagon out of here. Deputy Conley will hold the gate open long enough for you to turn your rig around. Next time, don't show up some place you can't get out of, else I will ticket your ass." The old cowboy sneered but walked over and stood by his rig.

"Your choice," Greenwood said to Conley, "Either go down to the Moon and pick up food for anyone left on duty or check out the lean-to. Ask Hoyt to do what you don't wanna do."

"Already took care of the lean-to, sir," Conley said and nodded at Hoyt. "He took up the watch while I went down."

"Okay then make the food run, would you? Let them know that I'll be back to settle the bill."

Conley touched the brim of his Lincoln County ball cap with the tip of his index finger and walked over to Smoot. The last thing Greenwood heard was Conley saying, "Sue me."

Greenwood looked at his radio and decided it was no risk to Leeland now. "Fay, would you see if you can get ahold of someone at St. Jude's and let them know I'm headed there now to pick up Investigator Magliaro?"

Fay was not being Fay. For a few seconds, she did not reply or even breathe into the radio, and then he thought he heard her say, "Crusade." Greenwood knew it for a signal. Quintana was no doubt hovering over the tall counter that kept Fay safe from the Lincoln County residents, who could get pretty hot-headed. Then she disconnected.

He was taking the road—bumps and all—both hands on the wheel and eyes straight ahead until he thought to look over at the lean-to. It was dressed in yellow tape as if ready for a May Day celebration, which he knew was out of fashion. And then the radio came alive suddenly and he heard Quintana shouting. Fay must have only had her thumb on the button to mute it.

"We have a double murder, my dear. Do I have to remind you?" The DA's voice said and Greenwood turned the radio off with a push of his flat hand. He didn't need to hear that.

"They have a parrot in there," Paula said as she stepped up into the truck. She had a Walmart bag that looked full, and she smelled of tacos. "You better pull over there and eat something."

"Fill me in," he said and pulled under a clump of juniper. He thought he might have put a scratch on the truck.

"Well, the parrot is Colombian. Mr. Salado's brother—he's a priest in Colombia—he sent the parrot up here and it only says one thing."

"Okay, so what does the parrot say?" Gosh, he liked this girl.

"It says, 'Why are you here?' "

Greenwood bit into a taco. It was half ground beef and half onions, and it made his eyes water.

"Alfonzo's wife brought the food. Lots of it. The DA called and screamed at Father Frank and wanted to know exactly where Leeland was. Sarah, Alfonzo's daughter, started crying about that time and couldn't stop, and another girl named Yolanda started in crying. Girls are like that—they cry in groups. I sat at the roadblock until the school counselor came up with his van and blocked the road. He said he knew everyone in the neighborhood, so that's when I came back to the church. The football coach was there to drive me. Father Frank doesn't have a car."

"Check," he said and felt himself able to focus. It was food he had needed.

"Here's the thing," she said. "Quintana is expecting us to haul Leeland into the Lincoln County Courthouse and press him."

"Yes, I know."

"So, I have a better idea," she said. "We take Leeland to CYFD in Ruidoso. I've called over there already, and the director is getting the safe room ready. The recording system is the best in the state. Of course, it's set up for victims of child abuse."

"Of course." He knew, and anyone paying attention knew, that was why Paula had come out to New Mexico. The safe rooms were her doing. "Okay, can we go now?"

She reached into the grocery bag and pulled out a Ziploc bag full of eyeglasses. "The counselor brought these. The Hondo School lost and found."

"What else you got in that bag?" he asked.

"More food and cards from kids. They kept showing up. Rosalie started a telephone tree. She kept saying, 'We're not losing this one.' And did you know that Leeland's real mother got custody of him a few years back, only to die in a car accident when she was taking him out to where she was stationed in the navy? Leeland was in the car." Paula stopped, and now she clutched her hand to her chest. "She was in the back seat sleeping."

"I didn't know that," he said and started the truck. Then he looked over at her and said, "So, a parrot lives at St. Jude's..." The words just came out because he was worried that his nerve was going to fail him.

"You know Catholics," she said.

"Leeland left a note and his bloody clothes in his closet. But he didn't run."

"Whipped dogs don't run," Paula said.

The Salado boys were at the gate as they pulled up, but Greenwood stopped them from pulling the gate open. He left the truck parked just outside the gate, and he and then Paula stepped around the gate.

"We need to see Leeland," Greenwood said to Mr. Salado when he came out. The Salado boys had been taught to wait for their father to speak first.

"Get Leeland," the man said. All five boys went inside, and then Joseph came back out with Leeland.

"His father talked down to him hard," Salado said before Joseph and Leeland had crossed the dirt yard. Leeland walked as if his feet were tender.

Paula put her hand on Leeland's shoulder. They matched in height. Greenwood saw what he hadn't before—green paint caked on the boy's skull right at the crown.

"Leeland, we need to read you your rights. You tell me if you don't understand."

Leeland nodded and Greenwood began. Leeland looked down and Mr. Salado looked away. Joseph had moved to Leeland's other side and stood steady, staring at Greenwood now.

"And now we need to take you into Ruidoso to do an interview. You can have someone go with you. An adult. You understand? There is the priest or your school counselor," Paula said.

Leeland didn't say anything. He had begun shaking and was making a little humming sound.

"You hungry?" Greenwood asked.

"No, sir," Leeland said.

"We fed him," Salado said with more anger than Greenwood would have imagined possible in such a gentle man. "I should have sent him to my brother."

There was no spite left in the man. He was putting blame on himself and Greenwood felt horribly sorry for him.

Greenwood nodded, and they waited.

"I'd like to have Mr. Salado be with me, but I am sorry to mix him up in this," Leeland said.

Joseph folded his arms in front of him as if he were taking on a new role in his family.

Greenwood cleared his throat. "Fine. That's fine, Mr. Salado. We'll have Leeland ride with us in the truck. Can you follow us to Ruidoso to CYFD?" he asked, and Paula started in with the address.

But it was Joseph who interrupted, saying, "My father knows the place. Every Christmas he goes there and plays Santa for the foster children." He took a step forward and it felt like a threat.

"Anything you want to bring with you, Leeland?" Paula asked.

"No, ma'am. I didn't bring anything with me."

"Dad, I'll go get him one of the new caps," Joseph said.

"Fine. And get your brothers," Salado said to his son in Spanish, but Greenwood understood. "Open the gate and tell your mother where we're going. You look out for her. Leave the gate open."

> *The best cowboys are usually ranch-raised. It's like getting a college degree, with Daddy being the professor. We start school at (or before) daylight, with the milk cows, and end at dark with the milk cows. We learn the worst parts of ranching along with the best, and the fewer times we get the seat of our pants dusted, the better "grades" we get.*
>
> Linda Pruitt, *Ranching Weekly*

Miss Alice

2001

Miss Alice was working as a sub at the Cloudcroft School that second week of September. Leaving the lunchroom where kids were eating—where it was sickeningly quiet for a Friday—she spotted Leeland standing in the hallway with his head down. He was alone. It was the fourteenth of September and the staff had been told by the school psychologist to check on any kids they found off by themselves. Anyone alone was a concern, but Leeland alone was an opportunity for Alice, and she took it.

"Leeland, hi."

The words weren't out of her mouth before he grinned. For a split second it might have looked to a passerby like she was going to grab him and run, or maybe just hug him good. But he was too shy for that, and so she said, "I'm subbing here this week. We miss you at church. We wish you would come back someday."

"I can't come back. We're moving," he said.

She might have forced him into that admission. He was always so respectful to her. Maybe he didn't want her to think she was the reason his parents had pulled him out of church activities. Or maybe it was a kid making an excuse for his father. There was no need to make excuses, she might have told him. But maybe Leeland needed her to stop advocating for him.

She was sure she'd made a huge mistake when she'd begged Luke Pruitt.

And then Karmen ran up. She appeared out of nowhere. In those next few moments, which Alice suspected were the last she'd ever spend with Leeland, it was hard not to see the little girl as a miniature Deona.

Karmen took hold of a strand of her permed hair, which was going to be ruined if Deona kept messing with it. She twisted it and started in on Leeland, threatening to tell their parents if he told.

"You better not be telling Miss Alice what we're doing. You know it's a secret and no one's to know where we are," she said, way too loud for a secret. And then she looked Alice in the eye and said, "He can't tell you where we are moving, and neither can I."

It felt like a taunt. And for a moment Alice wondered if these two young kids had been told much about what had happened at Ground Zero. It probably wasn't the worst thing in Leeland's life. Alice knew that for certain. It sent a chill up her spine that all her Bible teaching wasn't going to help her or these kids.

Hands on her hips, Karmen turned back to Leeland and added, "If you do tell her, Leeland, I'm telling Mom and Dad."

"He knows how to keep a secret," Alice said, and never regretted saying that.

Alice had always heard from the kids in her Sunday school that Karmen spied on Leeland. That had seemed harmless. But not today. Alice was a good Baptist, knew she was resilient in spirit, and believed she'd experienced salvation through her own personal faith. She'd made a genuine commitment to outreach, she told herself as she shook off the chill that had suddenly engulfed her.

To the ends of the earth, she reminded herself, and then thought again of smoke and dust, of people not obligated by any social consciousness. She thought of Luke Pruitt, father to two innocent children.

She knew she should keep reaching for Leeland, but today she didn't want to cause him any more trouble, and Karmen looked like trouble. It'd been a tough week up here at 9,000 feet. *Above the stress level,* was the town motto. She sure didn't feel above it today. And so Alice walked away and left the two children there, alone together in the hallway, and headed toward the school psychologist's office to tell her about things worse than 9/11. But we were way ahead of those two children and Miss Alice. Feed salesmen always spread the word from cloud country to ranch country, and so we all knew that the Pruitts were on the move again, this time to the Bounty Canyon Ranch in the Hondo Valley—on the dry side of the highway—near where Luke had grown up at the magnificent Diamond Crown Ranch.

And then, because Cloudcroft was tight-knit, teachers told teachers and teachers told kids and kids spilled their guts to their parents until it was no secret. It was a chant we thought we heard: *There is this boy, just started the sixth grade. He's bright as daylight but lives in fear of his own folks. Look out for him and spread the word.*

Word went out like an all-points bulletin: Luke Pruitt is heading back to the Hondo Valley. Watch him.

> *Not a fall works comes that two special animals don't come to mind. Not that they were the perfect examples of their breed, they were just special to me. One was a heifer that I named Julie. The other special animal was a bull. He never got a name, just a number: 930S. He was born here, fed out here, and grew into a herd sire. When the ranch company had the dispersion sale, I helped with all the work, and when I saw that bull climb on the truck, I thought my heart would break. I couldn't stop the tear from rolling down my cheek. A friend at the sale assured me that the people would certainly provide a good home and there was no need to worry. To this day, I think about 930S and hope my friend wasn't wrong.*
>
> Linda Pruitt, *Ranching Weekly*

Alfonzo

2001

The alfalfa field was a mile up the road to Capitan and so ripe for cutting that neighbors warned it'd go bad. "Stem rot," they all predicted.

Alfonzo walked across the end of the field with his new boss, Luke Pruitt, over to the hay-baler. They should have been here before sunup.

"Hondo—we're always chasing moisture," Alfonzo had said to Luke the night before, standing out at the corrals near the foreman's place. "Not so much the hay's wet."

"I know the Hondo," Luke had said and added, "Meet you at the alfalfa field at seven."

It was two hours too late to start. They'd be baked by ten.

That morning Luke left the two children—who were neither of them one hundred pounds—standing at the pickups. Alfonzo saw that they both had hats and gloves, but they were going to need bandanas to protect their bare necks. He carried extra in his truck; he'd dip the cloths in the ice water he always carried in the cooler.

We knew full well when Luke Pruitt arrived back in the Hondo Valley to take over as foreman at the Bounty Canyon Ranch—strutting around with superiority and authority that he took as his birthright—that he'd come back to the Valley to prove something. We didn't all agree on what that was. Maybe he wanted folks to know that his dad had been a monster who needed killing. Maybe he was here to turn things around for the Pruitt name.

We would have been lying if we said we were glad to have him back. "Welcome home," stuck in our throats. For Pete's sake, it was common knowledge that he'd disowned his own son, filed papers at the courthouse and all. And now he had taken the kid back and was milking him for Corinne's social security money while he hardened him. For what?

But here in Lincoln County, in the Valley, the motto was: "We take care of our own." Meaning family. Looking back, that didn't work out so good for Linda Pruitt. And it wasn't working for Leeland either. Luke was isolating his boy, fencing him in, and keeping him on a short leash. We should have turned that around.

Alfonzo was only half-listening to Luke as he fell into step with the man.

"Who screws up a herd that bad?" Luke asked as he stopped and looked up at the sky. Luke lit a cigarette but didn't offer him one, and then he coughed like a seventy-year-old.

La Culpa, Alfonzo thought.

It didn't matter. Alfonzo knew there'd come a time when this newest foreman couldn't blame others for his mistakes. Alfonzo could wait him out.

Not going anywhere.

After a minute at his cigarette, Luke went on, proud of the

half-facts he was spitting out, something about the one hundred acres they had in alfalfa.

Alfonzo knew for a fact that they'd get six—eight at the most—cuttings this year, and even eight would not be enough hay for the three hundred cattle and near to twelve hundred sheep they were running on the Bounty Canyon Ranch.

"No, sir, eighty acres," Alfonzo said in Spanish, because he'd been taught only that language as a child, and taught by his father and uncles that it was disrespectful to start out speaking English to the boss.

"English is prideful," his mother had always warned in Spanish, which was all the language she had needed with her eleven children. And then she'd make a spitting sound as if to get the bad taste out of her mouth.

Luke ignored the correction and shouted at the two children, "Welcome to the Promised Land." He looked at Alfonzo and said, "That boy of mine thinks he's Bible smart."

Alfonzo saw that Luke was nothing like his mother. Linda Pruitt had been a good neighbor to his two uncles who'd worked the Diamond Canyon, spoke only Spanish to them. They'd watched Stralin and Luke grow up and always said that Luke was a hard case just like his dad, Payton Pruitt— "A man mean enough to steal a coin off a dead man's eyes," was the way his uncles put it.

"That's fair," Alfonzo said when Luke finished up his next lecture about the hay.

Luke finished another cigarette and waved at the children, who darted over.

"A good day for haying?" the boy asked, but Alfonzo wasn't answering. It wasn't his place to be talking for the boss—he knew that. Besides, he had seen the flicker of hate in Luke's eyes.

Luke turned on his son, got real close to the boy, and said, "No, Stupid, we just came out here for fun."

Suddenly, Alfonzo wanted to get home to his daughter. She was his reason for all the hard work; she'd be helping her mother bake on a Saturday morning. "A mixture of sugar and chili," his wife liked to say about the girl.

The day felt June hot, not a bit like the October day it was. The sun, even at this late fall angle, was going to boil them bad.

Alfonzo squinted against the sun and spoke up without planning to. "Your father picked a good dry day. Wet hay can catch fire."

Alfonzo knew Luke hated him too.

Not going anywhere.

Alfonzo trusted himself to get along. It's what you did if you were from one of the original fifteen families come up from Mexico into the Hondo Valley; the families who'd named the creek. They came to farm and built acequias to share the water. His family's ditch rights went back to 1867. They were here long before the Anglos and never did mind the Indians.

I'll get along with this man.

It took time to learn the ways of a new boss, but he had ten years with the ranch owner, Mr. Duff. That counted for something. He'd seen four foremen come and go in that time— five, if you counted the ant of a man who'd called the ranch the Overlook and left in the middle of a minus-seventeen deep freeze in 1997. Alfonzo and the old cowboy, Tanner Granger, had been called out in that storm to look after the livestock. They'd counted fifteen head of cattle and twenty sheep frozen dead. The cattle had pulled up so tight in a corner of fencing that they'd smothered each other before they'd frozen. And there was that horse tried to make a run for it and froze.

It was getting late. The fall morning had exploded into heat. Alfonzo could smell the grass heating up in the sun.

"Now you listen and you listen good. This is no tea party," Luke said to the two kids. Then he made all three of them wait while he studied the field of alfalfa.

"Can I drive the tractor?" the boy asked, and Alfonzo didn't know if he saw Luke strike him or not. Luke had reins in his hand. They were leather. Luke had to have been carrying them since he climbed out of his truck. Alfonzo had never seen a man come to a hay field with reins. A cattle drive, yes. The boy went still and Alfonzo averted his eyes.

Alfonzo had seen the boy go still like that the first time he'd met him. Mr. Duff had asked him to come by after work in the hay fields and meet the new foreman. Alfonzo was the hand, not the foreman. He understood that.

"The Pruitt family comes recommended by Nathan over at the Diamond Canyon, across the way. Well, of course you know Nathan. I place stock in what he has to say." All-American family was the way Mr. Duff put it.

Alfonzo did know the manager at the Diamond Canyon. Everyone knew everyone in the Valley—not the way Mr. Duff knew folks because Duff never stopped at the post office. He always sent someone else on that chore. Alfonzo stopped at the post office daily—visited with Rosalie and had one of her cups of coffee, left his dime in the jar. Good to keep up with crops, missing calves, feed deliveries.

And so Alfonzo had driven up that night to the ranch to meet Luke Pruitt. He let himself in using the gizmo that opened the gate at the cattle guard. He and the FedEx man had those things. Coming around the hill Alfonzo spotted the boy in the evening shadows. He was in the yard playing basketball on the patch of cement. He was by himself in too-small work boots. As Alfonzo walked over, the boy pivoted, dribbled the ball, and then hooked it under one arm and put out the other for a shake.

"Ranch-raised," Mr. Duff had said when he told Alfonzo about the two kids Luke would be bringing. "One his. One hers," he'd said, not guessing that Alfonzo already knew all about the new foreman and his family. It was okay with Alfonzo. Most of the bosses he'd had thought they had the inside information on everything in the Valley.

Silly Anglos thought that way.

Alfonzo's wife worked at the Hondo School cafeteria. She ran it and could run a ranch if she had the chance. Plus his daughter was the same age as Leeland and had met him the first day he came to school.

"All the kids wanted to sit with Leeland at lunch," his wife said.

"In the schoolyard he had ten friends," his daughter added, all pleased. She was always pleased about something. But she wasn't pleased about Leeland being held back to repeat the fifth grade. "By his dad," she said.

"Punishment," his wife said.

Those two females had already decided a lot about the Pruitt boy.

"Ranch-raised?" Alfonzo asked in English.

They laughed. His wife and daughter did that a lot.

That evening at the foreman's place, Alfonzo and the boy spotted Luke up on the ridgeline. The sun had already dipped behind the hills and Luke Pruitt was only a square cut silhouette.

"Had your supper, son?" Alfonzo asked because he thought it might be best to send the boy inside.

"No, sir, not yet."

"Waiting for your father?" He switched to Spanish now because maybe it sounded gentler, and he knew the boy would understand him.

"Yes, sir," Leeland answered in English. "Deona gets supper when Dad is washed up." He pointed to the ridge.

Conceited, Alfonzo thought, as he and the boy stood there in silence watching Luke.

Luke was stalking coyotes at dusk, or pretending to,

balancing a repeating rifle across the back of his shoulders, his arms hung limp over the ends.

Proud.

Alfonzo knew Luke would have seen the dust he had thrown all the way up the road to the ranch. Alfonzo knew that Luke knew he was standing there with his boy past the supper hour. Alfonzo wouldn't tell his wife this part.

No sin in being poor, he repeated to himself three times.

The boy was fidgeting. He held the basketball out in front of him like he might hurl it out should something come at him. Luke came down the hillside slowly, stooped over, and picked up a rock. That's when the boy went still, like prey. Alfonzo put his hand on the boy's back and said, "Go on inside, son."

The boy tossed the basketball into the wooden bin that'd sat in the yard for years now and held other balls and things Anglo kids liked. And then Leeland got a doubtful look on his face that Alfonzo recognized as the same one his priest always put on his face when one of the village toughies showed up to take communion.

"Nice to meet you," the boy said softly. "I like your family."

Today in the blue-green alfalfa field, the boy stayed put, waiting to be hit maybe. The girl was at his side. She was no kin to the boy, it was clear. She had a way about her that made Alfonzo think her hearing was off. His wife would have heated up that oil she kept in the pantry and dropped little beads of it in the girl's ear. Alfonzo remembered the year his daughter had a cotton ball in her ear from October to March. That ear had healed up just fine.

Alfonzo heard Luke slap the reins in his hands. This man was in the business of showing off. Alfonzo gave his new boss his back. It wouldn't be good for his boss to see his eyes just then.

I am a worker, he reminded himself. *This is a good ranch to work.*

"You're so smart, you get up in the tractor and start it up," Luke said to the boy, who wasted no time climbing up. The girl ran off into the grass and did a few jumps straight up in the air like a fawn. Alfonzo thought he would head back to his pickup to get his gear, get the bandanas.

Alfonzo heard the tractor start. Smooth. Then it almost stalled. Then it lurched like it had a mind of its own and was going to take off for the hills. Then the lurch again and nothing, and so he turned to see what had happened.

Luke yanked open the door, grabbed his son, and said, "The next time you do that with the tractor I'm going to cut off your balls."

By late that afternoon, we started hearing that story, and more, about how Luke was working Leeland and even Karmen. We already knew he was keeping them out of school activities where we figured them for safe. Word was traveling up and down the Valley like a bird looking for a spot along the river to plant a seed that would become another tree.

Alfonzo never did know where the girl had gotten off to when Luke pulled Leeland out of the tractor. What he did know was that he hated himself right then. He should have gone to St. Jude's that first night to tell the priest about this man, his American rifle, and his son.

"Father of mercies," the priest always began after Alfonzo had given his confession. He should have gone to him.

Seventeen below, he prayed.

Alfonzo dropped a dime in the jar and helped himself to a cup of coffee that Rosalie kept hot and fresh. The weather had turned cold overnight, but then cold was past due. He nodded at Rosalie and Tanner and waited. Tanner was deep in his story and besides, it was early yet. Alfonzo knew Tanner prided himself on his stories.

"Been cowboying all my life," Tanner started in after taking a ragged breath.

Rosalie winked at Alfonzo. Rosalie was Alfonzo's cousin several times removed. Since that day in September, she'd been in a worried mood about her son Michael. Alfonzo had watched the boy play football for three years now for the Hondo Eagles. He was good. Everyone said Texas Tech was nosing around, UNM too, but the boy was set on the marines. Alfonzo had to feel for Rosalie; Michael was her only child, and he knew how it felt to have only one.

Tanner looked back over his shoulder at Alfonzo. They often met here and shared a ride to whatever part of the ranch they were working that day. Tanner put his hands on his bony hips and said, "Alfonzo can tell you what we see out there working with Luke Pruitt. I tell you I'm not turning a blind eye on that sorry excuse for a man."

Alfonzo let his eyes wander off out the side window. No one else was around to hear.

"We sat there horseback waiting for Luke to come down off the hill. Let me tell you, he was all wound up. He had a short rope in his hands."

"Reins," Alfonzo said.

"Reins, right," Tanner said and began acting out the part of wrapping the reins around his hand and said, "I've seen people taken apart with them."

Rosalie would spread this.

"That damn feed salesman, Smoot, was along for the gather," Tanner added. "Did nothin' 'cept what you can do horseback. Now I tell you, Luke's got that boy of his cowed. Talks him down pretty hard."

"So I hear," Rosalie said. Alfonzo knew she talked most nights with his wife, and when they weren't worrying over Michael's plans, they were worrying about the Pruitt boy.

Alfonzo watched as Tanner got comfortable—leaning up

against the side table with one skinny little elbow holding his weight, booted feet crossed at the ankle. Rosalie was doing some sorting. Alfonzo thought they'd be there a while longer.

"So...Luke says to the boy, 'You wuss. You stupid son of a bitch,' and other things I am not willing to repeat. We were out on a gather and Alfonzo and I took the outside—outside riders control the drive. Smoot was doing nothing but chatting up the boss. Am I right, Alfonzo?"

Alfonzo sipped his coffee and dug in his pocket for another dime, nodded for Tanner to go on.

"Leeland picked up a crippled calf and it was coming along slow. What you do is wait and watch in that situation, and I saw Luke coming down off the hill and he come at Leeland and cracked the kid's back with the reins and said, 'You're out of the drive, you little pussy...' "

Tanner hesitated, waiting like a worried cow that's making sure it has to move on ahead, ignoring all encouragement until it can't any longer. Alfonzo knew how Tanner told a story and so did Rosalie. Conclusions were Tanner's specialty, but they took time coming.

"It's like working stock—you can handle them rough or handle them gentle. If you handle them rough, there's problems." His voice turned raw. "Pulled Leeland down off that horse..." And then stopped.

He wasn't going to finish this story, not today.

"That boy is in hard shape," Alfonzo added. "Carries a lot of weight for an eleven-year-old kid."

Tanner tugged on the black silk neckerchief he always wore. Silk was best, better than wool in winter, and winter was coming.

Rosalie stopped what she was doing and said, "Michael said Leeland fell hard for basketball. Says he can run like a gazelle. But Leeland told him that his dad took that away from him too. Michael is going to talk to the coach about that." She nodded at herself and said, "Linda Pruitt was my friend. She came in here real regular."

Tanner went to the back counter where Alfonzo was standing and gave him his trademark cowboy hug. Alfonzo stiffened but it didn't stop Tanner, who said, "You're good people, patrón."

Tanner poured himself a cup of coffee that Alfonzo knew he wouldn't drink. "The Bounty is a good place to work," he said. "I ride the brand. Always have. Still...I'm thinking we take this to Mr. Duff."

Alfonzo nodded and then both of them saw the feed salesman pull up in his truck. Smoot was pulling a load of cotton seed cake and protein blocks. Ranchers in the Hondo expected a harsh winter. Rosalie saw him too and said, "Tell that man to drop a quarter."

Tanner laughed.

"What'd I miss?" Smoot said when he came in the door. He always said that and Alfonzo knew that he'd follow that up with his standard, "Where'd you get that hat?"

But today he walked right in front of them and took a look down the row of PO boxes like he was making sure they were alone.

Alfonzo nodded at Tanner meaning it was time to head out. They didn't have time for the backslapping salesman talk. The man would do anything and everything to keep his big accounts in the Hondo and the Bounty was big—not as big as the Diamond Crown but big enough to matter to a bootlicker salesman.

"Headed to Luke's place?" Smoot asked as he picked up the coffee pot, and when neither Tanner nor Alfonzo bothered to answer, he narrowed his little eyes and said to Alfonzo, "Cat got your tongue, boy?"

Alfonzo could feel the spit that Smoot had let fly.

Tanner glared at the salesman and said, "Pay your way. Do

your part." He jabbed his bent finger at the man. They all knew it for a threat.

Sure, it felt like a tragedy when Linda Pruitt killed her husband and then herself—right here in the Hondo Valley back in '95—under our noses. "That poor, unlucky woman," we'd whispered to one another, and then we'd gone on keeping her dirty secrets. We should have put it on the front page that she'd had no other choice, no other way to stop it.

"Ranch Wife Steps Up." That should have been the headline.

But when Luke came back to the Hondo Valley, it hit us that the murder-suicide was only the beginning, and now we were in the middle with no end in sight.

Salado

2004

Salado headed out to the Hondo Valley High School football field on a fall afternoon. The field had been recently renamed for the latest student lost in overseas combat—friendly fire, the marines reported. That half-fact gave his mother, Rosalie, no comfort. Leeland was wandering in the tall grass near the south end zone, hunting four-leaf clovers, Salado had to guess. "There's a lover in every clover," Salado's wife had taught their five sons.

The coach was on the sideline at the fifty-yard line, and when he saw Salado watching the Pruitt boy he said, "His folks won't sign the permission slip. We could really use him on the team." The coach put his clipboard under one arm and offered the custodian his hand.

"We ordered Leeland a tee shirt. Today's the day we handed them out," the coach said as he pointed to the boys in black and at his own tee shirt. There were only twelve boys

240

out there on the field today and Salado's sons, Joseph and Ramon, were two of them.

Get Your Wings the tee shirts said and featured a big eagle—wings spread—in negative space.

"Leeland said he'd get in trouble at home three times worse if he took a tee shirt. Said he wasn't allowed," the coach said.

Worse than what? Salado started to say, but both men knew what the boy meant.

"Give the shirt to Joseph. He'll save it for Leeland."

The coach moved his eyes up and to the left, and Salado followed. Leeland's stepmother was coming at them. Salado stepped back and watched while the coach magically got his whistle into his mouth, pulled in air, and let out a blast that would stop traffic. Boys came trotting over.

"Don't need that hyena going off at me today," the coach said to Salado out of the side of his mouth.

Mrs. Pruitt was waving her long arms at the coach. Salado watched as the coach found safety in the circle of boys. Salado turned to leave; he had work to get to. He didn't mind the work, liked being the after-school custodian better than he liked being the Roswell Walmart morning janitor, and he didn't mind that much either. He liked the early drive into Roswell on Highway 70, especially on pitch-black winter mornings. There was no better place to watch stars disappearing into daylight. And from above—to an alien passing over this part of southeast New Mexico—it had to look like a bottomless pit. Aliens must have had some real faith to land in these parts, Salado figured, or maybe just curiosity. All five of his sons were curious boys. It was one of the things he admired most about his boys.

Salado locked eyes with Joseph and warned him silently about Mrs. Pruitt. Joseph was in Leeland's grade and had seen some bad bruises on Leeland's back in PE when they showered. His son said it looked like someone had thrown rocks at Leeland. When Salado looked again for Leeland, the boy was gone. The stepmother was still there outside the circle of boys, slapping a paperback book in her big ranch-girl hands. She held her mouth in a tight little knot.

My wife is delicate next to her, he thought.

He was going to have to pass by the thick-necked woman to get back to work, but being Mexican sometimes gave a man a pass here in the Hondo Valley. Head down, he walked right past her. Hearing had always been his strongest sense, and as he passed the woman he was sure he heard her say, "Mexican."

If she were a man...he thought.

Salado saw that today Deona Pruitt was wearing Bermuda shorts, and he wondered how he knew the name for those. His wife would have cut the things up and used them to scrub the kitchen floor.

One evening, deep into winter the year Leeland and his stepsister had started school at Hondo, Salado had been mopping the floor in the cafeteria and saw Leeland standing outside in the lot where parents came to drop off and pick up their children. But it was long past dark and well into the supper hour. Leeland was crying, and when Salado suggested Leeland come inside to wait, he'd said only, "Not allowed." After that Salado had made it his business to watch out for the boy.

Salado knew he wasn't the only one watching out for the Pruitt boy—both Pruitt kids, really. But Leeland was so easy to like. Salado never sat and drank coffee in the teachers' lounge, but he'd heard the word around school. The latest story was about Deona going on the summer field trip to the Bottomless Lakes as a chaperone, and how she'd told one of the teachers, "When Leeland turns eighteen he's out of my house."

Joseph had been on that field trip, but Leeland hadn't. We

all knew he worked the ranch each summer. He was a hand now.

"The teacher told Mrs. Pruitt that Leeland would still be a senior when he turned eighteen," Joseph reported to his parents that summer night at the supper table.

"We'll take him and give him a good home," Salado remembered saying. "We already have his grandmother's dog. What's one more boy when you live in the country?" And Salado remembered looking out into the yard at Linda's Dog.

"It sure is a long trip out to those lakes," his middle boy had said, and his wife nodded and patted the boy's hand as if to tell him he was a good son.

Men for others, is what Salado's baby brother, who'd become a Jesuit, said when their mother cried about him leaving the Valley, first for Rome when he was only eighteen and then for Colombia. "Now you are my baby," his mother, who'd had eight sons, said to Salado. And now that he thought about it, he was sure his mother had patted his hand too.

On his way back inside from the field, Salado spotted the Pruitt kids out in the front lot, and so he went the long way to the front. "Goodnight, Mr. Salado," Leeland said and pointed his sister at their pickup parked in the lot. Salado waved and kept moving. He heard the girl say, "You know the truck's locked. Mom said to wait here."

At the janitor closet, Salado gathered his supplies and pushed the wheeled garbage can down the hall to the counselor's office. The counselor always worked late, and every afternoon his basket was filled with so many discarded papers that Salado had learned to finish up there. But today he headed there first.

Salado knocked on the doorframe and said, "Can I talk to you about a student? Not one of my sons."

"Sure, come on in, Salado. I'm not worth a teaspoon of sugar if I'm not a student advocate."

Salado explained the situation about Leeland and the football team. "If the coach can get Leeland on the team, at least he can look out for him after school. I can make sure he always gets a ride home." Advocate was not a word Salado felt comfortable using, but it was what he meant. He knew he was a busybody, but all those hours at his mother's kitchen table after his brother left had given him a lot of motherly insights.

Mexican boys do not leave their mothers. Salado remembered those words and the tears.

The counselor said, "Salado, my hands are tied. The brain trust up in Santa Fe has a new slogan for what we are going to do with our troubled boys: *Send them home.*"

Salado hadn't taken a seat—it wasn't his mother's kitchen—and now he ran his hand through his hair. His mother had said his hair was his best trait. She'd wanted a girl so bad— "Eight boys," she'd say in Spanish, and count them out slowly, name by name. They'd all lived and she was proud of that.

"Leeland's not troubled. He's motherless," Salado said.

A poster on the wall behind the counselor said Pull Together. Salado couldn't quite make out the black and white photo because his eyes were never so good. It looked to be the hands of an adult holding a little foot. It would make his wife Elena cry.

"Well...his stepmother is out there on the field now," Salado said and added, "In shorts."

"Yeah, she was here at lunchtime too. She's taken to having lunch with her daughter. It's out of line," the counselor said as he shoved his desk drawer in so hard that his desk wobbled. Salado wanted to shove something too.

"I'll give it a try. Let me tell you, though—pushing Deona Pruitt around just makes matters worse for Leeland. He's begged me not to call his parents for all sorts of things like black eyes. We are required to call home for those." The counselor held his hands together as if they were cuffed. He was looking for a smile and Salado gave him one. Sometimes Anglos were just plain silly.

"She won't smack a gimp," the man said. He had one of those walks where he swayed hard to the left each time he took a step. Nobody had ever said what his deal was, and Salado never remembered feeling sorry for him.

"Thanks, Santa," the counselor said. It was Salado's school nickname. He'd been the annual Santa at the Hondo School Christmas Fiesta for ten years.

There hadn't been any Santa at any fiesta when he was growing up. His family lived at the far end of White Goat Road in the home he'd grown up in with his seven brothers. The house was surrounded on three sides by a coyote fence. His sons knew how to strap the cedar posts together. Elena was particular about her fence. "Scatter the heights," she always told them when they went out to repair a place. "Only Anglos shave off the tops," she'd add. Her dad had been Anglo, and so she told her sons she could say such things.

The Rio Ruidoso bordered their place on the fourth side, and whenever the river got too quiet she'd send her boys down to roll in a couple of boulders. "Give it back its gurgle," is how she explained it.

Salado had found himself this pretty, happy woman when he was already thirty-five. Up till then he hadn't worried about time passing, because he'd been living with his mother. But now, married to Elena, he thought about it all the time; and he thought about being lonely when all their boys left home. So, he had the Hondo School to look after and all the children who passed through it.

If Leeland makes it through, he said to himself as he watched the counselor wobble down the hallway like the goat with all four legs different lengths that he and his brothers had bottle-fed and raised when its mother would not.

"Let's air it out before it becomes a bigger problem," Salado remembered saying to Leeland over the Christmas holidays the year before, when he'd found the boy on the steps to the Moon Café on Highway 70. It was darn cold that Christmas. The café was closed. Everyone in the Valley knew that the woman who owned the place took Christmas week off so she could take her twin daughters up to the crippled children's hospital in Albuquerque where they'd been cared for as little children. Salado had seen the now-grown twins before Christmas, decked out in matching blouses embroidered on the back with wildly decorated Christmas trees. The blouses had hung heavy on those two tiny women.

"Who you waiting for?" Salado had asked when he climbed out of his truck at the café.

"Nobody, Mr. Salado," Leeland said.

"Then I better wait with you." That got a grin out of the boy. Leeland had not come to the Christmas party, where every kid left with a gift. Salado and his wife always did the school Christmas shopping at Walmart and hauled the gifts home. Elena had taught her five sons how to wrap.

We all talked about how the Pruitts never showed up at parties. We knew that Luke and his brother Stralin had come to the Christmas parties with their mom back in the1970s. "It's only fair that Luke bring his kids," Salado's wife, who wasn't a Valley girl, had said.

It should have dawned on one of us that those gifts could have been delivered to the two Pruitt kids. It was stupid, easy stuff that we didn't do. Stupid that we didn't try just once to get inside that house that was such a big deal for Deona—and it wasn't even hers.

"I'm being punished," Leeland said after Salado got as comfortable as a fifty-year-old with no butt could get on cold steps. "I back-talked my dad, and there is no going back with him. He left me here while he went into Ruidoso."

They both looked that way.

The boy was slouching. He bent over with his head between his knees and fooled with the laces on his work boots. He wasn't wearing socks.

"How about I take you home for tamales? Christmas spells tamales at my house."

"Thank you, sir. I can't get you into this."

"Well, how long ago did your dad leave you here?"

"Twenty minutes, I'm guessing."

They sat there a minute or so in silence before Leeland said, "He just said, 'Get the hell outta my truck.' "

It was clear as a New Mexico day after a downpour that Leeland was sick. His nose was dripping. Well, that's how Salado saw it, and so he got up and went to the truck for the horse blanket he always kept in the back and the transistor radio he kept in the glove box, and a clean handkerchief— Elena kept him stocked in those, something her dad had insisted a man needed to carry. Handing the things to the boy, he said, "So you won't be lonely. I'll be back with Joseph and tamales. Just stash that stuff there under the steps if you see your dad driving up before I get back. He in the ranch truck?"

"No, sir, his truck," the boy said and used the handkerchief quickly as if he was ashamed of a runny nose.

I'm not gonna be shamed by doing nothing is exactly what Salado thought. He would come back to wait here with Leeland until that dog of a father of his came back. But on second thought, he would not bring Joseph.

"Who did that child see when he was born?" his wife asked as she was gathering up the food. She always asked that when she came across a child that no one loved enough. "Ghost Goslings," is what she called those children.

It would have been hard that Christmas season to find a single person in the Valley who didn't think Luke Pruitt was a monster, yet there Leeland sat on the frozen steps of that closed café, two days after Christmas—nose pouring and locked out. Sick as a dog. And the few of us who drove by, just passed on by. Simple as that.

Thirty minutes was all it took for Salado to get the food and some hot coffee and get back there. Coffee never hurt a boy. But Leeland was gone and the blanket was folded with the radio snug inside it, pushed so far under the steps that it could have gone undetected until some July downpour flooded it out. Luke must have gotten a change of heart is what Salado told himself at the time. It was only later that it came to him that Leeland had gone off someplace behind the café and hid. It was the missing handkerchief that made him realize this.

I'll have to live with this my whole life, is what Salado wrote his brother the priest.

You'll live, his brother had written back. It's the boy who needs some luck to survive this.

> *Cowboys expect a lot of their families because they expect a lot of themselves.*
>
> Linda Pruitt, *Ranching Weekly*

Salado

2005

Principal Norris was directing traffic in the school cafeteria when Salado arrived at three p.m. Salado stood in the doorway considering what all he'd need to do to get the place ready for the crowd they expected for the town meeting that night. A group of 4-H members—wearing tee shirts that said *Head, Heart, Hand, Health*—were collapsing cafeteria tables and stacking them in the back of the room in specially-made racks. Those kids always came out to help, and they were going to save him loads of time today. It was hard work dragging those tables when you were alone. Salado had been the sponsor for the 4-H Club a bunch of times when no faculty member was available. There was always one new kid who insisted one of the H's was for horses.

"How was the weather coming in from Roswell?" the principal asked. They'd had about six inches of snowfall in the Valley that morning, and a lot of it had melted. New Mexico was like that—snow never lasted—but the parking lot and walkways were on the north side of the building where, Salado knew, the snow could turn to ice.

"Clear coming in," Salado said.

"That's good news. I told the Albuquerque folks to get an early start, but you know Albuquerque people..."

Salado watched as the principal—who was standing proudly, arms crossed, under the huge banner that said A Convocation of Eagles—drifted off into his own thoughts. Actually, Salado didn't know. He'd never been farther north than Corona, and yet his baby brother was in Colombia. *I'm high now*, his brother had written on the card he'd sent at Christmas, posed in a hammock on a patio so full of green that it made Salado's eyes hurt. And suddenly, thinking of his brother made Salado know how his mother felt when she'd let her youngest leave for a life in the priesthood. "I'll die sad and proud," she'd promised and had.

Salado nodded at the principal. They both knew he'd get the cafeteria sparkling. The room smelled faintly of tacos like it always did on Taco Tuesday. But it was the sticky sweet smell of lemon furniture polish that was bothering him. It was not something he kept in the custodian closet. Salado could see through the little pass-through window into the enormous kitchen. The woman who ran the cafeteria, and two of the other cafeteria ladies, had stayed late. They wouldn't have been the ones to be spreading Pledge. It had to be some PTA committee member who'd been in after lunch. A big crowd of parents and town people was expected for the Hondo Town Meeting.

"I'll get to my rounds," Salado said.

"Okey dokey, as long as you trust us to do this setup right," Norris said, while some kid hoisting a microphone stand actually slapped the principal on his back. Salado would talk to his sons about that type of behavior.

It was too warm in the room, and if the cafeteria filled up the way the principal kept promising, it'd be blazing. That was Salado's first project—he'd get the heat down before he took care of the walkways.

Standing outside the cafeteria with the shovel and salt, he watched the sun as it was leaping and dying like one of the school homecoming bonfires. Afternoon light was bouncing off the moisture. A lifetime ago, when he was a Hondo Eagle, he'd always walked home for lunch and back. All the kids had done that, even on snowy days when the light bounced around like it was doing now. A cafeteria was not even dreamed of back in those days. *Things change*, Salado told himself, like he did several times every week it seemed. But no way was he going to have his sons slapping the school principal on his back.

At 5:45 p.m., Salado took a seat in the last row, near where the PTA hospitality committee had set up the beverage and refreshment tables. The two fifty-cup percolators were rattling and shaking like they always did at the end of their long routine. Salado was thankful to hear that sound. Those urns were old and were known to blow a fuse. Pies would be brought out after the meeting when people were visiting. "It's a fruit pie kind of town," someone would be sure to say as the pies were presented. There was always a PTA woman responsible for bringing the freshly laundered and pressed Hondo Eagles tablecloths to any school function where refreshments were involved and, like altar cloths, she'd gather them up and take them home afterwards so that she'd have them ready for the next convocation.

The Hondo School parents mostly showed up for school events in work clothes, and tonight, even with the CYFD officials coming in from Albuquerque, it wouldn't look much different in the room.

We were friendly here—*cordial* is what we called it—and

even if an alien had walked in people would still nod politely and wait their turn to wander over and say a few welcoming words.

Salado's Anglo father-in-law had taught his daughter, Elena, to look people in the eye, and she'd taught their five sons that looking a man in the eye was good manners. It was something Salado had never learned how to do, and so he sat quietly in the back while she visited and caught up with old friends. There was plenty of behind-the-hands talking going on about what was to be expected tonight. Elena brought him coffee.

He'd only been sitting here ten minutes, and already he'd heard three people say, "CYFD?" in disbelief.

And then the talk changed. We saw Luke Pruitt come in with his wife and Leeland. It was just wrong to bring a kid to a meeting for parents. We saw it as another stupid Luke Pruitt stunt. We watched as the Pruitts took their seats in the next-to-last row, and the two of them put the boy between them. We had to wonder if the statement they were making was that they couldn't leave the boy at home alone—he was fourteen. And if that was the case, where was the girl? "Brazen," we said as we began to take our seats.

Up on the riser at the head table, Principal Norris had seated a full team of teachers, along with coaches and the counselor. The president of the school board, however, was sitting in the front row, and Salado saw Mr. Norris walk over to him and insist that he come up to the head table. Near the center of the table sat a woman who was a member of the governor's cabinet. The governor had been calling her his Crown Jewel from the day he'd announced the appointment, or so the principal had reported in the flyer he had sent home with all the kids.

None of us in the Valley knew what to expect out of a Crown Jewel, who had come to tell us, no doubt, how the State of New Mexico was looking out for our kids. She was a husky gal with short hair the color of steel wool. We'd heard she'd been a nun.

"Welcome," Mr. Norris said as he stood behind the half-podium that sat dead center of the long table. "Let's stand for the Pledge."

Salado would have sworn that Luke, who was in the chair directly in front of him, had taken the opportunity right then to give him a sideways glance. Months later Elena said that she'd seen the look too and thought it was because Salado had nodded at Leeland when he sat down in front of them. Salado remembered how it suddenly felt as if the room filled with gloom. He wanted to take his wife's hand and lead her out, and if she had not been here with him he'd have gotten up to stand at the back door alongside his rolling trash bins.

"Welcome, neighbors. We are here tonight to welcome the State of New Mexico's Children, Youth, and Families Secretary. We will hear what is happening with the CYFD camp for boys, Camp Salinas, which is in our very backyard— a place of refuge for boys in need. We are, after all, a valley of families. First let me welcome Father Frank, who will give our invocation. Please stand."

Salado knew his wife loved the priest. She liked to say that he had brought Rome to the Hondo Valley. Salado wished it was his brother up there praying for them. He watched Leeland slump in his seat when the principal welcomed them, and now, before the boy could get to his feet, Luke reached back and grabbed the boy's hair at the nape of his neck and yanked him up. Elena gasped.

Father Frank took the microphone and, as if he were a stand-up comic, began with a big smile. "In nineteen eighty-six, Pope John Paul said, 'As the family goes so goes the nation, and so goes the whole world in which we live.' Believe me, I was sure, the way only kids can be sure, that the Pope was speaking to me personally and that my life's work would be with families of faith." He laughed as if he'd made a joke, and the crowd of nearly one hundred—Salado knew how many chairs they'd set up—mumbled.

We did not know if we should be laughing, what with the Crown Jewel sitting there and the Pruitt family smoking hate.

"The Church tries to strengthen Christian families. She reaches out with compassion to those families that are in difficult or irregular situations. Let us pray."

We could not turn around to look at the boy back there, but we hoped that Father Frank had him in his sights.

When Principal Norris again took the microphone, he began by saying that over one hundred years ago, right here in Lincoln County, in this very valley, people had protected Billy the Kid when a posse came looking for him. "That posse ransacked our village looking for him," he said as if it was of utmost significance.

Salado couldn't much concentrate. He knew the story by heart—knew everything there was to know about that soft-bellied boy hero and how the Valley folks had believed in him.

The principal switched to the story of the Hondo Valley boy who, three months earlier, had been sent to Camp Salinas. A half-native boy—we all knew him by name, knew he'd gotten sent to the camp for stealing.

"This boy now has a way out of a life of crime," the principal said as if he believed it, and Salado wondered if that was what the boy had planned all along.

We all knew he'd been a runaway on and off since he was six years old, and we knew his family was not here tonight. They'd never shown up for anything. Salado heard someone three rows up say, "He's just a plain Indian," and he felt ashamed.

"Camp Salinas is his home now and his family," the principal said. He nodded at the priest and said, "As the family goes so goes the nation." After a short burst of applause that confused us all he said, "Let me now introduce our CYFD Secretary."

Luke leaned back in his folding chair. The chair made the sound such chairs make when they are about to fold up on themselves. Salado put his hand on the back of the chair to right it and protect his wife.

The Secretary stood at the podium, and said into the microphone in a lullaby voice, "Every single child has value. We know that...and we especially know that at Camp Salinas." She settled herself like a pro and began a longer story. "Let me pass on some information for those of you who don't know about the camp. We treat low-risk males there aged fourteen to eighteen." She took a long pause.

Luke jammed an elbow into Leeland's side. "Fourteen," he said to his son. "You cry wolf, you better believe you're gone."

Salado got it—they'd brought Leeland here to threaten him.

And in her soothing voice, the Secretary said, "Make no doubt about it, we are at a crossroads. The camp is underutilized, and extensive repairs must be done to turn it around."

A big man, who Salado knew lived up near Ruidoso and had long ago sent his last child off to some big city, raised his arthritic hand that looked like a mesquite root and, without waiting to be called on, said, "The camp gives young boys an alternative to a life of crime. Close it and see what happens."

Principal Norris did not stand. He only nodded at the man and said, "Q&A follows the formal comments."

The Secretary nodded and said slowly, "When I took over CYFD last year, it was a big ship adrift in the night, no real captain, no compass to follow."

Luke leaned into Leeland and, loud enough for Salado and his wife to hear, said, "That captain must be a navy gal like your mother was, shipwrecked in the West after she gave up stripping."

Salado felt his wife flinch.

"We are righted now and committed to serving our most fragile families. The governor's philosophy towards juvenile justice is intervention and prevention, but he knows that our rural areas can get forgotten. We all know that."

It seemed to Salado that the Secretary got flustered when she didn't get applause for that.

"So, we looked at options, and, like the nation," she turned and nodded at Father Frank, "we will be concentrating on creating community-based programs for families."

Suddenly, as if orchestrated, the governor walked into the room. Salado had been reading the expressions on people's faces all his life, and he knew that this woman had not expected her boss. The governor had two men in suits following him. One of them had a heavy camera with a lens as big around as a baseball hanging around his neck. The governor was wearing black Levis and a tan cowboy hat that looked well worn. Salado expected him to take the hat off and wave it like he was leading a parade, but he didn't. He stepped up on the riser and went to the podium. His Crown Jewel put a frozen, closed-mouth smile on her face and kept it there. They shook hands, and she stepped behind him, where she stood like a statue.

Luke said, "Fucking shit."

And when Leeland looked at his dad—giving him a look of disapproval—Luke got the boy by the chin and said through a locked jaw, "Say one word and I'll beat you silly." Luke turned his entire body to look back at Salado. It was as if moving only his head would have been too relaxed a movement, too casual, and Salado saw in that moment that Luke was scared. And Deona suddenly turned to stare down Elena.

"It's great to be here in Billy the Kid country," the governor said and finally got the applause he had been expecting since he came through the door. Then he took off his hat and handed it to the Secretary, who took her seat.

"You folks probably know I am considering whether to give Billy a pardon."

A woman up front, who Salado did not recognize, said, "He was nothing but a gunslinger."

It was then that the town meeting plan to get things aired fizzled.

The governor nodded at the woman winningly and said, "But I am not here about Billy. I am here to tell you that as your governor, I pledge to keep Camp Salinas open." He had his right hand over his heart.

Salado watched as the Secretary tried to wipe the sour grapes look off her face.

After the governor's standing ovation the meeting broke up and only pie and handshakes were left.

Salado could smell the coffee, which for no good reason had begun to perk again. He knew he needed to check on those urns, but he had his eye on Leeland.

Those of us not so star-struck by a big cowboy governor were watching out for Leeland. We saw Salado move to the back of the room. Salado was a little man, not the perfect size to be Santa at the annual Christmas party. We saw what Salado saw—Luke had Leeland by his arm and was shaking him. We expected to hear something snap. Salado moved fast and got up real close to Luke, private-like.

"Hey, man, I know this is your son and all, but what I've been hearing all night doesn't sound like you've got much good to say about him, and I don't appreciate you shaking him like that."

"And you're Captain America?" Luke showed his teeth as if he were some sort of wildcat. He didn't back away, but Salado stood his ground and pointed his chin at the man. It was something all the men in his family knew how to do.

Stupid words; deaf ears.

"Shut up and mind your own business," Luke said and Salado thought of little kids taunting each other out in the play yard.

We heard that too, and we knew that the little gimpy counselor heard it because he said, "Dang, what the heck?" as he broke away from the Crown Jewel. Bobbing from side to side, he headed to the back of the room—a cripple heading over to put a stop to what had to stop, after we'd let so much happen.

But it was Salado who looked Luke in the eye and said, "I ain't gonna allow it, and if I see you doing it again, I'll put an ass-whipping on you."

Deona got that hyena look on her face. Leeland put his right hand to his mouth. All five fingernails were black. It was a sign, we thought, as if the boy said *stop.*

So Salado looked at Leeland and said, "We live down White Goat Road. The gate is never locked."

But it was Luke who said, "I know where you live."

Every single one of us, even those of us in the big hobnob around the governor, knew where Luke Pruitt lived, and not a one of us followed him home.

Leeland

July 3, 2005

When Leeland pushed open the barn door, the morning light jumped inside and the first thing he noticed was the filly's bleary eyes. She should have looked disgusted—her white tail mostly gone now from being tied to her back leg. Leeland knew it was no way to tame a horse. How easy it would have been to let her go.

"She's gone," he'd say to his dad.

There was a gentle rain falling. It had awakened him. It rarely rained like that here in New Mexico, where it usually took most of the day to build up to a storm that would tear the topsoil to pieces and be over so fast. Gentle was better.

Leeland was wearing his pull-up boots. They were already slick with mud. His dad wouldn't like that. He climbed up to the hayloft, missing a step. The filly looked embarrassed, as if she'd put him to extra trouble. He grabbed the hay hook and worked fast, tossing out more fine alfalfa hay than the filly had ever seen on this ranch. He came back down and carried the hay into her stall, looked into her pearly eyes, and said softly, "Go on and eat. Fast now."

Leeland figured that he could make it to the front gate, break out, and be down the road to his lookout before his dad burst out in the yard looking for him. Joseph said he'd pick him up.

"On Sunday morning, call me by six and I'll be there at the clubhouse by seven." Joseph said all that when they'd worked the alfalfa fields the week before. He meant the lookout and he'd be there, because he always kept his word. Leeland and Joseph had been stashing things there for two years now; survival things like water, blankets, old jackets, and a flare Joseph's dad had found.

Joseph was Mexican and Leeland's dad didn't like him talking to Mexican kids. But that day, Mr. D, the ranch owner, had been wandering around the alfalfa fields with his dad, admiring the not-quite-grown grass, and so Leeland figured it was pretty safe to talk to his friend.

But this morning it was different. Leeland had been afraid to pick up the phone in the kitchen, and the door to the ranch office was locked. That was a new thing this summer. His dad didn't want anyone messing with the computer, which was hooked to the Internet. Luke had a thing for the computer, which was okay with Leeland, because whenever he saw his dad's face lit up by the screen, Leeland knew he was safe to sneak by the office door.

In the stall, Leeland watched as the filly ate. His dad had sworn to Mr. Duff that he'd have the palomino broken by the end of the holiday weekend.

Leeland stayed clear of her flank. Her skin quivered—she wasn't ready to trust him. He could see that in her eyes. He thought again about letting her go. He'd ridden the fence line with Alfonzo for three days straight in June. Alfonzo knew the breaks where Luke had burned out the salt cedar, knew it was a place the filly might head to—to get free. So sure, Alfonzo would know where to look for her and would get her to safety.

"Never was a need for a fence here until your dad burned this stretch of salt cedar clear to the ground," Alfonzo had told him when they happened on that line of water-sucking invasive bushes up near the creek at the north end of the ranch. That had been Luke's grand plan that spring.

"Won't do no good to burn the salt cedar out," Alfonzo said, using the toe of his boot to point out the new fleshy green shoots to Leeland.

All the hands on the ranch knew that Luke had spent a week burning the cedars out. Luke even got into a big old fight with the hand on the ranch that shared a boundary line north of the Bounty Canyon Ranch. That hand was sure Luke was burning trees that were across the property line from the Bounty. It was like that with his dad.

When the filly finished eating, Leeland climbed back up to the loft and tossed down the right amount of hay for all the horses, the filly included, and got to work feeding them. He was on schedule now. The rain had stopped and Joseph would be on his way to the Stampede by now, hauling a truck full of friends. Leeland's day was going to happen, like regular. There would be work and arguing, and he would not be going to the Smokey Bear Stampede.

He hashed it over in his mind one last time. He didn't want to be a cowboy. He'd admitted that to his school counselor. "Nothing wrong with wanting to be your own person," the man who was always watching for bruises said. His office smelled like Bengay. But no one called the counselor gay, even though he probably was, and no one made fun of his funny-guy walk.

I trust the guy, Leeland heard himself thinking that morning. It was something he had to remind himself each time he went into that smelly office, and he said it now because he was thinking about the tube of the Bengay that he had hidden in his dresser. He had to be careful when he used it, because the time he'd used too much at home, Deona had torn his room apart looking for it.

"My house, my rules," she'd screamed.

Mostly he hadn't wanted to lose the tee shirt that he'd hidden in the dresser under the bottom drawer. She'd have to take the whole drawer out to find it and she hadn't gone that far, not yet.

Clever, he said to himself.

"You've got some mud to shovel when you finish feeding," his dad said from the door of the barn.

"Done feeding, Dad. I got out here early," Leeland said as he looked up from under the brim of his ball cap. He couldn't help being hopeful.

"Then shovel. And get that look off your face like you've gone and done me some fuckin' favor."

Leeland felt his shoulders twitch. He'd learned how to block a punch by pulling his shoulders inward, but he didn't dare make that move now.

It would go on like this all day, back and forth with his dad.

He decided right that minute that in the fall, he'd tell the counselor that he hated his dad. The man already knew about the social security money that was supposed to be his. Counselors knew all that legal stuff about a parent dying. Leeland decided he'd ask if the money could buy his freedom.

"Aren't there laws?" he'd asked his older friend, Michael, before he left for the marines. Michael was smart, but he'd still gotten killed. Leeland figured it wasn't always enough to be smart.

Stay strong, Leeland told himself.

"You damn well better have left that filly hungry. She breaks, then she eats," his dad said flatly. He was still there at the barn door blocking the light. Then they both heard the ranch owner's car. Today Mr. Duff was driving his Benz.

"Stay in the barn, asshole," Luke said, and Leeland heard his dad's footsteps heading across the dirt drive to the house.

Other kids would smell bacon and eggs on Sunday morning.

The car stopped and Leeland heard his dad making nice to Mr. Duff and then the car went on by and around the bend down to the gate. Leeland heard it pass over the cattle guard.

"Hush," Leeland said to the horses, and cleaned out all the evidence of hay from the filly's stall. And as he said it, Karmen came running into the barn—scaring the wits out of him and the filly.

"Uncle Stralin is on his way up the road and Aunt Trudy too. The whole family." She did a leap. "Dad said go open the gate, now."

Leeland knew that the first thing his uncle would say when he climbed out of his truck was, "Cross country would have been shorter than coming through Roswell, but there's always gates." Leeland knew he could count on his uncle to repeat his insights, but a visit was a good thing and maybe they'd all eat something. It was a hopeful way to feel. He patted the filly on her flank and even that was a good thing to do.

His uncle was pulling a horse trailer. He stopped and dropped his two boys off to walk back up the hill with Leeland, and then drove on slowly, popping sugar rocks.

Leeland hadn't known his uncle was returning the kid's horse he had been considering—might have bought from Mr. Duff. The rancher liked to trade in horses, even though he knew nothing about them.

"Out for a Sunday drive?" Luke said as Stralin and his wife and daughter piled out. Deona and Karmen joined them in the yard. No one was invited inside. Leeland liked his cousins and Karmen always babied the little girl who was not a baby any longer. Her brothers called her Little Flower—as if Pearl wasn't a sweet enough name— because their mom had turned them all into Catholics when she started the little girl in school at St. Therese of the Little Flower. Leeland knew that his dad hated Catholics. He called Father Frank a faggot just because he had a parrot, or maybe it was because he wasn't married.

The two families gathered in a circle all natural-like, and his Aunt Trudy said she was going to take some photos of kids roping at the Stampede, said she had a special lens for action shots. Stralin's oldest son said, "Let's play some ball."

It was Deona who said, "Leeland has chores."

Trudy said, "It's the Fourth of July weekend."

Stralin stood silent, mouth open. Leeland caught him looking at his dad with the same eyes the filly had—glassy and sad.

He's afraid of my dad, Leeland thought.

"Unload that horse, then ball," Luke said to the boys, and to Trudy, he said, "Not locking horns with you today."

His dad always called his aunt Tall Cotton, even to her face, but not today.

Little Flower started crying real tears, like her heart was broken, when the boys went to let the horse out, and she kept saying, "My pony, my pony." Leeland had to admit she was spoiled.

"He's too mean for you, Sugar," Trudy said as she walked over to their truck, reached into the cab, and passed Leeland a bag of wrapped burritos. Leeland could smell them. He hadn't eaten anything. "For the kids," she said real loud. And to him alone she said, "Angie wants to know if you need anything." And after what seemed like a full minute, she said real loud again, "It's the Fourth of July, in case y'all forgot."

Leeland smiled at her, wished she were his mother, and went back over to the small circle and handed the bag to Deona, who just stood there doing nothing. She was like that.

The boys had no trouble getting the horse unloaded and into the corral. Leeland knew he'd be in charge later of getting her back to the barn. He'd like that. He thought maybe that this horse would calm the filly.

The three boys then headed to the little beat-up spread of concrete that passed for a basketball court. "Play horse?" Stralin's younger son said.

"You crack me up," Leeland said. But he could see that his dad was about done visiting.

"I've got things to do," Leeland heard his dad say.

"So let us take the kids with us," Trudy said. "The Stampede's a community affair."

Leeland's heart did that little hummingbird thing it sometimes did.

"Like I said, things to do. Leeland has a wall to spackle in the kitchen. Don't you, Cowboy?"

It was true. There was a hole in the wall where his dad had pushed his head through after the town meeting months back. Leeland thought he'd always remember that total silence he'd heard after his head broke the wall. His dad had been waiting until Mr. D. wasn't around to work on fixing it. Leeland couldn't figure how his dad was going to match the milky green paint color on the wall.

Leeland let the two brothers play, said he'd play the winner. They weren't very good. Then he spotted two hawks circling overhead and pointed. "They can perceive more than they can see. And they have ultraviolet vision, and some can see a mile off."

Stralin said, "You don't say."

His dad said, "Einstein."

"Learned it in 4-H," Leeland added and knew he was not going to the Stampede.

"You'd have to watch that kid like a hawk, or he'd run off with his Mexican girlfriend," Luke said and smirked. Deona let out a laugh. Luke added, "I know my boy."

"Take Karmen," Deona said.

"Sure, and we'll take her home with us," Trudy said. "We might just keep her."

"Send her home when you get tired of her," his dad said.

Little Flower was doing a little dance with Karmen and said, "We have hummingbirds, lots and lots and lots of them."

"They're gluttons," Deona said. She was still holding the burritos.

"Well, if you're going, go pack a bag," Luke said to Karmen.

The boys stopped playing ball and the three of them joined the circle again. Leeland heard his uncle say, "You're not being fair, Luke."

He is brave, Leeland thought and was hopeful, but it passed, and he stopped listening. He was telling himself the poem he'd memorized all those years ago. His teacher had told them that if you memorized a poem, you'd always have something to think about.

I have been thinking, he began, because the poem began that way.

"Leeland, are you deaf or plain rude?" his dad shouted. It must have been because his aunt was trying to get a photo of them. He hadn't realized, because he'd been thinking.

Then his aunt said, "You three boys stand there. Let's get Leeland in the middle with the ball. Let me get this picture."

"You're too close, Mom," her younger son said.

"Nah. Unless I'm close, you all look the same. Now move in close together, boys," Trudy said and snapped one shot after another. Leeland was thinking he'd like one of those photos for his room.

That evening Leeland hit some clean baskets before it got too dark to see the rim, and when he held the basketball tight to his chest and let his breathing calm, he heard only silence, not even a coyote. In the first year they'd lived here, his dad had cleaned the coyotes out...killed the families off and used the bulldozer to clear out their dens. Alfonzo had taught Leeland how to translate coyote calls, said their short barks warned of danger, high-pitched barks were to warn their pups. Leeland missed hearing them at night.

The only lights coming from the house that night were the ones in his dad's office and their bedroom. Deona was probably in there reading.

"Sure, Mom, I'll be right in. I could eat a horse," he said out loud to amuse himself and because he was feeling sorry for himself at the same time.

In your dreams, he thought.

Suddenly he missed his stepsister. Karmen was probably on one of the lit-up carnival rides right now, or maybe they were all in the show barn watching the 4-H kids show their prize cattle and fancy goats.

A community affair, he thought.

He was going to have to eat something. He thought again about his friends hanging out at the rodeo barn. Joseph would have explained to Yolanda why he hadn't shown up.

"Hey, kiddo, you and Wes get in here. I have supper on the table." Leeland remembered Angie saying that on those nights back when he got to have a weekend at her place. What was it Wes had told him? Leeland was too hungry to remember, and there were tears in his eyes now. He stood there on the cool cement long enough to get under control.

"Save yourself," someone had said. He couldn't remember who.

One burrito had been left sitting on the counter. He removed the foil and then reconsidered. It was cold and mushy. He rewrapped it and put it in the toaster oven on broil.

He ate slowly, standing at the counter. It felt dangerous in the house without Karmen to spy on him, and he realized, with a surge of blood to his face, that she was his lookout. He hoped his Aunt Trudy had gotten her a cotton candy.

By nine he was showered and back in his bedroom. He'd gotten some of the spackle his dad had spread on his head out of his hair, but it had dried hard. At the beginning of the summer, Alfonzo gave him a Walkman and a handful of extra batteries. "From my daughter," he'd said. She'd sent cassette tapes too, and some of them she had made—a mix of oldies from the Rolling Stones and the Beatles. But it felt even scarier with the earphones on. He remembered he had summer reading to do, which made him think of Robinson Crusoe and his Island of Despair. He'd loved that story.

He saw the light still shining from his folks' room out into the yard, and heard the TV. But the sounds of Deona's squealing told him they weren't watching; they were rough-housing, making their own reality show. He really wanted to close his door, but it wasn't allowed.

Sitting on his bed, he put his earphones back on, turned up the volume, and tried with all his heart to read. He had a choice of six books piled up on the floor next to his bed. He picked up *The Life of Pi* because he had already read the first part of the book, up to where tragedy struck. Leeland started up again at the place where Pi was alone with the man-eating tiger.

He was a clever boy.

"Get in here and prove you aren't a pussy," is what Leeland thought he heard his dad say. Then he heard him coming down the hall toward his door. It was the sound of something that smelled its prey. Leeland turned off his lamp and lay still. The music played on.

"Get in here," his dad shouted.

Leeland knew he'd lose the Walkman if he didn't get it stashed away, and so when his dad hit the doorway, Leeland had his back to him. Luke flipped the overhead light on, and Leeland turned, empty-handed, and said, "Sir."

Survival skills, Leeland said to himself.

Luke was holding the torch they kept in the kitchen drawer to light the stove when the electric went out. Luke waved it at Leeland to follow him, the way a cop waves on traffic. Luke was only wearing boxers, and Leeland was thankful he'd pulled on both his basketball shorts and jersey—from the team he'd never joined.

Luke held the torch out, and the flame struck Leeland on his arm, and when he shied back, Luke stabbed him again, herding him toward the door and down the hallway. Leeland felt the burrito about to blow up in his throat. He swallowed and stumbled forward, even though his brain was saying, *Run. Run now.*

There was only a bedside lamp on in his dad and Deona's bedroom. It was enough light to see that Deona was sprawled out on the bed.

"Naked," Leeland said aloud before he'd thought it through.

"You get the idea," his dad said and swept the torch across his bare arm. Leeland's skin hissed.

"I've got nothing to prove, Dad. Besides, you said she's my mother."

Deona said in a stupid, gritty voice Leeland thought he'd hear forever: "Come on. I'm not your flesh and blood."

Slut, Leeland thought, because he knew what slut meant.

"You don't know what to do with the real thing, do you? You miserable coward. Get over there," Luke said, and Leeland pushed past him, shoving him up against the bedroom door, looking him straight on in the eye.

Then he ran, but he didn't need to. No one came after him. He slammed his door shut and wedged himself in the space between his nightstand and the closet. There was no moon, no noise anywhere, and if he hadn't been too afraid to move, he would have gone out in the yard and rolled in the dirt. He' seen his grandmother's dog do exactly that, roll and shake.

It was the wrong thing to do to a boy.

He didn't sleep. He couldn't stop his heart from pounding and he thought—when he finally began to think—that his ears were damaged from all that pounding. And so, he let himself cry, and when he couldn't stop the crying, he began to think he'd gone blind because he couldn't open his eyes, and he kept seeing his mom flying across the road—her hair flying loose, shining in all that afternoon glare.

Of course he wanted to save someone—most of all himself. It had been in the poem.

He found his way by touch down the hall to the bathroom, and he retched, over and over. Which started up something like crying, but unlike anything he'd ever done before. He went back to his room and closed the door and pushed his dresser under the doorknob. Then he slept.

Deputy Greenwood

Afternoon July 6, 2005

"How about we wait here in the truck for Mr. Salado?" Greenwood said to Leeland.

Paula slipped out of the truck with the Walmart bag and went inside the CYFD building. "Don't want these tacos to go to waste." She explained that there was a kitchen in the back for when kids were staying there. Greenwood checked Leeland in the rearview mirror and saw the boy nod. Greenwood opened the glove compartment, took out a pair of glasses, and reached back to hand them to Leeland.

"I believe these are yours, Leeland," Greenwood said and paused before going on. "I was born and raised here," Greenwood explained as they sat waiting. He cracked the windows and let in the mountain air newly washed by rain. "Believe it or not, my mother graduated high school with your grandmother Lindalean Pruitt, right here in Ruidoso."

He saw Leeland give into a hint of a smile because he was a polite sort of kid. Then the boy said, "Is your mom still alive?"

"Yes, but she moved to Mexico."

"My grandmother called me her sunshine, but she died. My real mother came for the funeral, but now she's dead too."

Greenwood looked away from the mirror. "Did you wear that shirt when you went to Joseph's house?" he asked.

"Yes, sir. I had it hidden in my dresser. My friend Michael gave it to me when he outgrew it and went into the marines. He's dead now too. I know lots of dead people." Leeland slumped and put his head on the back of the seat like he'd fallen asleep.

Greenwood remembered being able to fall asleep in seconds when he was a teenager. His mom said sometimes he'd fall asleep at the dinner table between bites.

Mr. Salado's Chevy kicked up pebbles as he pulled into the lot, and Leeland gave into a deep sigh of relief that Greenwood wished he too felt. There was so much wrong with this day.

"Sorry," is all Leeland said to the man as Greenwood held the CYFD door for them. Mr. Salado had changed his shirt and was wearing a long-sleeved, pearl-buttoned shirt that someone had to have ironed. As they all stepped inside, Greenwood noticed an inscribed plaque on the wall. It was a vision statement printed on a surreal depiction of a giant human eye. The vision statement was something about how children in New Mexico would live in family environments free from abuse and neglect. Greenwood felt his very skin turn cold.

A woman wearing nurse scrubs decorated with groups of bears sitting in chairs greeted them, but she was there really to block the way into the building. "I need your gun, officer. It's for the safety of the children." She pointed across the reception room at a gun safe, which had a potted plant on top of it.

Greenwood handed her his gun, and she said, "Wait here." He heard Leeland begin to hum. Then the receptionist returned smiling and offered her hand first to Mr. Salado.

"Santa, welcome." Then she shook Leeland's hand and said, "We provide protective services and investigate reports of children in need of protection from abuse and neglect by parents."

Finally, when she shook Greenwood's hand, she said, "Paula hired me and brought me out from Hoboken, New Jersey." And then she said, "The DA is waiting in the AV room."

She led them down the long hallway. The first few rooms were offices with new computers on old metal desks. No one, however, seemed to be working today. As they passed a room with a Dutch door she said, "For toddlers," and Greenwood spotted a basket full of stuffed toys—bears mostly. There were always bears in these parts. At the end of the hallway, she directed them into a room she called "the safe room," but held him back, pointed, and said, "Paula's next door with the DA. We'll get settled here and wait for you and Paula." She looked him in the eye and said, "Your name is?"

"Deputy Greenwood," he said.

"We use first names here," she said.

"Robin," he said softly. "Rob is fine."

"Oh, I much prefer Robin. I'm Mitzi, and don't tell me you know a dog named Mitzi. Heard that one about fifty times," she said and closed the safe room door behind her.

Paula and DA Quintana sat at a high counter in front of a special one-way window. The DA looked pissed. He was still wearing his sunglasses in the dim room. He turned to Greenwood and said, "About time. I'll be recording the interview. We've tested the sound and video, but get him to speak up. And just so we understand each other, I've seen the evidence bags, and all I need now from that kid is a confession. Get the story. It's simple—a rebellious kid who lays in wait and kills his family."

"We don't know that yet," Greenwood said and went to the window to look in on Leeland, who was seated in the chair positioned to face the glass.

Quintana pointed at Leeland and said, "He's a murderer. We've got him. We've got his bloody clothes at the scene. And we have his note. Is that clear enough for you, deputy?"

Greenwood said, "Let me be clear. He's a suspect. I'm not going into that room with a conclusion in hand."

Quintana took off his sunglasses and stared at Greenwood. "So, who's the man with him? He's in on the whole thing. Am I right? Hiding a kid and all?"

"Nope," Greenwood said. Paula picked up one of the blank legal pads that had been left sitting on the counter and said, "It's not fair to keep them waiting."

"Fair. Shit. You two kept me waiting all day. It's got to be at least three p.m. by now." But then he took his seat on a tall stool at the counter, hit the button that controlled the recording, and began to roll up the sleeves of his dress shirt.

Greenwood followed Paula into the safe room and was blinded by the sun that flooded the west-facing, floor-to-ceiling picture window. It looked out onto a peaceful scene—a yard carpeted in pine needles dropped by three thirty-foot Douglas firs. Paula took her seat at the table, but Greenwood walked up to the window and tapped it. A group of blue jays, which were really scrub jays, were feasting on a mixing bowl of peanuts still in the shell. In the afternoon light, the birds were sailcloth blue. Greenwood didn't know how he'd come to learn such things, but he did know that the safe room was a John Gaw Meem look-alike. From the center of the small room hung a pressed metal light fixture they didn't need to click on, and the table where Paula now sat was a smooth, dark oak. He'd heard that it had all been donated from a local with a home designed by the southwestern architect. If Leeland had taken note of the décor or the jays he didn't show it.

"See those scrub jays?" Greenwood said. "They often act as lookouts for each other."

Leeland focused on the yard and said, "My dad shot a bunch of them when we first moved to the Bounty, and he hung them on wire on the corral fence. He said the birds would stop coming. My 4-H teacher said scrub jays have funerals when they find a dead bird."

"Well, I'd say someone is taking good care of these birds," Greenwood said, and took his notebook out and put it on the table as he took a seat. The window to the AV room was directly behind him. Greenwood glanced at the clock over Leeland's head. It read 3:15. He penciled it in his notebook. Leeland was sitting on an upholstered easy chair. It had squared-off arms where Leeland placed his own arms. Mr. Salado had been directed by Mitzi to sit in the folding chair that backed up to the picture window. Greenwood knew that he, Paula, and Leeland would be on camera that afternoon.

Greenwood heard the air conditioner click on. Quintana wouldn't be liking that. Leeland was at ease, not shaking now. He was wearing a pair of round wire-rimmed glasses.

"Can you see with those glasses?" Paula asked and Leeland nodded and pushed the glasses up on his nose. He was wearing the ball cap that Joseph had brought out to him. It was black with a gold eagle front and center. There was a big H on the eagle's chest for Hondo, Greenwood knew. Leeland's Levis were old and baggy and there were holes at his knees. Most ranch kids in the Valley wore stiff Wranglers, but the boy in the chair didn't much look like a ranch kid. He was tall, but his shoulders were narrow.

"His friend Michael, Rosalie's son, passed that tee shirt down to him," Greenwood said to Paula by way of getting started.

"Sorry about your friend," she said. "He was brave to volunteer for Afghanistan."

Leeland nodded and Greenwood wrote in his notebook that the shirt said, "Only the strong survive." It was black, and a mean-looking scorpion crawled across the front of the shirt.

"You a Scorpio?" Paula asked and Leeland nodded with what was only a tremor. "Good secret keepers, aren't we?" she said, and Greenwood thought maybe it was a cruel thing to say to the boy.

"Okay, let's get started," Greenwood said. "I need to read you your rights again. Mr. Salado, you and Leeland need to tell us if there is anything you don't understand or follow." He read off a list he kept in his notebook. "Okay...now let's start with your birthday and address."

Leeland gave the information in a soft, polite voice. Greenwood couldn't imagine the boy in handcuffs.

"You have any neighbors?" Paula asked.

"No," Leeland said.

"No one drops by to visit?"

"Mr. Duff keeps the place locked up. Only the hands come in the gate and UPS and FedEx." Leeland did a little shake of his head again.

"Got ya," Paula said.

Greenwood heard the knock on the glass behind him, which was a stupid thing for the DA to do because it caught Leeland's attention and he sat back in his chair and pulled his cap down just enough to shade his eyes. Greenwood ignored the knock and confirmed Leeland's age by saying, "So you're fourteen?" Greenwood knew his New Mexico criminal law, knew a boy of fourteen had different rights than a fifteen-year-old. And while Leeland's age was already on the record, he wanted Quintana to hear it.

Greenwood went on, "Turning fifteen after school starts, I guess since you're a Scorpio like Investigator Magliaro, you're going into the tenth grade then?"

He knew the answer to that too but just wanted to hear Leeland explain it.

"No, sir. I'll start ninth. My dad and mom held me back a grade."

"I'm wondering, Leeland, if the lean-to down the road from the ranch is your place."

Leeland flashed a look of distrust at the two of them. It was going to take some time to earn back the boy's trust, and Greenwood regretted his wording. But Leeland still nodded and said, "Joseph and I built it." Mr. Salado nodded too, and it was clear he knew about the place.

"Richard Parker—is he another buddy of yours?"

Leeland took his hat off and propped it on a knee and said simply, "No, he's a man-eating tiger." He hesitated, then said, "From a book."

Greenwood crossed out the name in his notebook, and Paula said, "Got ya."

"Okay, Leeland, I need you to write me a sentence or two on this paper." He nodded at Paula to pass Leeland her yellow legal pad. "You can write anything really, but why not write two sentences about Billy the Kid."

Leeland slipped out of his chair and gently dropped to his knees to get closer to the table to write. It was a very childlike thing to do and Greenwood felt his stomach clench.

Leeland hesitated before he started writing. After he finished, he said, "I wrote about Pat Garrett, the lawman who killed Billy."

Greenwood studied the sentences, then tore off the page and folded it four times until it was a perfect inch square. He put it in the back of his notebook.

"Do you know why we're here, Leeland?" Paula asked.

The boy didn't really answer. He had begun to pick at loose threads where the fabric of his jeans was ripped at the knees.

"Do you need anything? More water?" Paula asked because Mitzi had left a tall pink plastic glass of ice water for the boy. It was weeping on the oak table.

Leeland shook his head.

"Do you want Mr. Salado to stay?" Paula asked, and her

voice had such a sweetness to it that it made Greenwood want to reach out and hold her hand.

"Yes," Leeland said.

"Okay, let's get started," Greenwood said and knew he was repeating and might never get past this part.

"When did you get to the Salados place?"

"Monday," Leeland said softly.

"About what time?"

"Noon...maybe noon."

"What were you wearing?"

"These clothes," Leeland said.

"So, on Monday you got up and did your chores first. What time? Your dad wake you up?"

Greenwood knew, and Paula knew, he was leading, but he didn't much care now that he was into it.

"It was right at five. I always set an alarm."

"Then what?" Paula asked and Leeland listed the chores and the animals he had fed.

"After that?" Paula continued.

"I wanted to eat something, but my dad came into the kitchen and told me to get the hell out of his house and his face, and he threw the keys at me."

"Can you describe your dad?"

"He's hard, and he's mean, and he wished he'd lived in the Old West days where you can kill people you don't like," Leeland said in a rush.

Greenwood heard the knock on the glass behind him, and he stood and said he'd be back.

Once in the AV room, Greenwood heard Paula ask Leeland if his sister got up early too.

"Usually, but not on weekends because the girls sleep in on weekends. But anyway, she wasn't home."

Paula nodded and asked Leeland to describe the house and where his bedroom was in the house. Suddenly the DA stood, walked Greenwood back up against the door, and slammed him up against it. Greenwood had an urge to call out to Mitzi. But Quintana began pacing the room like a watchdog kept chained up too long.

"You and that New York woman are sniffing around for a victim. I get it. Like I told you, I have bloody clothes. His clothes. I have the note he wrote. What proof do you have that he was victimized?" The DA stopped his pacing and came back at him.

"That's our job. We investigate," Greenwood said. "But in case you didn't notice, how about a scabbed head caked with green spackle, or those oozing blisters on his arms? How's that for proof?"

It was now a standoff with the two men inches apart.

"Let's be clear, deputy. Right now in that room, that kid is a murderer. Not a victim."

Greenwood reached to push the DA. It'd be the end for him, he knew that. But Quintana turned his back on him and returned to the bench, where he perched again on the high stool.

"Show me a guilty mind," the man said.

When Greenwood left the room to return to the safe room, he spotted Mitzi at the other end of the hallway, arms folded across her chest like a sentry.

Greenwood sat, and Paula pointed at her legal pad, which said, "Luke owned nearly two dozen guns."

"Let's go back," Greenwood said. "Why'd you change your clothes?"

"I didn't want to be smelling like a barn," Leeland said, but Greenwood knew he had lost some sort of momentum.

"Where'd you leave those dirty clothes?" Paula asked.

"They're in the bottom of my closet," Leeland said, and Greenwood knew he was hearing truth.

"Tell us about the places you lived," Paula said. "And the

schools you've gone to."

Leeland spoke carefully, and from everything Greenwood knew about the Pruitt family, he knew the boy had his facts straight. Paula interrupted now and then to clarify, but Leeland brought them up to the present.

"And your family...you have a stepsister and stepmother and your real mother. Tell us about her."

Silence hung in the room until Mr. Salado said, "This is a hard thing for a boy."

"She died in a car accident. She flew through the air. I didn't see her do that, but I saw her on the ground, and her hair was all electric and popping like it was a live wire."

"Who is Angie?" Paula asked.

"My first stepmom. She had rights for me to visit her after my dad divorced her, but then he moved us to Weed."

Paula looked up from her mostly blank tablet and said, "Tell me, Leeland, what size pants and boots you wear."

Leeland answered and she wrote it all down.

"Talk to me about lying," Greenwood said.

"I used to lie when I was a little kid, but it made things ten times worse."

Paula said, "So you've been honest with us today?"

"Yes, ma'am," he said. "I went down to the café when I left the ranch and washed up."

Paula raised the eyebrow Greenwood had not seen raised all afternoon.

"That would have been when?" she asked.

"Well, it was in the morning...maybe around ten."

"Who'd you see there?"

"Lots of people were there—holiday and all. But nobody really. Just Valley folks."

"You see the twins?" Greenwood asked.

"No, I went into the restroom. The door is on the outside of the building. I washed up."

"Okay, so after that you drove to the Salados'?"

Mr. Salado leaned forward in his chair and said, "We fed him a big lunch."

"When were you going back home, Leeland?"

"Tomorrow, when things cooled down."

"But you left home, and we need to understand why."

"Because I wasn't going to wait for my dad to bash my head through the wall we'd just fixed. And there was no one to save me from him, not even my sister. I could never please him. It just got worse. And that day he said he'd kill me if I ever told anyone what he was doing to me." Leeland pulled his hat down.

"Did you want him dead?" Greenwood asked because he knew he had to.

Leeland took a minute to answer. "No. After I saw my mother die...I didn't want anyone else to die. I love him maybe because he's my dad, but I hated him. I hated him bad."

"How would you sum up your stepmom?"

This time Leeland answered quickly. "She's mean like my dad, but she's cruel too. If she gets mad, she'll grab a rock and pitch it at me. A rock can break a rib." He stirred in his chair.

"Okay, let's take a break, why don't we?" Greenwood was out the door before he finished that last part. He headed to the restroom to splash cold water on his face like his mother had taught him. It was a small room, and when Quintana pushed his way in there was no space for the two grown men to move. Greenwood was thankful for a reason to lay into the man. He hit him flat-handed. Greenwood knew he was overweight, but he was strong, and the hit took the breath out of the slight DA. Mitzi pulled the door open and said in a smoky voice, "For the love of God, cut it out."

Quintana left and Greenwood locked the restroom door using a lock high up on the door meant to keep little kids from locking themselves in, he guessed. And for the slightest bit of time, Greenwood found that lock reassuring.

When he came out and went back into the AV room, he found Paula with the DA. "We're ready to wrap it up," he said to the DA. "But you call in for an attorney for Leeland. You know which attorney I mean. If he's not up next on the public defender list, you put him there. And you get him to meet us at the courthouse in Carrizozo tonight. I know you're not aiming to show Leeland one ounce of mercy, but we all better show him justice or we will pay."

Back in the safe room, Greenwood took his seat. Mr. Salado had been standing, and he sat too. Leeland's eyelids were swollen, and through the glasses they looked huge. None of this was the way to break a kid.

"Leeland, we are sitting here watching you, and I thought you might pass out just now. You've got tears in your eyes. We need to know why. You need to tell us what happened." Greenwood was whispering by the time he finished speaking.

"I got tired of it. I couldn't take it anymore and Sunday night..." Leeland was speaking only to Paula now. "He tried to make me have sex with Deona."

Greenwood could see that Paula was taken back.

"She was naked, and my dad was trying to force me." Leeland covered his face with his hands and said, "He said, 'Get in here and prove you aren't a pussy.' "

"Slow down, kiddo." Paula leaned forward with both her elbows on her knees.

This was going to mess them all up and also tie them up together, Greenwood knew. He fought back the bile in his throat. They couldn't leave this boy now—not for the restroom or fresh air or time out.

"I shot him in the head." Leeland was getting it all out.

"Let's go back," Greenwood said, because he knew precision mattered now, and besides he'd broken the boy. It was over for Leeland.

"And your mom, your stepmom? Where was she when you shot your dad?" Greenwood went on.

"She was on the sofa reading. I shot her first."

"One shot?"

Leeland nodded.

"Anyone else hear this or help you?"

Leeland gave Greenwood a look that said, *I'm being honest here. You be honest with me.* And so he stopped with the stupid stuff. "Did you ever have to reload?"

"No, except I first took out the snake shot in the barn and loaded something that would do the job."

"Where was the gun?"

"In my dad's saddlebag."

"Got ya," Paula said. She took over, but she was shaking. "Where's the gun now?"

"It's in the river over at the alfalfa farm.

"You tossed it? When was that, Leeland?"

"I left the ranch and went to the fields...and then I went to the café to clean up." He took his glasses off and put both the palms of his still-small hands on his face and began to sob. The clock on the wall said it was fifteen after four. Greenwood wrote the time in his notebook. Once Leeland got control of himself, Greenwood started all over again with the boy, getting the precise timeline of the killings. Leeland never once backtracked. He remembered every little bit of Monday, July 4, 2005. He was trying to be helpful, which was his nature, and Greenwood wondered where he'd learned such behavior.

"I know that this is tough...and if you need a break, we'll take one," Paula said. "We aren't bad cops."

They sat silent while Leeland got control of his breathing.

"He might need an attorney," Mr. Salado said. "He's still a minor."

Greenwood stepped out of the room because he knew it was better not to answer. In the AV room, Quintana rolled his eyes at him and said, "Didn't know when to quit, did you? How long you been doing this line of work?"

"I've never brought in a child before," Greenwood said and wanted to kick the man.

They stopped their messing with each other long enough to listen to Paula, who was kneeling now in front of Leeland, holding tight to both of his hands. "It's totally up to you, Leeland. But if we can finish up here, I can promise you a public defender at the courthouse—tonight." She rolled back onto her heels and took her seat.

"I can sell a piece of family jewelry," Mr. Salado said, and Leeland looked up at the man and then back down at his lap.

Paula turned and stared into the glass, holding her hand up as if to say wait.

"Okay, might as well," the boy said.

Then Salado said," The world is a better world without Luke Pruitt in it. We can all tell you that."

Greenwood came back in the room, this time with Mitzi, who carried a tray of fresh water for everyone. She handed the glasses out and then stood there watching them all. She was there to check on the boy and check she did.

"I'll get some honey salve to put on those burns," Mitzi said. "A little goes a long way." Hers was the better job, Greenwood decided.

It was nearly five in the afternoon by the time Greenwood had finished getting Leeland to nail down the timeline of the murders and the night before. Nothing changed in his story. It was Leeland's story of his own telling. Greenwood wasn't going to change a word of it.

The boy was emptied out.

Paula stood up and said she needed to find a phone.

"I regret it," Leeland said when she was gone, and sat up very straight. "Please tell my sister that I'm sorry. Tell her she'll be okay with Aunt Trudy, once she gets used to it. It's not her fault that Deona was her mother. Tell her I didn't do it to disgrace her."

"Okay, I will. I promise. I will go see her myself."

"Maybe with the lady, 'cause my sister will cry a lot."

"Okay, we're going to go get something to eat now on our ride over to the courthouse in Carrizozo," Greenwood said and added, "My treat." Which was a stupid thing to say.

"I should have turned and run," Leeland said.

Greenwood had his face in his hands now; thoughts were running through his head and then scattering. "Could have, should have," he said in a faint whisper.

He didn't know if the tape was still running then or if Quintana had stopped it when Paula left the room, when he had everything needed to nail the boy. Greenwood could only hope that the rest had not made it to the tape. It was between him and Leeland. But it didn't matter really; it was his guilt now.

We

February 2007

We sat stone silent as Leeland was escorted into the Lincoln County Courthouse in Carrizozo, New Mexico by Deputy Greenwood, who was no longer a deputy but rather a simple transport officer. That man had lost so much weight we might not have known him. We'd heard that he'd moved to Carrizozo, which was on the far west side of Lincoln County, had taken an apartment above the old drug store. Who knew where in that one-café town he found his supper each evening?

Leeland had pleaded not guilty, and so his jury trial began on a winter day in a church-quiet courtroom. We sat there, hands folded in our laps, as if waiting for a robed choir to appear to settle our hearts and minds and make believers of us again.

We knew who all the players were in the courtroom—a boy now sixteen; a defense attorney in a brown, western-cut suit jacket and pressed jeans; a DA in a double-breasted, vested

286

suit. Leeland's stepmother, Angie, sniffed and said to the man seated next to her, "I thought they'd have Kleenex like at Corrine's funeral." And then she began playing with her long braid, making us fearful she'd use it to wipe her tears.

Leeland's public defender addressed the judge politely, requesting that the defense be allowed to hold their opening statement until after the State presented their case. The DA rolled his eyes at the request and objected but was told to get on with it or lose his turn.

Leeland wore a pressed dress shirt with a tie, and his hair had grown out so that we could see it was curly. And it was clear to us that now the boy had begun to shave. His glasses were a bit too small for his face. Most of the time, however, we only saw the back of his head, and we watched as sometimes his slight shoulders shuddered.

Sam Duff arrived, wearing polished, black cowboy boots, to take the stand as the first witness for the State of New Mexico. Greenwood directed him to a seat in the row behind the DA, but Duff never acknowledged the officer who had been first on scene, never acknowledged any of us for that matter. Investigator Paula Magliaro nodded at Greenwood as he stood in the aisle waiting for Duff to get settled. She'd been called to testify when Greenwood could not, now that he was transporting Leeland and looking after the boy. She would sit in the row behind the defense table for most of the trial.

In his opening statement, the DA presented photos of a happy family. One photo was of Leeland grinning with his cousins. It was taken on July 3, 2005. The photo was presented to the jury to be passed from hand to hand, and then it was projected on a screen to the side of the judge as if meant to illustrate some moral lesson about *family*. The next photo projected on the screen was of the iron gate of the Bounty Canyon Ranch flooded in blinding sunlight. We recognized that photo. It had taken up half the front page of the

Alamogordo Daily News on the day after Leeland was arrested. We remembered the caption too: "The landscape was serene in the early morning sun."

Reporters love murder.

"Welcome, Mr. Duff," the DA said. "Tell us, if you would, were you satisfied with Mr. Pruitt as an employee?"

Duff took command of the room and made eye contact with juror number three before answering, "He proved his worth by getting the ranch back on track." And then Duff started in on observations about the Pruitt family. The DA did a lot of nodding and agreeing.

"Your witness," the DA said as if pleased with how it was all going.

"Who managed the ranch—you or Mr. Pruitt?" Leeland's public defender asked.

"I managed it with the ranch manager. Hands on."

Duff crossed one booted foot across a knee, and as he answered he did a little knock on his shiny boot with his fist as if that settled that, as if we all didn't know better.

"Was the front gate on the ranch locked in July 2005?"

"It is now," Duff answered.

"Was it then?"

"It's a 40,000-acre ranch. It had better been locked," he said and did the knocking thing again.

"Who had regular contact with the Pruitt family?"

Duff didn't get a chance to answer that question because the DA was on his feet, spitting out words. But then suddenly Duff answered a question he had not been asked, saying, "I was shocked that Leeland turned on his parents."

"Really?" the defense attorney said, and when he was back sitting at his table next to Leeland he said, "No more questions."

The judge was too quick for the DA and said in his polite voice, "The witness is excused."

The DA gathered his wits and the papers he had scattered when his witness surprised him and put out his hand for a quick shake with Sam Duff as he left the stand. Sam Duff testified all of ten minutes. His wife had not joined him in court. But then we'd heard that she'd left him. He took big, heavy steps down the center aisle of the courtroom and took off for home in his Benz.

Next, the DA called on the Lincoln County Sheriff, who testified that his department had never been called out to the Bounty with any family concerns, not even one single time. He said, "If we'd gotten a call with any concern," he stopped to look at Leeland and then went on, "we'd have been out there. But let me remind those of you who've come from out of state to gawk at us, that in Lincoln County we take care of our own."

Between sobs Angie said, "My fault."

Leeland's attorney objected to the unsolicited western maxim. We should have begun to count those objections. For God's sake, someone was finally objecting for the boy.

"Did a neighbor ever call you with concerns about the boy on that ranch?" Leeland's attorney asked the sheriff when he got his chance in cross-examination.

"No," the sheriff said, as if it were plain stupid to ask that.

"Did the Pruitts have neighbors?" he asked.

The sheriff was easy to stump, and he said, "Not that I know of." And then he shook his head in disbelief.

The State rested after two days of testimony, and then the defense attorney presented his opening statement by beginning with a parable. "From the Gospel of Luke..." Lots of us nodded as he walked over to the fence that held in the jury and said, "And who is my neighbor?" He stood there and waited as if expecting an answer from one of them, or for a hand to go up.

Someone in the gallery whispered, "The Good Samaritan."

"Look at the man who acts in mercy," the attorney finally

MARTHA BURNS

said. He surveyed the panel and then turned and looked at each of us. At least it felt that way.

"And when we get done with that, with asking who my neighbor is, the decisive issue remains: What kind of person am I?" He pointed at himself and then at all of us—even the judge. He let those words hit us like a sudden downpour.

We were afraid to look at each other.

Leeland took the stand in his own defense, and only a clarinet could have mimicked the sadness of that boy's voice. Even when the DA took him apart in cross-examination, the voice was the same.

"It was too much to ask of a boy," the defense attorney said in his closing. "I wouldn't treat my livestock the way Luke and Deona Pruitt treated that boy."

Nearly one hundred of us had been called up for jury duty. So many excuses were made not to serve. And so when the jury filed back into the courthouse and squeezed into their box on that bitter February day, we saw, all in one glance, what the deliberations had done to them. Telling us, *time's up.*

The foreperson—who was an older ranch woman—read the verdicts as if she were on stage giving the performance of a lifetime. "I don't need any microphone," she said as she batted the bailiff's hand away when he reached into the jury box to pass her the silly thing. And then she read the verdicts while staring down the DA. "Guilty of second-degree murder for the death of Deona Pruitt. Guilty of manslaughter in the death of Luke Pruitt," she said and finally turned to the judge.

"Thank you, madam foreperson, for your service," he said softly, and she scoffed as if she were waiting for the opportunity.

What had we hoped for? Acquittal for Leeland, who was standing now to face the jury of his peers, or a guilty verdict for those of us who were huddled in our seats, which were really well-worn pine pews. *We should have stood with him while someone prayed.*

A woman near the back said, "Damn it all to hell," and then we heard the double doors slam shut behind her.

Leeland's attorney helped the boy to sit and then wrapped his arm around him for a minute or more as they both wept. The bailiff appeared and produced cuffs out of thin air. A woman of the hippy generation we all knew as Lark, who'd been seen going up the steps to Greenwood's apartment in the evenings during the trial, stood and said, "As if Leeland Pruitt is going to try to escape now."

Leeland's Aunt Sally yelled, "He's only a kid." And then she collapsed, and Robin Greenwood stepped forward to help Rosalie carry her out of the courtroom. Together they struggled under the weight of Sally's grief.

"Sentencing," the judge said over the racket, "will take place after the second phase of the trial. We begin tomorrow at nine a.m."

Well, we all knew that would be next.

In the two days of courtroom testimony leading up to the sentencing, many of us stood up and took the stand. For the duration, Officer Conley stood at the back of the courtroom, weaving from one leg to the other like a pendulum. We waited, fearing the judge would condemn Leeland to a life in prison by sentencing him as an adult.

"My decision will be dictated by law," the judge said to the courtroom before he took most of the next day to deliberate. We waited, watching the wet winter storm come across the county from the west. The judge must have seen a child, because he sentenced Leeland as the child he was.

It was Leeland who got the last word in the courtroom before being sent to the CYFD detention facility in Albuquerque, to remain there until his twenty-first birthday. The boy asked the judge if he could speak, and when the judge agreed, he turned and faced us. "I will not let you down," he said to the assembly of his neighbors, as if he was standing to give a benediction. "That's the kind of person I want to be. I won't disappoint you."

In the early evening winter darkness, we found our way across the muddy parking lot to our scattered pickups. The headlights of vehicles on the two-lane highway that passed through town bounced off the dirty snow and lit up our shamed faces before passing on.

THE END

Acknowledgements

I am indebted to my 'first reader/re-reader' Teddy Jones and to Doug Kurtz and Candace Simar who critiqued my work, coached me, and pushed and pulled me toward a better book. For writing lessons and encouragement, I want to thank Dr. Laura Winters, Robert Boswell, Dr. Robert Ready, Pam Houston, Laura Brodie, and Minrose Gwin. I am grateful for The Taos Summer Writers Workshop and grieve its passing and for the Pirate's Alley Faulkner Society for promoting writers and for granting me my first ever writing award. Without that award I might never have become an author. I want to thank Bobby Frank of *Livestock Weekly* for generously sharing with me the wisdom of Linda Posey and granting me permission to use her words on my pages. I am grateful for Mary Oliver's poem, *Lilies*, which my Leeland Pruitt memorized and used as a touchstone as did I as I wrote this book. I am so lucky to have found my way to Atmosphere Press where my enthusiasm for the writing life has been renewed and for that I am grateful. And finally, a thank you with my whole heart to my daughters Hayley and Evayn, who have listened to years of my storytelling, and to Dennis, who always reminds me that I am happiest when I am writing.

About Atmosphere Press

Atmosphere Press is an independent, full-service publisher for excellent books in all genres and for all audiences. Learn more about what we do at atmospherepress.com.

We encourage you to check out some of Atmosphere's latest releases, which are available at Amazon.com and via order from your local bookstore:

Nine Days, a novel by Judy Lannon

Shadows of Robyst, a novel by K. E. Maroudas

Dying to Live, a novel by Barbara Macpherson Reyelts

Looking for Lawson, a novel by Mark Kirby

Surrogate Colony, a novel by Boshra Rasti

Á Deux, a novel by Alexey L. Kovalev

What If It Were True, a novel by Eileen Wesel

Sunflowers Beneath the Snow, a novel by Teri M. Brown

Solitario: The Lonely One, a novel by John Manuel

The Fourth Wall, a novel by Scott Petty

Rx, a novel by Garin Cycholl

Knights of the Air: Book 1: Rage!, a novel by Iain Stewart

Heartheaded, a novel by Constantina Pappas

About the Author

Martha Burns, a native of New Mexico, was always a story-teller, who embraced Albert Camus' theory that *"fiction is the lie through which we tell the truth."* She earned a Doctor of Letters with distinction from Drew University and won the Faulkner-Wisdom Gold Metal Award for Short Story. She and her husband have returned to live in New Mexico where she is at work on her next novel, the story of a woman in the 1930s sued for adultery who loses custody of her six children. *Across the Narrows* is both a mystery and a story of redemption. More can be found about Martha at MarthaBurnsWriter.com.